PLUS ONE BONUS

Table Topped #4

Alex Silver

COPYRIGHT

TABLE OF CONTENTS

BLURB

Our relationship is fake, but my feelings are growing more real by the day.

Max sweeps me off my feet at our bus stop. He becomes my friend. Then, just when I think he might be into me, he throws me a curve ball by asking me to be his fake date to a wedding. He claims his buddies won't leave him alone about finding a plus one. The catch is, the ceremony is months away, so we'll have to be pretend datemates for a while.

I suspect there's more going on than Max's inability to handle confronting his meddlesome friends. Especially once I meet them all and see how much they care about Max. I'm spinning in circles trying to figure out how he feels about me, all the while trying not to fall for him.

Plus One Bonus is the fourth book in the Table Topped series. It is an M/X (genderfluid) romance between Max, the newest member of his gaming group who misses home, has a secret penchant for manties, and can't handle confrontation and Si/Simon/Simone, a snarky genderfluid tea seller.

CW: History of neglectful parents and parental abandonment, a side character's infertility struggles are mentioned.

CHAPTER 1

Max

"**H**ey, Max, have you found any potential plus ones for our wedding, yet?" Theo asks me, not for the first time. We're walking to the bar after our VentureQuest game. The folks in my gaming group are my closest friends. Even if they are all settling into lovey-dovey romantic relationships. It's not that I begrudge them their happiness, it just makes me feel even more like an outsider to see them all so settled. If I wasn't the new guy to the group, I might not feel so insecure about my position with them.

"I'm not sure yet. It will depend on if I'm seeing someone. Why, did you guys settle on a date?" I ask, hoping to redirect Theo into talking about his latest wild ideas for the wedding. And away from my kilometer-wide insecurities about finding a date. I wish I had someone to bring to the wedding, but I'm not holding my breath.

Jude, Theo's fiancé, is the romantic out of the pair. Theo likes to get creative. He's been having a field day coming up with off the wall ideas for their wedding. Gems like getting married underwater while scuba diving off the coast of some overpriced seaside resort. Or on a helicopter flying over an active volcano. For that one, he suggested instead of exchanging rings, they could drop them into the caldera, like something out of Lord of the Rings.

The one about exchanging vows while bungee jumping off a building sounded particularly awful to me. I'm pretty sure Theo's got to be joking about most of his wild ideas. Jude seems less keen on making their day some sort of unique spectacle. I suspect it will more closely resemble a scene out of one of the rom-coms Jude loves than anything Theo has come up with so far.

"We're leaning toward New Year's Eve for the wedding. With a second reception in LA over the summer for my family," Jude supplies. He gives Theo a big sappy smile, which Theo returns with a meaningful smirk and one of his goofy eyebrow waggles. I suppress a sigh at their overt affection as Jude kisses his fiancé's cheek.

"My folks live out in the country so we can have a big all night party. Set off firecrackers and ring in the new year as newlyweds," Theo adds. That's his most realistic plan to date. "Champagne toast at midnight, and it's an anniversary for us. What's not to love?"

"You guys didn't start dating until the spring," Laura points out, tossing her hair over her shoulder.

Theo flashes a devilish grin and says, "Not that anniversary.

"Dude, TMI," Gui groans, shoving Theo into Jude. Theo cackles and Jude sighs.

"Seriously, though, it's the day we first met," Jude says defensively, his cheeks pink. He's sweet.

I'd have been interested in pursuing him, if he hadn't already been hung up on Theo when we met. They're totally stuck on each other. And they've become one of those infuriating couples who are so happy in their relationship that they insist on trying to pair off every one of their single friends. So we can share in their coupled off bliss. Or something.

In theory, that doesn't sound so awful. I would love having someone to share my life with, but their match-making skills leave something to be desired. And since they've already paired our other single friend, Laura, off with Paz's cousin Alice, that leaves me the primary target of their meddling. Laura and Alice both seem fine with being shoved together at every opportunity. I'm less cool with the whole arrangement the longer it lasts. Needing their help to find a date taps into every part of me that hates asking for things I want and fears it will be what makes the people I care about walk away.

It doesn't help that the last several dates that I let them convince me to try sucked. The first guy was someone Paz knew from work, Bob the Barista. Jude suggested it because he claimed Bob was flirting with me when we went in for drinks. We had nothing in common, except that Bob makes coffee for a living and I enjoy drinking it. I enjoy most of the menu at Sin and Chocolate, to be honest. Bob spent the entire date glued to his phone. I got all paranoid that he was live-tweeting about how much our date sucked in the style of a nature documentary. *'Behold, the gamer geek—taken from his natural habitat and forced to socialize.'*

Naturally, I'd started spamming our group chat with the sort of messages I'd convinced myself the guy was posting to his social media. If you can't have fun, at least laugh about it, right? Yeah, that was fine, until I realized that I'd sent the messages to my date instead of the group chat by accident—oops. His text that he'd arrived at the restaurant was my most recent one, re-placing the usual group chat at the top of my message history.

So, I sent Bob my play-by-play of how horribly awk-ward the whole date seemed. All the while he sat op-posite me, acting increasingly uncomfortable. Until he excused himself to the washroom and walked right out the front door.

So, I got stuck with the bill and an upset text from Paz asking why I was an asshole to his work friend. To be fair, he spent the entire date fiddling with his phone, even before I started the disastrous play-by-play. I still felt awful that Bob thought I was making fun of his so-cial skills instead of mocking myself. I apologized and explained I'd meant the texts about myself, not him. But it was super awkward.

I haven't shown my face at Paz's workplace in weeks thanks to that incident. Gui doesn't mind mak-ing coffee runs for me, at least. More chances to make googly eyes at his boyfriend.

That was the worst disaster. Errol's attempt, once again, at Jude's prompting, to set me up with an animator he knows at another studio wasn't bad. We had a pleasant, if bland, chat about work. There just wasn't any chemistry.

And then there are Theo's attempts. Jude came up with the plan, but I think this all esclataed when Errol bailed early on us for post-work drinks a while back. Pia let slip how she helped nudge Errol into giving Rene a second chance. We all agreed that he seemed happy with Rene and Mo. Theo somehow took the exchange as a personal challenge to help Jude find me the love of my life, no matter how miserable the entire process makes me.

"You know, if you don't bring a date, my buddy Paul's still single. He'll be at the wedding," Theo suggests. "He mentioned he thought you were cute when you met at that con last month."

"Paul? Oh, the Link cosplayer?" I take a minute to place the name. When I do, I suppress a sigh. Paul was a decent guy. I'd enjoyed hanging out with him after Theo insisted on introducing me to his old high school buddy. Paul was visiting the city for the gaming convention, and we'd all gone together as a group. The Link outfit was a little weak. It didn't hold a candle to Theo's Hiccup, from How to Train Your Dragon, with custom-made armor.

Jude had dressed up as another of the viking youths. I hadn't bothered with a costume, though most of the rest of our group did. When pressed, I flipped up the hood on my black sweatshirt and declared that I was Toothless, Theo's dragon. He thought that was hilarious and cracked a joke about riding me, and how he and Jude should have stolen the idea as a couples costume.

After that, Theo and Jude spent the day inventing excuses to keep ditching me with Paul. It got old fast. Subtlety is not Jude's strong suit. It was obvious he wanted Paul and I to hit it off, which was a bit of a bonding moment for us. But Paul lives in Squamish and has no interest in moving to the city. The mere suggestion had appalled him. Bit of a deal breaker, considering the industry I love working in exists in the city.

There are a couple smaller studios scattered around the province, but I'm most likely to have stable employment in Vancouver. If I was going to move anywhere, it would be back home to Toronto.

This city is an amazing place to live, but it's lonely here. I miss the GTA. Even hearing a familiar Ontario accent makes me homesick some days. I don't want to give up on my dreams, though. So, Vancouver it is, working my way up through the ranks of production at Eye-On Games. Game development is as fascinating as I'd hoped when I moved out here to find work in the industry. Once I accrue more experience, I might move back out east. Montreal is only a five-hour drive from where I grew up, but rural BC isn't in the cards for me.

"And he's coming into the city with Jacob for that independent film festival in a few weeks. Bet it's not too late to score tickets," Theo is still talking about Paul. I resist the urge to roll my eyes.

"Um, I might pass. Work is busy," I hedge. An indie film fest sounds like not my cup of tea. More accurately, I'm not into the sort of people such festivals

attract. Nothing wrong with smaller budget produc-
tions getting a chance at a big break and bringing
unique perspectives to the screen. But there isn't much
that screams 'cooler-than-thou' hipster louder than an
indie film festival date.

I guess it just seems pretentious. It's possible Theo's
old friends just want an excuse to come into the city
and spend a weekend away from the boring tedium of
rural life. At least, I assume that's what people who
don't live in cities do. Theo's sister takes any excuse to
come into the city.

Maybe if it was an animation expo, I'd be more keen.
It's always fun to see artists exploring distinct new
styles at those sorts of festivals. That could just be my
bias from the fact all my friends are in animation. Even
back in Toronto, my first PA gig was working at a television studio that made low budget shows for kids. When
they closed last year, after some legal issues with the
company founders illegally exploiting tax incentives,
I'd followed the work out west.

"We could all do dinner together instead. If the film
festival isn't your thing," Jude suggests.

"Yes!" Theo bounces around like an excited puppy.
"Or, if Paul's not your type, you can meet Jacob. He's
also into dudes."

"Or our cousin Julian is flying in for the wedding,"
Gui adds, his tone more mild. Jude has roped him and
Paz in on this 'find Max's soulmate' scheme, too. Not
that they're getting married, yet. I think it's just a matter of time before they do. Dollars to donuts, Gui's putting it off so as not to steal his baby brother's thunder.

Jude is such a sappy romantic, and Gui is protective of him.

"Yes!" Jude nods with clear enthusiasm. "I think you'd like Julian, Max. He's a financial planner, but he's also a gamer. And he's ripped from doing CrossFit."

I suppress a groan because my idea of a date from hell is listening to my potential partner discussing the intricacies of his CrossFit workout regimen. Perhaps with a dash of mansplaining my job to me, since he's a gamer. Half the time people say that, it means he's played the occasional round of Halo or Call of Duty with his frat brothers or something. Then he can round out the dinner conversation by judging me over my less than stellar financial situation. That might be uncharitable. I'm sure Gui and Jude's cousin is a perfectly wonderful guy.

I just can't take another date using my preference for cheap date spots and public transit over cabs as a jumping off point to offer me patronizing investment tips. Like cool, if I could afford to stash money in an emergency fund and max out my RRSP, I wouldn't be broke all the time. Not that I'm bitter about that failed date with Theo's fellow lighter's husband's friend who works in finance.

As to the CrossFit, sure, muscles make a pretty picture, but they aren't everything. Sort of hot for a one-night stand, but not my ideal of what I want in a longer-term partner. I find Jude's lean swimmer's build more appealing than what he's describing. Not to mention, most ripped guys seem unimpressed by my preferred workout routine of nope.

If I was looking for a relationship, it would be with

someone softer around the middle for cozy weekends spent snuggled together under the covers. Not that I'm looking for forever. Just because my friends are all finding love, doesn't mean I'm ready to settle down. I'm not. Or rather, I'm not sure it's in the cards for me. If I did have someone, at this point, it would be a relief to get the gang off my back about dating. If that also meant having a partner to fill the long lonely evenings and weekends in my crappy basement apartment, far from home and family, so much the better.

I can usually count on Errol to defuse these conversations, before they go too far, but he's skipping drinks tonight. That sucks for me, since I'll need to pay attention to the bus schedule if I want to get back to the North Shore without him to drive me home. Oh well, Errol doesn't owe me rides or buffering from the rest of our group's rabid romantic recommendations.

If I protest their meddling enough times, they might get the hint and drop it. Or I could gather my courage and tell them I've had enough. I'm not holding my breath for that outcome, conflict is hard. And, in truth, I do want to find someone.

This all started when I was hanging out with Jude last summer to get his mind off missing Theo while Theo was staying with his parents. We got drunk and Jude asked how I was doing, probably just to get the topic away from how much he missed his boyfriend, and I blubbered all over him about how lonely I've been since moving to Vancouver. I told him that I want to find my person the way he found Theo. Ever since that night, Jude has made helping me find love his mission. And recruited all our other friends to help him find potential dates for me. Theo in particular wants to help. The others haven't been nearly as pushy. I swear Jude infected Theo with his love of romantic comedies.

It wouldn't be so bad if I had the guts to tell them why their picks for me are way off base. I mean, Jude asked what I look for in a guy, but I don't think I have a type. I'm not into things like muscles and stereotypical beauty. But I'm not NOT into those things. It's just, how do you describe someone's energy? There's a vibe I get from some people, and that's hard to pinpoint. It's harder to find someone who sparks my interest and likes who *I* want to be with a partner. And I didn't know Jude well enough at the time to explain all that. I'm still not sure if I would.

I know that I act relaxed and kind of brash, but it's all a front to cover up my insecurities. People *like* confident people. So I act confident. At least until it's something actually important.

"Don't worry, Max, we've got your back," Theo claps an arm around my shoulders. And they do, so I can't risk fucking it up and driving them off like I always seem to do.

Jude nods, earnest as ever. "Yeah, Theo's right. You're in the wedding party, and we've got plenty of eligible bachelors to invite. You'll have your pick of dates. If you don't meet anyone you click with before then."

Well, fuck me. Guess I better meet someone before Theo and Jude's wedding. Otherwise, I'm going to be spending a week in the mountains with my buddies throwing every single guy they know at me. Like they're plotting their own amateur take on the bachelor. No pressure.

It'll be like a revolving door of first dates. Or like a weeklong speed dating event. Count me out. If only I knew any convenient single guys who could pretend to be my plus one. Yeah, as if anyone would go along with that sort of ridiculous scheme IRL. Still, if I had more friends outside our immediate group, I'd consider giving it the old college try.

CHAPTER 2

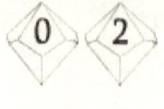

Si

Today is going to go my way. I repeat the mantra under my breath as the overcrowded bus that ought to take me to work whizzes past without so much as slowing down. It passes close enough to splash my legs with cold rainwater from the gutters. The electric placard above the windshield that announces the route only reads, "SORRY, BUS FULL," in shouty all caps, quashing any hope of making it to work on time.

"Today is a shitty ass fucking craptastic day that can suck my fucking cock," I growl. Icy cold water seeps up my pant legs, leaving me shivering at the curb. More steady rain drums down on my head, soaking the hoodie I pulled on over my work shirt and the compression vest I wear for my social anxiety.

I'm not the only one waiting at the bus stop. I am the only one who didn't bother with an umbrella. Rookie mistake, but I thought I'd only be waiting at the curb a few minutes, at most. It will be at least another ten minutes before the next bus arrives.

I resist the urge to slump in defeat. Shoulders back, head held high, I will overcome this setback. My hair drips water into my eyes, the universe mocking me for my optimism.

Shit happens. I'm not about to get fired a few weeks into working at Celine's tea shop. I hope. Crap. I cannot lose another job right now. Celine, my boss, will understand. Perks of working for my favorite cousin. Better text her to say I'll be late once I'm out of the rain.

"Back to school. It's always like this during the school year. That's suburbia for you," the guy waiting behind me grumbles. Then he holds up his umbrella and raises a brow at me. "Want to huddle in and escape drowning?"

"Uh, yeah, thanks, mate," I say, shuffling close enough to share his umbrella without getting all up in his personal space.

I can't help but notice he smells nice. Some sort of citrus and vanilla. I shiver from the cold and he shuffles closer, his body heat tantalizingly near. I stand my ground. Neither giving in to the impulse to crowd close and inhale his scent nor the warning bells telling me to retreat before he realizes I'm checking him out. In my defense, the stranger is a hottie.

"Thanks for giving me shelter. Headed to work?" I ask.

"Yeah."

"Cool. Me too. I mean, I guess, duh, why else would I be out here freezing my balls off in the rain so early in the morning, right?" I ramble. Ugh, did I really just bring up my balls? Big, stupid mouth. Why can't I shut up?

"Right," his lips twitch like he's fighting a smile and his eyes dance with suppressed mirth. Great, he's trying not to laugh at me. Great going, Si, scare away the hottie who's nice enough to share his umbrella with a schlub like me.

"So, what do you do? Like for work," I clarify the question, sounding like a dumbass.

"I'm a production assistant," hottie says, that smile still not quite forming on his full lips.

"Oh. Nice. Like for movies? They were filming a show outside my job all last week. Something with a bunch of zombie extras. It was freaky," I say. Great. I'm going to scare him off by rambling about seeing zombies and have to go back to getting soaked to the bone.

"Video games," hottie corrects me. "It's a step up from unpaid intern. I'm learning how the studio runs and I'm hopeful I can work my way up from being a lowly PA. What about you?"

"What about me?" I ask, could I sound any more clueless? "Oh, you mean my job? I just started a new gig working at my cousin's tea shop." I wince as I say it. Way to admit the only way I nabbed a hybrid barista slash retail job was by being related to the boss.

"That's, uh, cool?" He sounds unsure. He's not the only one.

"Yeah. It's not the worst job I've ever had. So. Yeah." I shrug.

"What is?" He asks with a twinkle in his eye.

"What?" I'm thrown off kilter by the unexpected question.

"You said it's not the worst job you've ever had, so, what is?"

"That would be my very brief stint on a farm back home, backbreaking labor in the dirt with heavy machinery from sunup to sundown is not my cuppa tea." I give a theatrical shudder, then pivot to more interesting topics. "Anyway, what's your name?" I wouldn't blame him if he refused to answer. What am I even doing? Chatting up strangers at the bus stop is so not the norm in Vancouver.

"Max," hottie replies with a sunny smile.

"Nice. Max. Cool, I like it. Max. I'm Si," I say. I don't add that it's short for Simon. And sometimes Simone. Just Si today, though. Definitely a Si day. I hunch my shoulders because the nice stranger already has to regret offering me a spot under his umbrella. No way that outing myself all over him will make him regret his life choices any less.

"Nice to meet you, Si. I've seen you around," Max says.

"Oh, yeah? Guess we're neighbors. You know, ish."

I hunch more. Great. So he noticed me. I don't know if that's a positive thing. I've noticed him too. How could I miss the hottie I see most mornings at the bus stop? Some lucky evenings I see him going home, too. Not that I'm keeping tabs or anything. I just notice attractive people in my vicinity.

"Yep," Max says, sounding amused.

"Cool. So, uh, thanks for sharing." I gesture at the umbrella, almost thwacking it out of his hands. Smooth.

"No problem. Something happen to yours?" he asks.

I wonder if he intends the question to sound pointed or if he's just making conversation. "Lost it."

"That sucks. Hope you have time to replace it soon; it's been pouring all week," Max says with a wry quirk to his lips.

I chuckle; it rains a lot in Vancouver. Not as much as people joke about, but not an insignificant amount of the year's weather necessitates huddling under umbrellas. If losing mine is what it takes to talk to my hottie sort-of-neighbor at long last, it seems a fair tradeoff.

"Yeah, I'll have to pick up a replacement on my break," I agree, keeping the conversation moving. "Of course, as soon as I buy a new one, the old one will inevitably turn up again, that's just science." New low achieved, I am officially so much of a loser that I am chatting up strangers on the bus trying to make friends. That last line only gets an agreeable grunt out of Max. The bus will arrive soon, ending my moment with Max. "So, got any big weekend plans?" I ask. God, could I have strung together a cheesier line?

Max gives me an assessing look before he says, "hanging out with some friends tonight. We have a standing thing. Afterward, if I know them at all, we'll either grab a beer and head home or hit the clubs so they can grind on their significant others."

"Oh. I know all about being the last lonely single standing. They couple up, get married, have kids. Then you're sitting there alone on Friday night while they bitch about not being able to find a sitter. Or worse, they decide to throw pretentious dinner parties instead of having actual fun. Or they realize the city is no place to raise a family and they move away. Ugh. Gross. My condolences." I wrap up the rant, cheeks ablaze as I realize I just unloaded on the guy about all of my friends moving on without me.

It's not like I blame them for growing up. Sometimes it just seems like I'm years behind them. I'm still figuring out dating and being an adult when they got to start that shit years ago. Even though most of them went to university while I jumped into the labor market with both feet after high school. Too bad most of my jobs haven't stuck for long.

I can be what employers call flaky. I'd call it needing a mental health day every so often, but most corporations disagree on that point. At least, they do once you go beyond what their less than generous paid time off policies dictate as allowable.

Nevermind that I'd need less of those days to recuperate if I didn't have to choose between hiding being Simone or dealing with harassment on my girl days. It's not as though it impacts customers' lives that I sometimes present femme. Too bad that fact never stopped some of them from being assholes to me. Sure, there are gender related labor protections, but fuck if I have the money, time, or energy to fight some faceless corporation for my basic human rights.

"Wow." Max shifts his grip on the umbrella. That draws my attention back to the cutie and away from the soul-sucking realities of life. "Um, tell me how you really feel, Si." There's a teasing tone to his voice, but I think I've overstepped the bounds of polite waiting-for-the-bus conversation.

"Sorry, do I sound bitter?" I try to play it off as no big deal. A joke.

"Just a skosh bitter, yeah," Max agrees, but he's grinning at me now. "Anyway. They're not like that. It just gets lonely. Like you said, last single standing. Well. Except my friend Laura, though I'm pretty sure it's only a matter of time before she and Alice stop dancing around their feelings for each other. So, yeah."

"I hear you, mate. Gets lonely," I commiserate. Where the hell did I pick up that verbal tic? I'm not British, and he's not my mate. Time to lay off binging on the BBC. Or it might just be a thing I do. Why am I over-thinking this?

"Yeah. Doesn't help that my other friends, Theo and Jude, are planning the wedding of the century and they want to pair me off, too."

"Oh. Gross." I pull a face for comedic effect. "I hate

it when happy couples want to infect you with their lovebugs. Like, great, you found love; no need to spread that shit around."

"Right?" Max chuckles.

"Right. Are they trying to set you up with every eligible, uh, person, they know?"

Max's lips quirk again, and he fills in the answer to the unasked question for me. "Guys. They're trying to set me up with guys. I'm all about the dudes."

"Oh. Cool." I nod, ruthlessly stamping out the thrill of possibility zinging through me at that little nugget of information. If Max is gay, he might be into me. Most of my casual flings have been with gay or bi dudes. It's easier to just hook up with no strings attached on my Simon days than trying to navigate the minefield of more than casual dating while trans. "That's, uh, cool. Have they roped you into any dates?"

"Several. They've been—not great? If I'm still single at their wedding, they're going to fling every single eligible guy they know at me. Jude has some distant cousins coming up from the US. Theo's got a group of friends from his hometown who are all going to be there. It's as though they want their reception to be some sort of speed dating thing to couple off all the singles in their lives. Jude has watched an unhealthy number of rom-coms, and I think they've distorted his view of reality. It's ridiculous."

"Ouch. Yeah, my friends Gina and Cal did that at their wedding. Gina tried to set me up with her gay co-worker because we're both into dudes. What could make us more compatible?" I roll my eyes. Sometimes I wonder why Gina and I were ever friends in the first place. We never had much in common, other than attending the same grade school and being the outcasts on the cheer squad for being chubby, and in my case, queer.

"Oof, yeah. Tell me about it. I guess that's where it pays to hang out with other queers. They at least realize that having a sexual orientation or gender identity in common isn't enough basis for a relationship." Max chuckles as he gives my back one of those solidarity slap things that dude-bros do. I force a grin, weirdly dysphoric about it.

Normally, I wouldn't mind a hot gay dude thinking of me like a guy. Except today I'm *so* not in guy mode. Too bad. If I could turn on Simon mode to cozy up to Max, I would, but my brain doesn't work like that. I kind of want to disappear into my sodden hoodie and stop having to people.

The drumming rain beating on the umbrella and the pavement seems like it's getting loud enough to swallow me whole.

Max looks puzzled at my sudden withdrawal. He glances away down the road. I stare fixedly at the growing puddle under my feet.

"Oh, looks like our bus is finally coming," Max observes.

This bus pulls up to the curb, and the door opens onto an aisle that's already packed with teenagers to the point of being standing room only. I board, swipe my fare card, and elbow my way toward the back until I find a place to cling to a handhold. Max shakes off his umbrella before following me into the press of people. The crowd does nothing for my prickling anxiety, and I'm glad for the tight squeeze of my compression shirt to ground me. Max ends up standing beside me. A few stops later, when all the teenagers disembark at their school, he slides into the vacated seat next to me.

"Fancy meeting you here," he teases.

"Hey," I return the greeting. We ride in tense silence. Max fidgets.

"Did I say something wrong back there?" he asks.

"Oh. No. You're good," I say, forcing another tight smile.

"Because I get some people aren't cool with being called queer. I mean, I'm good with it, but if you're like, not, I can avoid saying it." Max stumbles over his apology.

"No, I'm queer as fuck, mate. Really, no worries," I say. I hate how snappish my tone is. Today is sliding downhill fast. If I let myself get pulled into the spiral of hyperawareness over how others might perceive me, it won't improve anytime soon. I can't afford to be late and then act short-tempered with all our customers.

"Cool. That's, uh, cool. Yeah. So, did I say something else that upset you?" Max presses.

"I'm just having a crap day, mate. Nothing you could have known. It's fine." And yep, there it is, the part of the conversation where I have to all but apologize for my dysphoria. Fuck my life. Max's face pinches as he tries to figure it out. Sheesh, why do I feel compelled to give him more emotional labor when he's just some random on the bus?

"I did something that upset you, then?" he asks.

"You clapped me on the back. Like 'hey, bro'," I explain, since he isn't dropping it.

Max blinks at me, totally not getting what I mean. "You don't like to be touched?"

"No. I don't like to be touched like I'm a dude." I lay it out, bracing for his reaction.

"Oh," he says, sounding like he still doesn't get it, then the lightbulb goes on. "Ooooh. Shit. I'm sorry." Max bites his lip then blurts, "I should have asked. Or, I mean. Do-over? Hey, I'm your sort-of-neighbor, Max, he/him pronouns. Who're you?"

I can't help a small smile at that. He's obviously trying. "Si. Today is a Si day. Um, I don't like pronouns when I'm in Si mode. Just Si. Some days I'm Simon and he or they are both okay, I'm not particular. Rarely, I'm Simone she/her."

"Cool. Nice to meet you, Si," Max offers me his hand and we shake, quick and casual.

"Nice to meet you too, Max."

"So, you never said if you have weekend plans?" Max asks.

"Nah. If I get through work today without wanting to crawl out of my skin from getting misgendered one way or the other all day long, it'll be a miracle. I'm going to go straight home. Might order something with obscene amounts of cheese for delivery and drown my sorrows in a bath."

"Oh," Max looks taken aback.

"Not drown myself, mate. Just a hot soak. My cousin's place has a killer jacuzzi soaker tub. She's letting me stay on her pull out couch while I save up for a new place."

"Good. That you're not, I mean, that's good. Well. If you wanted to do something else to forget your troubles, I think we're due for a dancing night, after our game. So, like, if you wanted..."

"Are you asking if I want to grind up on you at a club?" I ask. He's endearing, this cute boy who tries so hard, even when he's obviously out of his depth.

"If you're into that." Max shrugs. "It's a queer club. You won't be the only not cis person in the group, let alone the club. Might get my buddies off my back about dating. And Errol and his partner usually give me a ride home, so it's better than taking the night bus, right?"

"I'll think about it. It's been ages since I had a proper night out. Could be fun."

"Cool. Let me give you my number and then you can text if you decide to meet up with us?"

"Sure," I agree. And if nothing else, the conversation takes my mind off the dysphoria. The weight on my chest lessens. I can breathe. Max might have stumbled a bit, but he seems to respect what I told him about being genderfluid. No intrusive questions about my identity or pressing me about the no pronouns thing.

Max gives me his number and his phone pings when I send him a text to make sure he has mine. We talk about random crap for the rest of the ride to downtown. Part of the conversation is about the distance from our little corner of suburbia to the SkyTrain. We commiserate over how much faster our commute would be if we weren't in North Vancouver.

We could take the SeaBus, but I'm not a huge fan of the boat. It's too enclosed, like if I ran into trouble, there's no quick escape. Besides, the wait times can be a hassle during the morning commuter rush. We engage in idle chit chat as we drive over the bridge and through Stanley Park with the bus bypassing most of the traffic.

As we enter downtown, Max asks, "So, if I chat with you again, should I ask if it's a Si day or not?"

"Yeah. That works," I agree with a tentative smile. It's not perfect, but it's the best option I've found for conveying how I'm feeling on any given day.

"Cool," Max grins at me. Not long after that, the bus pulls up to the Granville stop and we exit, along with almost everyone else who's still aboard. Max waves before the bustling crowd separates us. He jogs to catch another bus and I head in the other direction, sending a text to Celine apologizing for being late to start my shift.

It's only a few minutes past my start time, but she opened the shop hours ago to catch any early morning caffeine seekers. I'm supposed to be there for the rush during the morning commute. Still, after my chat with Max, I'm more optimistic that today might turn out alright.

CHAPTER 3

Max

I can't get Si out of my head. It might be silly, but our exchange of stumbling flirtations keeps playing on a loop in my mind. I wish there was a better way to make it up to Si that my actions made Si dysphoric.

This no pronoun thing will require practice. Even in my head, I keep catching myself and having to sub in Si's name instead of the pronouns that want to slip into my thoughts. I intend to put in the effort to make Si feel seen and accepted, though. I assume that's what Si meant by saying no pronouns. Maybe I can ask Theo. Or Pia. Or heck, half my friends here aren't cis. In Toronto, I mostly knew other cis gay dudes, so I've learned a ton just from listening to my new friends. Should I already know this? Probably.

I debate whether to bother anyone, but in the past Theo said he'd prefer I ask him if I have questions rather than assume things. If he isn't up to teaching me something, he can at least point me toward trans friendly resources to learn more. I hesitate a moment longer, battling with the voice at the back of my head that says asking will only make Theo lose respect for me. Drive a wedge between us and make it clear I don't belong. The mental image of Si's expression closing when I screwed up earlier floats to the surface of my thoughts, I want to do better. I open a new message to Theo.

Max: Stupid cis person question incoming, if you've got the spoons.

Theo: Shoot.

Max: If someone says they don't like to use pronouns, does that mean I should just use the person's name instead?

Theo: Pretty much, yeah. You meet someone new, Max?

Max: Ugh. Do not start teasing. This is the reason I didn't ask in the group chat. It's nothing. Just a maybe sort of friend.

Theo: Defensive much, Max? ;) I didn't mean it like that.

Max: Right. My bad. Jude's been asking if I've met anyone I'm into and it can be a bit much sometimes. Sorry. Tone is hard over text... So. Another question for you, oh keeper of all the trans knowledge.

Theo: LOL, am I your identity guru, now? Go ahead.

Max: So. If a person goes by different names and pronouns on different days or whatever, is there a word for that?

Theo: You mean like this person is genderfluid or bi-gender? Rene or Pia might have more insight into that. I'm not even a little non-binary.

Max: It's fine. No big deal. I don't even know if this person wants to talk to me again. If we might become friends, I want to know what to avoid to not be a dysphoria inducing asshole.

Theo: Sounds like you're doing what you can, Max. Let me loop in Pia? They've got a better idea about what sucks to hear when you don't fit in the binary.

Max: Yeah. Okay.

Pia: Theo says you're crushing on a genderfluid person and you don't want to fuck up on pronouns?

Max: There is no crush. Just a new friend. And I already fucked up by assuming that masculine clothing and a touch of stubble meant I was chatting with a dude.

Pia: That's why we don't assume things.

Max: Yeah. I know. I think I fixed it. Just hoping to avoid screwing up again. So. What's shit that people do that makes you think they're just plopping you in a gendered box?

Pia: *snort* Are you kidding right now?

Theo: Bro, seriously? Do you even interact with people?

Max: What?

It didn't seem like an obvious question to me. People are just people, right? I horse around with all my friends. We shove each other when we're joking around. Like I did when I upset Si this morning.

All of us have messed around with Theo's animal hoods when he wears his PJs to dollar donation days. It's not like I treat Pia or Laura any differently than I treat the guys in our group. But I'd said and done stuff that made Si assume things about my perceptions, so I must have missed something.

Pia: So, for funsies, take a day to pay attention to the way people interact. Then you won't have to ask idiotic questions. Obviously this is all broad stereotypes, but, for instance, cishet dudes hold doors for not-dudes and let it slam on other dudes. Or they'll walk down the middle of the sidewalk and expect anyone else to just make space for them. Not-dudes don't do that. Or if we do, it's something we had to decide consciously to claim for ourselves.

Theo: Or like on the bus, pay attention to how people sit. Observe who takes up their entire space. Versus who shrinks to accommodate others. Also, most cishet guys aren't huggy with each other. They might slug another guy in the arm to show affection, but they won't hug without making it a backslapping bro-off to prove their masculinity.

Pia: It's all in how we're told we should behave. Girls should act delicate, be gentle. Boys should be all rough and tumble. Sometimes just having someone hold the door for me feels like they see me as a woman.

Theo: Or like, getting smacked on the back can be hella validating that I'm being accepted as one of the guys.

Pia: A lot of it is subconscious stuff. Like I might not even realize why something makes me dysphoric until later.

Theo: Yes. That. Early on, I sometimes had guys tell me to smile or offer me the seat next to them on a crowded bus. It took me forever to realize it made me all miserable because they acted like they were trying to flirt with a girl.

Max: Okay. I guess that makes sense. What does it mean? As far as day-to-day interactions. Should I just not touch this person?

Pia: Consider starting with asking permission before touching people? Consent matters.

Max: *sigh* I know. Never considered asking about casual touches before. It sounds kind of exhausting to have to second-guess every interaction.

Theo: Worth it not to hurt people, though, babe. It gets easier with time.

Pia: It *is* exhausting. Think how much more exhausting it is for your new friend when reading the signs wrong could mean risking a violent reaction from a stranger.

Max: Do you two worry about violence from strangers?

The thought horrifies me. I don't like the idea of my friends worrying about being hurt for who they are. Not that I've never worried while with a guy in public.

You always hear things. And sure, I've had my share of slurs thrown at me out car windows. I've felt the trepidation over whether it's safe to be out in certain places. But I can always take off any pride merch I'm wearing or drop my date's hand if it seems like our acceptance as a couple is in doubt. It helps that Toronto and Vancouver are LGBTQ2+ friendly cities, I rarely have to worry too much.

This conversation sort of puts Errol's insistence on playing designated driver to the group whenever we go out into a new light. He's always making sure everyone has a safe way to get home. Pia and Laura more so, but the rest of us, too. They take a long time to reply. Which makes me think I'm being hopelessly naïve about the state of the world.

Theo: Not as much now. I mean, we live in a pretty accepting area. I pass reliably unless someone knows enough to piece together what my scars are from, or they figure out why I'm wearing the compression sleeve over my arm. And I'm not hooking up with randoms now that Jude's got me all domesticated, so that reduces my risks, too.

Pia: I'm not visibly trans, so like Theo said, the risk is lower. I worry about Emil more than me. Not to say we've never gotten harassed. Especially when the three of us engage in PDA.

Theo: Yeah, that's a thing that happens.

Max: Why do people suck so much?

Theo: Sucking is one of my favorite things to do with people, Max. ;)

Pia: Keep the sex talk to Jude, lover boy.

Max: Ugh, you're impossible. Thanks for answering my questions. You two rock.

Theo: Anytime.

Pia: Happy to help.

I get back to my work, heart lighter for knowing that my friends have my back. It occurs to me I haven't had friends this close before. Friends I can admit my ignorance to without judgment. All that's missing is someone to go home to at night. I push that thought away. I shouldn't be lonely with all the people who care about me in my life. That makes me sad for Si.

I got the impression Si doesn't have many close connections these days. Not many people to turn to on their bad days. If my friends have a bad day with their dysphoria, they have no shortage of listening ears to vent to about it. On a whim, I pull up the text Si sent me and shoot off a quick message.

Max: Hey! It's me, Max. From the bus. Just wanted to say I hope your day is turning around after the rocky start.

I don't expect an immediate reply, so I tuck away my phone and get back to work. I need to fill out the weekly supply requisition forms. To do that, I have to track down a production coordinator for *Battle Fox* to check whether they really need a hundred new pens. It looks like they marked down 10 boxes when they meant a single box of ten pens. My phone buzzes before I get the reply about the pens.

Si: Better now ;). Rough start of the shift, but the customers are thinning out, so it'll be pretty dead until the lunch rush. How's your day going?

Max: Busy. It's Supply Day Friday. Got to put in the order before noon so everything arrives on Monday. Ugh. I've got a supervisor trying to order some sci-fi thing that doesn't exist in our current reality.

Si: LOL. What did they order?

Max: A power glove. Had to google it. I guess it's a prototype thing, that or a vintage gaming device that's no longer on the market. No way I'm getting one from the office supply store. I *think* they meant a wrist brace?

Si: That's probably a more realistic bet.

Max: Yeah. Now to convince them of that fact. ;P

Si: Good luck with that. I need to go serve a customer. Wish me luck.

Max: Luck.

We text back and forth more throughout the day. I almost suggest meeting up for our lunch break, but I don't know how far away Si's work is from the studio. Then, after lunch, I have to accept delivery of a couple dozen cupcakes for a birthday celebration for one of the *Battle Fox* animators. It's someone on Jude's team.

That means sucking up my desire to avoid Bob the barista. I trudge through the light rain to pick up a sugar-free treat from Sin and Chocolate for Jude. I also need a gluten-free offering for the team lead who has an intolerance.

While I'm there, I'm sorely tempted to grab a latte for myself. Too bad I don't have more hands to carry everything, but at least Bob doesn't seem upset with me when I see him behind the counter. We don't interact, but he isn't giving me a death glare like I'd feared. Paz mentioned he's seeing someone now, so I hope that took the sting out of our awful date.

While I wait for one of Paz's other coworkers to box up my order, I wonder what Si's warm beverage of choice might be. I snap a selfie in front of the bakery display and send it with a caption bemoaning how hard my job is with a winking face.

Ugh. That right there is the sort of thinking that will lead me to yet another hopeless crush. Still. Si looked so cold huddling in that flimsy hoodie this morning. I kind of like the idea of warming up together over a steamy mug. Or something cozy to go with that cheese feast Si mentioned wanting after work. Jude's romantic streak is infecting my brain. I'll have to bitch at him about it tonight. Or when I give him his peanut butter cookies.

I get back to the studio to find the big bakery boxes stacked with cupcakes still stashed where I set them. Piled high on my workstation, they've got plenty of people eyeing the confectionary logos on the lids. I stack the smaller boxes from Sin and Chocolate on top of the others. The *Battle Fox* production supervisor enlists our entire team to distribute the treats. When I return to my desk after sugaring up the artists, I've got a new message waiting on my phone.

Si sent me a return selfie. Framed to show only Si's eyes and forehead with a display of various teas as a backdrop. I wonder if the angle is intentionally cutting off everything below the nose because Si isn't comfortable with being pudgy and shorter than average. People can be assholes about that stuff and it was hard to tell just how big Si is between the bulky hoodie and the slouched posture. I wish there was a socially acceptable way to say "I find your body esthetically pleasing." Better not to comment on how cute the subject of the photo is, I don't want to scare off my bodyshy new friend by coming on too strong. No matter how much I want to feel Si's curves pressed against me while I gaze into the mischief-filled eyes that the selfie captured. Those eyes can say a thousand words and I want to hear them all.

Si: Wish we got baked goods. Just tea here. So much tea. I can make a mean tea latte after working here. Too bad I can't stand to drink the stuff.

Max: More of a coffee person?

Si: More of a cold beverage person.

Max: So iced coffee or iced tea?

Si: Are you a secret caffeine pusher?

Max: More like I can't comprehend how anyone functions without the stuff. You should see the coffee setup at the studio. There's an espresso maker in the break room.

Si: So why were you at a cafe to get your fix?

Max: Sin and Chocolate makes the best fancy drinks. Besides, I suck at operating the thing. It's got as many settings as a spaceship. Plus, my buddy's boyfriend makes all the baked goods there, so we're loyal to the shop.

Si: You're close to your friends, huh?

Max: Yeah. They're great.

And they are. I just sometimes feel like I'm not quite one of them. I know Theo didn't want me to join the group at first, and Errol pitied my inability to make friends here because I can come off as abrasive. Most of them have been friends with each other for years, or dating someone who has been part of the group forever. Sometimes, when they reminisce about the past or refer to old VentureQuest campaigns, I feel like I'm just a tagalong. Someone they tolerate having around.

Si: What time is your thing tonight?

Max: Game? We get done between ten and midnight most weeks, if we're going out after. Why? You thinking of coming out dancing?

Si: Ugh. Not anymore. I don't think I'm up to hanging around town until that late, and I don't fancy an added round-trip on the bus. Another time? When you don't have other plans?

That's more disappointing than I'd have expected,

considering I only officially met Si this morning. If I'm honest, I've been noticing Si at my bus stop for weeks now. Ever since the first time I spotted the cutie with the tousled hair ahead of me in line. Sun-bleached locks bared to a drizzling warm summer rain, as though Si was unaffected by nature's wiles. I hope suggesting a rain check isn't just a polite way of fobbing off my attempts at nurturing a friendship.

Max: I'll hold you to that. ;)

CHAPTER 4

Si

Max's first text after I get to work makes me smile. His offer of friendship seems genuine. Maybe we can even hang out sometime. Probably. Unless he's just being polite. Still, if he were just being polite, he wouldn't have followed through on texting me, right?

I enjoy talking with him. I've noticed he's trying not to gender me, and I like that too. Not that it means anything. Just that he's a decent person. Someone with whom I could strike up a genuine friendship.

Despite my earlier mantra, it's not a great day. Other than those texts to brighten it, my day stinks. I have to strip out of my bulky dripping sweatshirt at work. Its lack leaves me too exposed in only the damp t-shirt I'm wearing underneath. The outline of my compression vest is visible through the wet cotton, just inviting prying eyes and nosy questions.

My vest clings to my skin, too tight now that it's soaked. It constricts my ribs until I have to remove it. The lack of it leaves me hyper aware of my jiggly gut. I'm aware of every passing stranger's eyes searing into me. I wear the vest on Si days because people make me anxious. It's not as bad when I'm not being constantly misgendered in my more binary presentations. The pressure from the shirt eases my nerves around social situations and I pretty much always wear it if I have to leave the house on Si days. I know I'm going to get misgendered and stared at, so it's like walking around with a big hug as a deflector shield.

I still don't love dealing with customers, but I can tolerate them better with the reassuring pressure surrounding me. The ridiculous work apron I'm supposed to wear over my clothing helps some. An added neutral layer buffering me from the public. I cinch it tight at my waist so that the top part billows and obscures my flabby figure, making me an interchangeable retail drone their eyes can skip right over.

"Good morning, si-ma'am?" My first customer of the day can't seem to decide whether to call me sir or ma'am, stumbling between the two before squinting at my name badge. "Si?" they ask.

"That's my name, how can I help you today?" I say with false cheer.

"Oh, let's see, can you recommend a good herbal tea?"

I want to say 'no, I can't,' because that's a freaking

oxymoron. And herbal tea isn't even technically tea. I don't, though. Instead, I ask, "What sort of flavors do you enjoy? We have several popular fruity options."

"Oh, I just want something relaxing for the evening."

"How about chamomile?" I try to mask my frustration with the unhelpful reply.

"Hm, no. Do you have any blends with lavender and mint?"

I get down two blends that each fit half of that description, and a third that's one of our more popular bedtime blends.

The customer doesn't like any of them upon sniffing the tiny samples of the leaves. On a whim, I grab a decaf mint green tea with raspberries that my cousin wanted me to push since the berries aren't a seasonal flavor heading into fall. That gets me the sale, and I soon have the customer rung up and on their way. Not before another awkward fumble over how to gender me that has me gritting my teeth, hunching my shoulders, and wishing to run off and hide.

Lucky for me, the heavy rain keeps foot traffic by the store light. There aren't a ton of gawkers wandering in off the street. We often get folks wandering in to see if they might suddenly have an interest in loose leaf tea, if only I answer all their burning inane questions. Like how it's different from the bagged stuff they can buy at the grocery store. Not that I'm at all bitter about my cousin's business.

Today, most of the customers know what they want,

purchase it, and leave. I deal with the usual rush of morning caffeine seekers. After a lull, the lunchtime crowd comes in to refill their tea supply or grab a drink to bring back to the office during their break. Then we get a handful of folks looking for afternoon pick-me-ups.

A new parent group comes in during the mid-afternoon lull, each with a baby or toddler strapped to their person in carriers. They all order beverages, then sit at the two little bistro tables at the front of the shop and chatter amiably. None of them pay me much attention, preoccupied with their little group, but they're friendly if exhausted looking, and they tip well.

I'm getting the hang of the job and doing better than my usual at not saying the parts you're supposed to keep to yourself in customer service.

Celine seems to agree that today is going better. She gives my shoulder an approving squeeze after the parent group leaves. Then, smiling, she asks me to stay until closing so she can train me to close up on my own soon, if I'm comfortable with it. I am. It still means I'll end my shift way before Max and his buddies are ready to go out, so it doesn't change my plans. But it sort of makes me feel less shitty about mooching off Celine that I'm doing a decent job and making her life a little easier, maybe. At the end of the evening, Celine is her usual chipper self.

"And that's about all," she wraps up her rundown of the closing routine.

"Cool. Seems simple enough. I still say you should get

pastries to sell with the tea. Make it a full on cafe instead of just drinks. Or at least cookies. Something to nibble on," I say. It's not the first time I've suggested adding to the menu. Max's selfie in front of a cupcake display earlier has the idea fixed at the front of my mind.

"You volunteering to bake for me, coz?" Celine shoots back. "You know there isn't room in my budget for a trained pastry chef right now. Let alone a full on kitchen reno. Adding baked goods is in the five-year plan, though. So get your butt trained and working in a proper kitchen for me." She winks to soften the command, but I'm pretty sure she means it.

"We'll see. I cook more often than I bake," I hedge. She's got a point, though. I might cook more, but I prefer baking. The precise recipes relax me.

"You know, if you went back to culinary school like you used to talk about, they'd teach you both," Celine says. As if she has a clue how competitive professional kitchens are. For the scant weeks before I dropped out of school, I'd been miserable in that world. I was lucky that I had my anxiety fueled freak out early enough in the term to get a refund on my tuition. The timing meant I returned my loan money before it started racking up interest.

"And you know why I won't do that," I say, snappish and short-tempered at her poking the old sore spot.

Celine sighs meaningfully, but she knows me well enough to notice I'm at my limits, so she drops it. "Well, you know best," she says in a dubious tone. "If you change your mind, we can work out a deal. I'll help you with tuition on the shop's dime, in exchange for you agreeing to supply us with confections once you graduate. You're good, Si. I want to help you succeed."

"I'll think about it," I agree, with no intention of taking her up on that generous offer. The culinary school I'd briefly enrolled at a year after moving to the city doesn't offer part-time courses for dabblers. Adult ed classes won't make me into a pastry chef, even if Celine hadn't just finished a major renovation that didn't include a kitchen.

If I knew what I was doing, I could rent space to bake elsewhere or even work out of a home kitchen. Supply other shops. That's a pipe dream. The amount of work involved is too daunting to even contemplate right now. Celine gives me a sad smile that says she knows I'm only humoring her. She pulls me into a quick hug.

"I mean it, Si. I'm here for you, if you decide you want to pursue your passions again. We can work out a part-time schedule around your classes. If you sign some papers agreeing to work for the shop once you graduate, I can even have the business help with your tuition."

"Thanks," I say, getting all choked up and emotional from knowing that her concern is genuine. "I should get going so I don't miss the bus, if that's all?"

"That's all. Anyway, I'm spending the night at Harvey's," Celine tells me on my way out the door. "Don't wait up." She winks before we part ways.

I force a smile and a wave. I'm glad that Celine is

happy with her boyfriend. She deserves every happiness. I'm just gun-shy after all my closest friends found love and faded out of my life over the past few years. Doesn't help that I'm living on Celine's couch. The writing is on the wall. If her relationship with Harvey continues to progress, I'm going to be out on my ass when she inevitably moves in with him. That's a problem for another day. Celine will give me enough notice to figure shit out. It will be okay. I will be okay. I snort.

"Today is going to be a good day," I mumble the affirmation under my breath as I head toward my bus stop. That and five bucks might buy me a sandwich.

CHAPTER 5

Max

"**M**ax, right?" The guy who must be Jacob holds out his hand in greeting. I stand to shake, then we both sit. "You look just like the picture Theo sent. How are you?"

"Good," I say. "Ready to demolish some wings. Theo said you were in town for a film festival?"

"That's right. Paul and I have attended to support local indies for several years now. It's too bad he couldn't get the time off this year. It's been great so far. Another two-and-a-half days of viewings, then I'm heading back to Squamish on Sunday night. It's a bummer Theo and his fiancé had to bail at the last minute, I was looking forward to meeting Jude. Never thought I'd see the day Theo settled down with anyone. I guess potential water damage is nothing to sneeze at, though."

I splutter. "Yeah. It's a real shame. Did Theo mention

why he couldn't make it?"

"Something about a pipe bursting in their apartment," Jacob says, frowning at me like I should know that already.

"I'm going to smack him," I fume.

"Why?" Jacob looks taken aback.

"Because Jude texted me to say he has a headache, and that's why they aren't here. He's got it in his head that he's the meddling BFF from some bad nineties rom-com and he needs to find my one true love before his wedding or all is lost. Dollars to donuts there is no burst pipe or illness. They just wanted to set us up on a date." I knew to expect this, but it still stings that even my friends think they need to go to such lengths to revive my dating life. Am I that hopeless? Apparently so.

"You think so?" Jacob asks.

"Yeah." I heave a defeated sigh and run a hand through my hair. "This isn't the first time Jude's pulled a similar stunt. I can't tell whether he thinks this 'oops, we didn't show up and now it's a date!' thing is hilarious or how people are actually supposed to help their friends find romance." I put air quotes around the last word. "I've been dealing with his matchmaking pretty much since they got engaged in August."

"That's rough," Jacob says, shifting in his seat.

"Yeah. Super awkward. Not that I didn't want to meet you! I'm sure you're great," I blather, belatedly realizing I'm coming across like a bit of a jerk. Why do I turn into an asshole the minute I'm on a date? Never fails to bring out the worst in me. "Besides, we're here. Might as well enjoy our evening, right?"

"Right." Jacob hides a smile behind his hand, so maybe I'm not bombing this social interaction too badly?

"Tell me more about the film festival?" I ask. Jacob obliges. I tune him out as he goes on about the films he watched before our meal and the ones he plans to see over the rest of the festival. A server interrupts to take our meal orders. I don't need to look at the menu to know what I want, half price wings and a pint of the cheapest beer on the menu. Since I had Jacob meet me at The Taphouse, I get my work discount on food, so it's an affordable ambush date, at least. And the crowd isn't too rowdy at suppertime on a weekday.

"Sounds like a packed schedule," I say when Jacob runs out of steam.

"Yeah. It's a pity Paul had to cancel on me. The screenings take up most of the time I'm in town, but it's always fun to meet new friends. Theo said you're in his gaming group?"

"Yeah. I was the party's sorcerer."

"Was?" Jacob arches a brow.

"It's complicated? I don't know if you've played with Theo much, but he does a lot of house rules."

Jacob snorts. "Sounds like the same old Theo, then."

"Right. Well, he has me playing a recurring villain."

"A PC villain, huh?" Jacob asks, then takes a swig of

his water.

"Yeah. Maximus hates all dragons, so instead of help-ing the group rescue the dragon prince, I bailed on the party after using them to get rare spell components. Now I'm helping evil mercenaries keep the dragon heir captive, and we're doing magical experiments on them to xenomorph all the dragons into humans. Do you still play?"

"I do. Paul and I have a regular game with a couple other people. You met Paul, right?"

"Yeah, Theo hoped we'd hit it off," I say, taking a sip of my water.

Jacob chuckles. He has a pleasant laugh, rich and heartfelt, but I can't help thinking I like Si's warm smiles better. "Sounds familiar, sort of like how he wants us to hit it off?"

"Yeah. I think so?"

"I still can't get over the idea of Theo getting mar-ried." Jacob shakes his head.

"You'll get it when you see him with Jude," I say. "They're both head over heels. It's sickeningly sweet."

"I'll take your word for it."

Our food arrives, and I take the reprieve from having to make awkward conversation with Jacob. He seems nice enough, but I don't see us staying in touch after to-night. We might see each other at Theo and Jude's wed-ding, but it's not like we're going to strike up a friend-ship from meeting twice. Jacob seems to agree. We both devour our meals without further chitchat. When the server returns to check on us, we settle up the bill, each paying for our own tab. We exchange stilted pleasantries about the food.

"Shall we go?" I suggest. Jacob nods and we weave our way between packed tables and out to the street.

"Well," Jacob says as we stand awkwardly on the sidewalk. "I'm this way." He gestures down the street. I breathe a sigh of relief that my bus is going the opposite direction so we can part ways and not deal with anymore awkwardness.

"Ah, I'm headed back the other way. Guess this is goodbye." I give him a half-hearted wave.

"It was lovely to meet you, but yeah, I've got a packed day tomorrow. We could catch up the next time I'm in town?" Jacob offers.

"Sure," I agree, though I'm fairly certain neither of us will follow through on that. It's just the polite reply. "If not, I'm sure I'll see you at the wedding of the century." I wink and Jacob snorts in amusement. I've had worse dates, so I summon up my manners. "Nice to meet you, Jacob. Enjoy the rest of your visit, I hope you have time to catch up with Jude and Theo while you're in town."

"Me too, thanks for a lovely meal, Max."

"Likewise," I say. Then we part ways. I watch Jacob go, admiring the view. Theo wasn't wrong that Jacob is an attractive guy. There wasn't any spark, though. And his interests sort of bored me over dinner. Not the guy for me. I make my way to the bus stop that will take me home. As I'm waiting for the next bus, I pull out my phone to check my messages.

I consider calling Jude and Theo out on their matchmaking, but I don't want to talk to either of them after the stunt they just pulled. Not only was it super awkward, but I'd wanted to see them, not Jacob. I realize Jude and Theo meant to be helpful. But that isn't how it feels. My ever present self-doubts worm their way into my head with whispers that they did it because I wasn't worth their time, so they dumped me off on someone else.

My conversation with Si catches my eye.

The bus pulls up and I board along with the rest of the straggling evening commuters. At this hour, the bus isn't too crowded and I find a seat near the back. I open Si's chat thread and glance back at the messages we exchanged about me having dinner with friends tonight. I sent my last message right after Jude canceled on me. There's a new unread message waiting.

Si: So, how was the surprise date?

Max: Ugh.

Si: That bad?

Max: Not bad, just frustrated that my friends are meddling.

Si: Want to vent?

Max: Nah, tell me about your day?

Si: Not much to tell. I sold a bunch of tea to indecisive people. Most of them weren't memorable. How was your day?

Max: Could've been worse. Ran around delivering new game scripts I can't discuss and collecting and shredding the old versions for most of the morning. An artist yelled at me about the policy for standing desk requests. They need a doctor's note that they have to stand because we don't have enough desks to accommodate all the requests.

Si: Ugh. Not like you're the one setting the rules.

Max: Right? That's what I told her. She was not impressed. Went full Karen on me. Luckily, Errol's got my back. He took the complaint and got her settled down. He referred her to a walk-in clinic close to the studio that will write a note for back pain.

Si: Errol's in your gaming group, right?

Max: Yeah. He's also my supervisor and the guy who referred me to HR for my position. He's great.

Si: You into him?

Max: Ha! No. I mean, I was for a hot second, but he shot me down. I think he felt bad about it, so that's why he helped me get the job? Worked out for me, got my foot in the door at Eye-On and a great gaming group out of the deal.

Si: If only every failed flirtation turned out to have those sorts of perks, huh?

Max: If every guy who wasn't into me ended up being a new best friend, my social calendar would overflow. Heck, if that were how things worked, I wouldn't mind if Theo and Jude set me up on dates with new guys every night.

Si: LOL. Sign me up, too! I'd have bucket loads more friends in that case.

Max: Same. g2g, catch you in the morning?

The long commute flew while I exchanged texts with Si and browsed my social media between messages. My stop is coming up, so I need to wrap up the conversation.

Si: See you in the morning.

Si sends a kissy face emoji at the end. The sight of it makes my insides all warm and tingly where the cold lonely spot usually resides. This feels like flirting, the buzz of excitement over a new crush. Are we flirting? No, just friends. It's only an emoji, after all.

I tap back a matching emoji, hit send, then pocket my phone before I can overthink it. Other than the gang at work, Si's the first new friend I've made in Vancouver. I will not screw up our tentative bond by bringing an unrequited attraction into the picture. Si has been on my mind since we started chatting. That doesn't have to mean anything.

Once I get home, I plug in my phone and strip out of my work clothing. For all that I didn't have high hopes for tonight, some small part of me wanted the night to end on a different note. I knew Jude and Theo wanted to set me up with Jacob, so I'd worn some of my nice underwear. Just in case. Only my subconscious can say for sure whether I chose the satin and lace because I wanted to get laid or as a way of scaring Jacob away before I got attached.

Now that I'm home, I might as well get something out of spending the day with my junk cradled in the silky dark satin briefs I wore. Each shift in my posture as I sat at my desk came with the delicious thrill of the soft fabric sliding over my sensitive flesh. I don't wear my nice panties enough to get too accustomed to them.

Lounging in my bed and stroking myself through the fabric feels decadent. It only takes a few strokes to have me hard. I stifle a moan with my free hand. My housemate is home and I don't want to give him a performance. But, knowing he could overhear, or even burst in and find me fingering myself only adds to my pleasure. Not that he'd enter my room, but that's not the point. My fantasy is more about the thrill of threatened exposure. That he might see me with my crotch framed in satin and lace.

I speed my stroking, imagining an anonymous lover watching me from across the room. I'd be on display for him. With my head tipped back in pleasure, my hand working my shaft through the soft fabric.

I need more friction, a firmer grasp, but I don't give myself that luxury. Not yet. Instead, I ease my dick free of the waistband, looping it under my balls. That makes my briefs stretch tight across my thighs, digging in enough to make their presence known. Just looking down at my dick straining up from the silky panties makes me horny as fuck.

I tease my fingers through the pre-cum leaking from

my cock. From there, I stroke idly down my length with one hand while I reach further back to press the soft satin against my hole. I press against my opening with a fingertip, tracing my rim with a silky smooth touch. Like I might fuck right through the flimsy barrier.

I indulge in the familiar fantasy of a lover so hot for me he tears through the delicate panties to gain access. He'd shove in hard and deep and fuck me until we were both a sweaty, cum covered mess. The mental imagery has me bucking up into my hand. I want that. I want my imaginary lover to fuck me with my panties forming a tangled ruin, still caging my cock.

There's another fantasy, too. One I've barely let myself believe is possible. A lover who lets me fuck into him with my panties still framing my thighs as I bottom out inside him.

Caught up in my flight of fancy, I tighten my grip. Hard, fast strokes with a little twist at the end of each move drive me toward my climax. I'd take my lover hard and fuck in as deep as I can go. Join our bodies together and empty my balls inside him.

As if most of the guys I've slept with haven't seen my penchant for pretty lingerie as a declaration of my status as a total bottom. I refuse to dwell on the improbability of my fantasy. In my imagination, I can have whatever I want in a lover.

I cant my hips upward, spreading my thighs wider. The lace-trimmed satin pulls tight over my thighs and ass. I move the fingers from my hole to the spot just behind my balls to massage the sensitive nerves there as I thrust into my tight fist. I picture my cum leaking out of my imaginary lover's body. So good.

I can't hold back any longer, my balls tighten and my dick surges with my release, cum hot on my fingers. As waves of pleasure roll over me, my imagination fills in Si's face smiling up at me.

CHAPTER 6

Max

"How was the date with Jacob?" Theo asks, all excited innocence as he intercepts me on my way to my desk first thing Friday. Since his workstation is on the first floor, he must have been lurking to ambush me. That or I'm paranoid and he was visiting with Jude, who sidles up to stand beside him, cradling a steaming mug of tea from the break room in his hands.

"Awkward, considering I thought *we'd* be hanging out? I skipped my video chat with Gramps and Grandad to see you two. Sure, I agreed to meet Jacob, but I wanted to hang out with you guys, too. You realize he lives hours away, right? Not exactly conducive to developing any sort of lasting friendship," I say as I hang up my jacket on the back of my chair. I get that Jude was trying to help, but it stings that he ditched me to stay home with Theo, no matter the intent. That hits me where it hurts, even if Jacob had turned out to be my insta-love soulmate.

"He visits the city plenty. And it's not a terrible drive for weekend visits," Theo points out defensively.

"Theo and I made it work," Jude adds, completely missing my point. On purpose. This is why it's so hard to tell him that I don't want to be set up. He's just so exuberant about it, and I know he cares about me, and it's kind of a way to connect... even if I'm his project.

I roll my eyes. "That's not the same at all. You made it work for like a month and a half while Theo recovered from his surgery. And you'd been practically living together in all but name for months before that. It's different to meet someone long distance."

"Two hours barely counts as long distance. Some people have longer daily commutes than that," Theo insists. He moves aside to let me pull out my chair and get started on my weekly supply requisitions.

He's not completely wrong. Gramps and Grandad loved each other from oceans apart for decades with nothing but letters to sustain them. My morning commute takes almost an hour most days, and there are suburbs further out than North Van. But the distance isn't even the real point. Jacob and I barely had enough to talk about to last us through a casual meal. Besides, I'd have rather spent the evening relaxing with my friends than pressured to feel chemistry that just wasn't there.

"We didn't have that much in common," I explain, hoping they'll pick up the hint.

"You both play tabletop games," Jude points out, sipping his tea.

"And you're into visual media," Theo adds.

"He likes artsy indie films, and I'm more into CGI and animation. And much as I love our game nights, Theo, I'm more into video games than tabletop."

Theo sighs dramatically. "Is that the reason you just wanted to hit stuff at our first session?"

"Pretty much. I figured it would be more like *Baldur's Gate*, where you go around smashing rats to get XP and treasure and level up to smash bigger baddies. Don't get me wrong, I'm having a blast with your game and the group is great. But yeah. I won't date your old high school buddies just because we both play Venture-Quest."

"What about a newer friend?" Theo wheedles, leaning a hip on my desk to keep chatting despite my pointed efforts to show him I'm too busy for this nonsense. "Kevin's back from Montreal. He worked at Eye-On on *Day Dreamer*, then took a contract out east. But he's back to work on *Dreamer 2*."

I groan. "No more surprise dates." There. I said it. Kind of.

"Fine, fine. No more setting you up," Theo agrees, hands raised defensively. "We'll tone it down. Right, Jude?" He nudges his man, tugging him away from my workstation.

"Right. I'm just saying, if you change your mind,

Kevin might join us dancing next week. And if you two happen to hit it off, he's bi and single..." Jude persists.

"Good to know." I sigh, and despite my frustrations, I'm weirdly disappointed that they'd give up on me so easily. The rational part of me realizes it's just respecting my choices, but emotions don't care about rationality.

"Right. Well, don't give up, the right guy for you is out there, Max. You look busy," Jude gives me an easy out from the conversation and I nod, latching on to the excuse.

"Yeah, I need to get the supply order placed by noon."

"We'll leave you to it. Come on, Thee," Jude drags his man away.

"See you at lunch!" Theo winks at me as he goes. We have plans to discuss my role as major supporting villain in tonight's game session. I only hope that talk of VentureQuest will keep Theo from turning our meal into more prying about my love life. Or lack thereof.

I remind myself that my friends mean well. And rack my brain for potential dates I can bring to our next night out to get Jude off my back. Otherwise, I just know I'm going to end up thrown together with this Kevin dude. Relegated to sitting next to him at the end of the table. I'll end up dancing next to him at the club as the other couples all slip away to get funky and leave me behind.

That settles it, I need to bring a buffer. If only all my friends weren't either already dating or in on Jude's machinations. Then, it hits me, I might have one friend I can ask. This might be a terrible idea. Si will probably turn me down, but what do I have to lose? As soon as I consider inviting Si, I know I want a date.

After Theo and Jude's meddling last night and this morning, our game session tonight reminds me why I appreciate my friends. Even if they are over-invested in my love life. It's fun to play with them, especially when everyone gets into the roleplay. Our time together holds my growing loneliness at bay.

Theo and I laid out the basics for tonight at our lunch together. So we're agreed on how to greet the adventuring party when they arrive at the mercenary stronghold. We also mapped out how my character and the NPCs under Theo's control will respond to the most likely scenarios tonight.

For all their planning and preparations, the warrior contingent of the party doesn't fare too well once they get inside the camp. Gui and Errol's characters fail their will saves against my sleep spell, ending Theo's planned combat almost before it starts. After Carl and Zelphod's capture, we take a quick caffeine break before Sin and Chocolate closes for the night. Now that we've returned with our magic brew, Theo is paging through his notes, looking for where we left off. I sip my latte while he searches.

"You two were waxing poetic about xenocide while locking the entire party into your dungeon," Errol reminds Theo as he gestures between Theo and I.

"Right, Max, did you have anything else to add to your villain monolog?"

"Nah, I think I hit all the keynotes before our break." I mark off the highlights on my fingers as I recap in my Maximus voice. "I'm on a noble quest to unmake all the dragons for their wicked ways. We shall force them to live as humans as recompense for all the evil their kind has done to my people in the north. All it took was a clever reimagining of some old spells and liberating the key ingredient from the citadel's gardens. I harvested the fire phlox, or to put it in colloquial terms: Dragon's Bane, at the full moon when the blooms were at their peak potency. At long last, my lifetime of planning is on the brink of coming to fruition. Soon all dragonkind will know human frailty and suffer as my people have suffered under their rule!" I end the recap on a triumphant evil cackle, then go back to my normal voice to say, "That about covers it."

"Alright, you're getting bonus experience for the killer monologuing, we'll hash out details after the session." Theo smirks at me and we bump fists. "Since Maximus got his say, the mercenary captain has a bit to add."

"Hey, wait a minute, don't the dragons only rule in Ethar? Do humans even live in Ethar?" Laura asks.

"A few, and they have all the same rights as dragon citizens thanks to the treaty with Laud, same as the rights of any Laudan dragon free-holders," Theo explains.

"Maximus is from the Northlands, over the forbidden seas. Where dragons have dominion and all other species fall under their rule." I explain the backstory Theo helped me flesh out for my evil sorcerer's motivation. Dragons killed my family and forced me to tend their flocks and fields. I served them until an elderly sorcerer discovered my innate aptitude for magic while he was gathering spell components near my home. Once he saw I had magic, the old man spirited me away for training as his apprentice.

"Ah, okay, that makes more sense. Have you considered enacting your vengeance on the Northlands dragons who are actual dicks to other creatures and leaving our peaceful dragons alone?" Laura suggests.

"It's only a matter of time before the dragons here break their treaty and show their true nature," I insist in my snooty Maximus tone.

"Bardic Persuasion?" Laura asks.

Theo nods. "I'll roll it for you." This is where playing a villain gets dicey. Laura's roll might railroad me into doing something I otherwise wouldn't, but not allowing her to use her abilities on me limits her actions.

Theo balances these situations to best preserve free will for each player. Sometimes that means rolling against each other to see if a spell or attack hits. Other times, Theo rolls for us. It's a delicate balance, but Theo's proven apt at navigating the challenge while ensuring we all have fun.

Theo rolls a few times, hiding the results, then consults his copies of our character sheets. We all watch as he clucks his tongue and shakes his head. "You can try to convince him, Larris," Theo says in a tone that implies she has a slim chance of success. Considering my character's obsession with retribution against all dragons, any effort to change his mind seems doomed to failure, even if Maximus wasn't a player character. It might still be fun to hear what Laura comes up with to convince me.

"The dragons in your homeland might be as wicked as you say. I don't know what your country is like, but here in Ethar dragons and humans have coexisted in peace for generations. Ever since our treaty ended the war. Your attack on the dragon heir jeopardizes that peace. Your vile spell may very well lead to a renewal of the sort of devastating dragon-human enmity we've fought so hard to overcome between Laud and Ethar." She ends the impassioned plea by singing a few bars about being friends, a cantrip that has Theo snorting with laughter.

"Plus two bonus for that on your next skill check, since it won't matter here. Nice song choice." He and Laura fist bump, then Theo turns to me to ask for my verdict, "Maximus?"

"This is but a ploy to serve your dragon over-lords, Your empty words shall never sway me from my course," I say, flapping a hand imperiously toward Laura. "After telling her that, I sweep from the room, unwilling to hear anything else that might convince me to abandon my path when success is within my grasp. There is no room for weakness when fighting reptilian tyranny."

"Are dragons reptiles?" Laura asks. Her brow furrows.

"They're magic dinosaurs with wings, right?" I say flippantly. "Ergo, overgrown lizards."

"Actually," Errol says, pushing his glasses up his nose. "Some dinos are more closely related to birds. Scientists think they might even have had feathers like modern birds. So calling them vicious overgrown magic chickens might be more accurate."

"Fine, so no weakness when fighting avian tyranny either," I stick my tongue out at Errol for being pedantic.

"Sorry." Errol shrugs, not looking very apologetic at all. "Mo has me reading all about dinos. He found out there's a non-binary T-Rex at the Field Museum in the states and he's all about following Sue on social media now."

"Sue is a badass. I'm not even sorry that Emil showed him their twitter feed." Pia grins, nudging Errol's shoulder.

"Anyway, back to the game?" Theo prompts and we all apologize for the tangent. "Maximus leaves the prisoners in their cell. The mercenary leader has a few more choice words about the treaty and dragons for you all, though," Theo declares. He launches into a spiel about the cleverness of the plot to use my new spell against the dragons. I sip my latte from Sin and Chocolate and wait to see how the others respond to their dire situation. What with the entire party locked up, it's not looking great for the heros.

After noting that the mercenary underlings are locking the party up snug in their cell, Theo finishes his villain monolog. None of the adventurers manage an escape. Laura reminds everyone that she sent her dragon companion away to safety in the chaos of her capture. By then, it's time to call it a night. The others confirm that the scared young human huddling in their cell truly is the kidnapped dragon prince, but that's as far as we get. We've got post game plans with people, so there's not much point in drawing things out tonight.

I'm tempted to text Si a last-minute invite to join us. Too bad bussing in from the North Shore at this hour is a pain unless you hit the schedule just right. Besides, we've been texting a lot, and chatting on our morning commute, but that's as far as our fragile new friendship has gone up to now. If I am actually going through with my zany half-formed idea about asking Si to pose as my date, then I should wait and ask in person. Preferably before introducing my new friend and potential fake date to my buddies.

CHAPTER 7

Max

When I don't see the familiar blue-hoodie-clad figure waiting at the bus stop as I turn the corner Monday morning, it's a bigger let down than I'd have expected. It shouldn't be a big deal. But it feels like I've missed out on a special treat I was looking forward to. I trudge the last block to join the waiting line of commuters.

"Yo, Max," someone calls from behind me.

I whirl, breaking into a grin when I see that it's Si. Or, maybe not Si today? The outfit isn't what Si typically wears. No bulky hoodie or baggy pants. Today, Si is decked out in fitted slacks and a button up dress shirt under a blazer, complete with a snazzy bow tie. The ensemble is almost nerdy. It reminds me of something Errol would wear, if the studio were less casual. In comparison, I feel downright underdressed in my faded graphic tee. Not that anyone at the studio minds. The dress code in my industry is super lax. Most of our artists prefer to be comfortable when they work. The studio rolls with their preferences. It's always fun to see the nerdy fandoms, viral memes, and obscure visual puns represented among my coworkers' wardrobes.

"Hey, is today a Simon day?" I ask, part of me cringes, hoping I'm not overstepping by asking in that leading way.

"It is," Simon flashes me a sunny smile. He's cute, and the more fitted clothing shows he is softer around the middle, though he's partially hiding his bulk with a boxy blazer. What I can see of his figure looks perfect for cuddling. Or for the far less PG things I want to do together while I hold him tight.

"How was your weekend?" I ask before I can think too much about why his smile makes my insides feel all gooey like a melted marshmallow. I try not to fixate on getting up close and personal with him; that won't do at all if my plan is going to succeed. Best to keep things friendly.

"Pretty chill," Simon says. "Celine spent most of it with her boyfriend, so I had the place to myself."

"Nice."

"Yeah. It was. Got to take full advantage of the jacuzzi and uncontested control of the television." Simon's voice is as bright and cheery as his smile. Guess he's having a good day today. I can't help noticing his tone sounds a little deeper than when he was presenting as Si.

I bite back a crack about watching porn with the volume up. Sure, that's what I do when my housemate isn't home, but that might be TMI. Somehow, bringing up sex with Simon at our bus stop seems like it's crossing into bro territory. He didn't like the last time I treated him like a bro. Or—Si didn't. Simon might prefer it? And is this a situation where Si and Simon are different people, or just unique ways of expressing who Si is inside? I don't know, and I don't want to upset him by asking. Then again, not asking might be worse. I'm pretty sure my buddies would tell me I should ask Simon about Simon instead of them.

"So, probably a stupid cis person question, but how do you know today is a Simon day?" I ask, glancing around to be sure no one is paying us too much attention. There aren't many other commuters waiting with us. A canoodling couple, too wrapped up in each other to care about us, and a teenager with pods in their ears. None of them so much as glance our way.

"The same way you know you're a cis dude," Simon says with a shrug. "I just know. Today, I feel good about the masc parts of me. Content in the boy box. My skin fits me right. If you call me dude, or bro, that would be okay. Good, even."

"And on Simone days?"

"I spend a lot of time on my makeup and hair," Simon deadpans. "I mean, that's actually true. But it's not just that. It's about connecting with a distinct part of me. Sort of like an internal compass. Most of the time it points toward Si or Simon, but occasionally it swings around and I feel more at home with my feminine side and the masc stuff chafes. It's not that I'm a different person. Just different ways of expressing myself and wanting others to perceive me. I know it can seem hard to wrap your head around. It took me forever to realize that other people have a more static sense of their gender."

"So, you're genderfluid, right?" I check.

"Yeah. And you're cis?" Simon asks.

"Pretty much. I mean, I'm not super into conforming to gender stereotypes or anything, but I'm comfortable being a dude with some traditionally feminine esthetics. My first roommate at university was a total ass because he didn't like that I used: quote 'a girly body wash'. It smelled nice and the guy I was seeing liked it, so I went with what made me happy. Still do," I say, flashing the chipped glittery rainbow polish Errol's son painted onto my nails. That was a couple weeks ago, when we were hanging out at his and Rene's place for video games.

I don't bring up my less than conventional underwear preferences. Few know about that. A couple exes and several hookups I met on dating apps find a man in lace and satin sexy for the occasional fuck, but not good enough to date. That's one of the many reasons I gave up on finding love, for now anyway. If we were together, I'm convinced I could tell Simon about my penchant for panties without fear of judgment. He gets the difference between presentation and identity, probably better than me.

"Nice. Sometimes I add a hint of makeup on my Simon days. So, you're cis and a gender rebel, huh? I can dig that," Simon gives me a flirty little nudge and I grin at him. I like this guy. More than I've liked anyone in a while. Sure, I've all but given up on finding the sort of happily ever after like my friends have, regardless of Jude's conviction my perfect guy is out there. But, if it falls into my lap while I'm waiting for the bus, then who am I to pass up a good thing?

I could ask Simon out. Take a chance on love. It would be so easy, just open my mouth and ask. "Hey, Simon?" I start, then I freeze. What if he says no? Or thinks I've only been friendly because I wanted a date? What if I fuck everything up under the pressure to impress him with fancy dates? It wouldn't be the first time dating killed a connection for me.

Simon watches me expectantly. "Yeah?"

I lick my lips to buy a second to think. Ever since last week, I can't get Si out of my head. I want this, so of course I can't bring myself to ask for it. My stupid brain is frozen, telling me I'm not enough to make him stay. If I can't manage to ask Simon out, maybe I can at least spend more time with him?

"I had a thought," I say.

"Oh, no, was it your first one?" Simon teases me. I stick out my tongue at him.

"Yeah, it really hurt my head. Think I should see someone about that?"

"Can't hurt," Simon says with a twinkle in his eye.

"Just don't google it, or you'll end up convinced you're going to die."

"Oh, man, yeah," I exclaim, then pause as I realize I shouldn't have used that wording. A quick glance at Simon confirms it's okay when he gives me a subtle nod and a, 'go on,' wave of his hand. Right, so on Simon days it's fine. Not so much when he's presenting as Si or Simone. I can handle this, 'not making him feel like shit,' thing. I hope.

I take the conversational shift for the gift that it is. I need more time to think, and I'm kind of distracted now anyway. "So, my gramps is constantly diagnosing himself off Google. He had a rash over the summer. The internet had him convinced it was some rare cancer. He called me up in a video chat to give me and Grandad the bad news at the same time. Turns out it was shingles. He had a miserable couple months, but it wasn't fatal."

"Oh, wow, that must have been upsetting," Simon says.

"Yeah. I mean, it's not the first time he's had that type of scare, so we took it with a grain of salt, but yeah. Grandad was ready to book me a plane ticket home, in case I needed to be there."

"Wait, so, hold up, he told you and your other grandfather? Like are we talking about both of your parents' fathers?" Simon asks, leaning in close for my answer, eyes alight with interest.

"No. Never met my father's family. Grandad is Mom's father. Gramps is his partner. They raised me after my mom bailed on having a kid. I mean, for most of their relationship they pretended to the world they were just good friends, but they've been in love since long before my mom was even born. Served overseas together. Grandad came home, got married and subsequently widowed young. After that, he raised my mom by himself."

"Wow, that must have been unusual back then," Simon says.

"It was. I guess everyone expected him to remarry." I shrug, Grandad didn't talk about my mother much after she left. It hurt us both too much.

"Except he was in love with your gramps, right?" Simon presses.

"Yep. Gramps stayed in the army for his entire career and when he retired he moved in with Grandad. Technically, they told everyone he rented the garage apartment, but damned if he ever slept a night out there alone. I first met him as Grandad's old army buddy. I don't know if they'd intended to tell me they were more. Gramps caught me kissing a boy behind the bleachers after a soccer game when I was twelve, and I froze up, terrified of how he'd react. That's when he told me he was gay, too."

"Aw, that's sweet." Simon nudges my shoulder, offering his comfort and understanding of how formative that early experience of seeing a happy gay couple model a loving relationship was for me. It made me feel safe and loved. Taught me I didn't have to settle for less than someone who could treasure me, quirks and all. Seeing the way they loved each other made it impossible for me to settle for the many guys I've dated who couldn't embrace all of me. My grandfathers tried to give me the confidence to pursue my dreams, no matter how improbable. It's not their fault I seem to have some sort of broken circuit when it comes to keeping people in my life.

"Anyway, it wasn't hard to put it together after that. They share these long swoony looks like something out of a blockbuster romance. Like you said, they're sweet. And they gave me an incredibly supportive home." I'm in danger of getting choked up with missing them.

"Where's home again?" Simon asks, like he can tell I need a subject change.

"Ontario. Just outside Toronto, what about you?"

"BC born and raised," Simon replies. "Small border town. Celine ran off to the big city for university right after high school. I followed her as soon as I was old enough to hop a bus, taking whatever retail jobs I could find. The plan was that I'd save up for school, but it didn't work out. What was that idea you mentioned?" Simon deflects the focus away from his past fast enough that I suspect there's more to the story, but I don't pry.

Oh, shit. This is it. What do I say? I could ask him out and he could say no and that would suck. I could ask him out and he could say yes, and then it wouldn't work, and then it would suck even more. I could not say anything and pitifully ride the bus with him every morning wishing I had the guts to ask him out.

That's when it hits me. The perfect idea. I'd thought of it the first day we met: if Simon came with me to hang out with my friends *like* a date, Jude and Theo wouldn't keep throwing men at me. Without even having to risk making them upset with a confrontation. *And* I could see more of Simon. All the time. He would get to know my awesome friends and I wouldn't be so alone, and neither of us would have to worry about the complexities of actual dating.

Yeah, I can totally see it working. It would be like... all the benefits of dating with none of the stress. Well, maybe not *all* of the benefits of dating, but also none of the drawbacks. Right? I'd get to see more of Simon, which is the biggest benefit.

Now I just have to convince him, if I can figure out what to say. "I was just thinking, we talked about how neither of us is into serious dating at the moment, right?" I hedge.

"Right?" Simon agrees, drawing the word out until it almost sounds like a question.

"It occurred to me, you need people in your social circle. So your big weekend plans include more than a cheese jacuzzi party for one, because dude, that's just sad. And I need to get my buddies off my back about coupling off, preferably before Theo and Jude's big day. So, what if we tell my friends we're seeing each other? I can introduce you to the group without Jude trying to meddle and get us together," I blurt out the half-baked plan before I can overthink it.

"You want to fake date me?" Simon asks, giving me a puzzled look. "For months?"

"Yeah? Only until after Theo and Jude's wedding.

Then we can stage an amicable split," I rush to reassure him. This is not going well. I'm already fucking everything up, and I didn't even ask for a real date. Ugh. Why can't I rewind my mouth? I'd take it all back. *Just a joke. Haha.* Fuck. Too late to go back, now. Confidence. Stick to my plan, such as it were. I can brazen out any situation by exuding enough confidence. Even if that situation is possibly the stupidest idea I've ever had. Simon's got to see right through me, right?

"So, I need more details, mate. Is the wedding here?" he asks. At least he's not shooting me down?

"No. Theo's family lives near Whistler, so they're having the ceremony near there." I suppress the urge to fidget as I answer.

"What about Jude's family?"

"California. They're probably going to have a second celebration in the states so his entire extended family can make it. We joke they just want another big feast with a massive chocolate cake. Theo's got a major sweet tooth."

"Are they hobbits?" Simon jokes.

"Right?! What about second wedfast?" I recite the line from the LOTR movie, altering it to fit the joke. Simon chuckles. "I don't mean to complain, I'm just feeling weird watching my friends pair up, I guess. While I'm happy for them, we're all young and queer. Guess I figured they wouldn't all settle down so soon? I don't want to be the sad token single at their family board game night, but I'm not ready to settle down either."

"That's what happened with my friends, too. We just don't have as much in common as we used to, and we drifted apart." Simon sighs.

"Yeah. On the bright side, we still get together. Their relationships haven't stopped the others from hanging out and doing the stuff we enjoy. Just, it's hard always being the odd guy out, with no other plans and one to flirt with, you know? It's lonely always going home alone," I say, then immediately regret unloading on Simon like that. We're just bus-buddies, I shouldn't expect him to give me the emotional support I've felt lacking in my life.

"Okay. I see what you stand to gain. Explain how this is supposed to benefit me. I mean, your friends might not even like me," Simon asks, sounding skeptical. But the look he's giving me is full of compassion. Like he gets what it's like to be lonely among friends.

"Are you kidding? They'll love you," I say, because Simon is great, of course my friends will like him. Even though it's a totally valid point. I could just introduce Simon to my friends. They'd get along. I know they would. But I want him and this is the only way I can think to get around the fact that I'm a total disaster when it comes to dating. Fake it till you make it, right?

If I ask Simon out for real, this will fizzle before it even starts. It always does. No one ever sticks around for long. Not even my own mother thought I was worth staying for. But if we pretend to date, then I can at least get a taste of what it might be like to have someone other than Grandad and Gramps love me.

"Because I'm a disaster? Or because you have a few trans friends and we're just supposed to bond over not being cis?" Simon arches a skeptical brow.

"Crap, no! That isn't what I meant. You and Paz both sell warm beverages to the caffeine deprived masses, so I figured you'd have that in common. When we were texting, you said you like dancing, but you don't go to the clubs because it's awkward not knowing anyone or being unsure about your reception. My buddies like to go out together. We all watch out for each other. We do dancing at least once a month. The more the merrier. Theo's bringing a friend, too. I was hoping you'd come with us on Friday, regardless."

"Ah, so you want me to fend off another date ambush? Is that all I am to you? A human shield to ward away your one true love?" Simon teases, hands on his hips, he's smiling so I don't think he's actually upset at the notion. Guilt at the idea of using him twists my belly. Except he knows that's what I'm asking for.

"You got me." I spread my arms in defeat as I admit, "I just wanted to use you like a meat shield to fend off all Jude's well-meaning attempts at wing manning me."

"A meat shield, huh? Pretty sure there's a lewd joke in there, just waiting to get sprung." We exchange juvenile smiles at the potty humor. "Okay, I'll bite. If I date you, that means months of hanging out with your closest friends leading up to the wedding. What happens when we fake break up?" Simon asks, arms crossed.

"We'll wait until they get to know you well enough that you're their friend, too. I mean, the wedding isn't until New Year's Eve. That's almost four months away, plenty of time to cozy up to them, if you decide you want to be friends with my friends after meeting them. We'll say we agreed to stay friends, then it won't be weird if you keep hanging out with us after the split."

"How many of your friends' exes hang out with you all?" Simon asks, unconvinced.

"There's Rene. Errol's ex. Or, former ex? The two of them got back together. But Rene met everyone when they were just co-parenting their kid with Errol."

"That sounds complicated," Simon says, mouth quirking toward amused.

"It totally was. I had my doubts when Rene waltzed back into the picture, but Errol seems happy, so all's well that ends well. Anyway. If you'd rather meet them as my new friend, that's fine, too. Or you and I can go out," I offer, my big mouth finally saying the words that would have saved me a giant heaping pile of stupid, if only I'd said them in the first place. Simon doesn't reply right away. I can't take the silence, so I chicken out again. "Like, as friends. Either way, I'd like to know you better. No pressure. It was only a thought I had."

"You'd really want to introduce me as your date?" Simon asks, adjusting his bow tie in an unconvincing attempt at nonchalance. Does that mean he likes the idea? Should I have asked for real? Too late to back-pedal now.

"Sure." I shrug, aiming for casual. I've been enjoying our text chats. Simon is funny, and he gets what it's like to be lonely in a city full of people in a way that my other friends don't seem to worry about. Maybe because they built their own family. One they've welcomed me into with open arms. So why do I still feel so alone most days?

Simon lets me forget that gnawing ache for something more when we chat. If I had any faith in my ability not to crater a relationship before the big day, I might've asked to take him to Jude and Theo's wedding for real. This feels safer, no strings or messy feelings to navigate. No risk he'll run when he sees more of me. No broken hearts on either side. "Or as my boyfriend."

Simon's brow furrows, his smile dims, alerting me I've touched on a sore spot.

"Sorry," I raise my hands in emphasis, then feel like a jerk for making this into a big deal. "Is it the level of commitment implied, or is there a different relationship title you prefer?"

"A little of both? Datemate is what I'd go with, if I had a long-term romantic involvement," Simon says. "Though, on Simon days boyfriend would be okay, too."

"And girlfriend on Simone days?" I check.

"Yeah," Simon's smile goes soft and affectionate. "But datemate works all the time. Same with calling me Si, FYI. As long as you aren't using the nickname to avoid gendering me properly, I'm good with Si all the time."

"Noted." I nod, mulling over the new word in my mind so that I won't forget it—datemate. Si is my datemate. The thought makes me grin.

Simon gives me a soft smile as he says, "Okay, Max, I'll do it."

"You will?" I ask, incredulous. I know the whole scheme is a flimsy pretext, but now that Simon has agreed to go along with it, maybe I can convince him I'm worth sticking around for.

"Sure." Simon nods. "We can fake date to get your buddies off your back. Worst case, they leave you alone for the wedding, and I have Friday plans that involve other human beings for the duration of our little ruse."

I pump my fist in victory. "Perfect! I'll text you the deets about dancing before Friday. You won't regret it!"

Simon's amused smile at my exuberance makes me suspect I might regret not offering him an actual date instead of this charade, though. I might have screwed this all up, big time. I shove those doubts away, like I've learned to shove away every doubt I feel about every-thing. Confidence. Confident people don't second-guess their choices, they just deal with the consequences as they arise.

CHAPTER 8

Simone

F riday, I wake up well before my alarm to a crushing weight on my chest. I take a minute to assess myself and realize why. It's not just the anxiety over my pretend date with Max. The mild euphoria of waking up in a body that fits from top to toes for most of the week as Simon has vanished.

Simone. Today is a Simone day. Sometimes I forget how much these days throw me off balance. It's not that I don't like this part of myself. I resented it for a long time, but girl mode is as much a part of me as Si or Simon. There was a stretch of time where I thought if I could push a magic button and just be cis, whether girl or boy, I'd do it. Now, I don't think I would. Not after experiencing the world as I do by virtue of never fitting neatly inside society's boxes. Over time, I've learned to embrace every side of myself.

It's not that I can't be femme and still be Simon,

the gay boy. This goes deeper than that. It's not about my outward appearance. Though I do wear makeup and dress in traditionally feminine clothing on Simone days, now that I'm in a place where I have the freedom to express myself. This is a bone deep sense of myself. As sure as I know when I'm hungry, or horny, or need to pee, I know I'm operating in girl mode today.

When Celine sees me out of bed early and hitting the makeup hard, she gives me a soft smile. "Simone today?" she asks.

"Yeah," I confirm as I apply mascara.

Celine props her hip on the counter. "You need to borrow anything, girl?"

I perk up, because Celine has the best wardrobe. "Really?"

"Sure, what's the point in having a roomie the same size as me if we can't shop each other's closets, right?"

"I guess so." When we were teenagers, it sometimes chafed that I wasn't taller. Now, I appreciate having a similar height and build to my cousin, even if I'm rounder than her in the middle. "Do you still have that one blouse that makes my chest look fab?"

"The floral one? Think so, let me go check." Celine stands. Before she goes, she hugs me around the shoulders, leaning down to kiss my head. Then she leaves me to my makeup.

I'm nervous to see Max this morning. The two of us

have been bonding ever since our first conversation. We now exchange texts throughout the day. The messages have only gotten more frequent since he cajoled me into being his dance partner and meeting his buddies as a fake datemate.

To be honest, it took very little convincing. I like Max. The only reason I haven't already asked him out for real is that my life is a disaster right now, living on Celine's charity. For a minute, I thought he was going to ask me out for real when he suggested this fake dating plan. The joy swooping in my belly at the thought told me everything I needed to know. I'd have said yes if he asked, despite my trepidations about starting anything serious right now.

In fact, I still don't really understand what's going on. He just looked so nervous for a couple minutes there. I can't untangle how much this fake dating idea was about the thing with his friends setting him up versus the maybe, hopeful possibility that he wanted to ask me out and chickened out at the last minute. I've been getting the sense that he's more nervous around me than most other people, which is kind of endearing.

So, for better or for worse, I said yes. At least this way, I can see how things might develop between us, if my situation were to change.

Max hasn't seen me as Simone, yet. I pray it doesn't ruin everything between us. A cynical part of me wonders if this flip to the girl-side after months fluctuating between Si and Simon is my subconscious trying to eff up a good thing.

It's obvious Max likes me as Simon. We've been sort of flirting on our morning commute and texting throughout the day. He seems into me as Si and Simon. But he's gay, and I'm anxious that seeing me as Simone will change things for him. Make him ghost me. Or worse, want to ghost me but remain stuck with a shared morning commute so he will literally pretend like I'm a ghost he can't see.

I get to the bus stop early, despite fussing over my makeup and styling my hair into a feminine style. An artful application of hair extensions lets me walk out of the apartment with a full messy bun atop my head. The details matter; I prefer not to draw attention. My goal isn't to pass as a cis woman upon closer inspection, and medical transition isn't for me. But most people don't bother giving me a second glance in passing to see beyond their preconceptions that makeup, a dress and long hair equal a woman.

I lean into presenting femme on my Simone days for me, noone else. This is how I feel most authentically myself. Clothes that flatter my body and emphasize a feminine shape, my gaffing underwear to flatten my bulge. My chest is never exactly flat—I'm a bit of a big person—but my bra shapes my chest and modest breast forms fill out my borrowed blouse in more feminine curves. Smooth cheeks and full makeup mean that most strangers see what they expect at a glance, a woman. It's safer that way than on the Si days when I dress femme without going all out like I do on girl days.

Max isn't there yet when I arrive. When he approaches from up the hill, at first his eyes skate right over me. As though he doesn't see me. My heart lurches with the fear that he's going to pretend I'm not there. It stings as I brace for the rejection.

Then Max's gaze lands on me again. His eyes widen with surprised recognition. His face lights into his familiar smile.

"Hey, Simone," he says without missing a beat as he comes to stand beside me at the back of the line.

"Hey, Max," I grin at him, pleased that he noticed the shift and that he doesn't seem put off by it. It sucks that I've lost friendships over having Simone days. Or Si days. But it happens, and it's a relief that Max is treating me like I'm still the same person.

"How's it going?" Max asks.

"Good," I say. It takes a little concentration to keep my voice pitched higher. Softer. That took years of practice and online voice coaching to perfect for when I'm Simone. I still slide into a lower register if I'm not mindful when I'm upset or stressed, but it's second-nature on Simone days now. Something that I slip into along with the flowy garments I favor on girl days. "Not running late for once. Celine's talking about letting me close the shop on my own soon, so that's cool." And it's amazing to be working for a boss who I know will have my back if anyone has a problem with me being myself.

"Nice." Max shifts his bag on his shoulders. "That's good, right? Celine letting you close on your own?"

"Yeah. It's good, means I'm not screwing up the job," I say with a smile.

"Cool. That's cool. We're still on for dancing tonight?" Max checks.

"Yeah. Unless there's a reason you'd want to cancel?" I ask, silently praying that he won't back out on me at the last minute. The bus pulls up to the curb and the line shuffles impatiently forward.

"No, not at all," Max assures me. We make our way onto the crowded bus. "You're you no matter how you're dressed, right?"

Max and I grab handholds midway down the aisle, standing amongst the crowd of school kids taking all the seats.

"Right," I agree, trying not to wince at the acknowledgment that he's not unaffected by my changed appearance. Our conversation lapses until we get to the school and slide into the vacant seats after the students leave. I cross my ankles, focused on my posture because it's been a while since I wore a skirt and I don't want to flash anyone.

It's not that I wish I was different, but tonight would be simpler if I could just choose to be Simon. Or Si. That isn't how my brain works, though. Most of the time, my internal sense of self doesn't shift much during the day. It happens, but it's rare.

A sexy date, even one that's only meant to get Max's buddies off his back, is unlikely to make my brain flip into Simon mode. If anything, it's more likely to make me feel more firmly like Simone. Experience dictates that my internal sense of self will stick in girl mode until I either scare Max off, or convince myself that just being Simone isn't a deal-breaker. My subconscious is a jerk like that.

I'd be lying if I said this side of me hasn't driven away potential love interests in the past. Fuck, do I want Max to be different. Someone who can see that I'm still me, no matter how I'm presenting. That Si, Simon, and Simone are all parts of me, but none of those parts define me on their own. It's been a while since I had a date of any kind, I'm looking forward to tonight, even if it isn't real.

"Great. I'll text you with the address where to meet us once we settle on where we're eating."

"Dinner and dancing?" I bat my mascara-enhanced lashes at him and his cheeks darken in a flush. "You know how to spoil a girl." I wink at him.

"Anything for my pretend datemate," Max teases.

"You're sure you want to introduce me as your date?" I fret.

"Unless you changed your mind? You can still come as my new friend. I meant it when I said no pressure."

"No. It's fine. I want to help you out. That's what friends do, right?" I touch my fingertips to his forearm. The delicate gesture isn't one I'd use as Si or Simon. Outside of girl mode, I'd go for a heartier back-slap or conspiratorial elbow nudge. It's the minor details I've picked up from years of studying people and being steeped in the strict gender binary of our culture. The way Gina and Celine interact with their gal pals versus how the guys I know rough each other up to show affection. Thousands of subtle cues that constantly surround us. A lot of it has become subconscious over the years. Sometimes I change how I move intentionally to match how I want people to perceive me, even if I think it's stupid to gender affection. But today it feels right. I like being a bit delicate and leaning into that body language.

"Yeah, pretending to be your new bus-buddy's fake date is right up there in the friend code next to not sleeping with your BFF's ex," Max jokes weakly.

"Bus-buddy code," I wink at him. "So, how are we telling them we met and started dating?"

"I planned on sticking with the truth. Since I already mentioned meeting you to a few of them. I figure, they might put two and two together. After I asked them how not to be an asshole to my new genderfluid friend a couple weeks ago, and now I'm introducing them to my new genderfluid datemate tonight."

"That's fine, but we need to work out more details. We can say we met at the bus stop when you saved me from showing up to work looking like a drowned rat, but that only goes so far. Which of us asked the other out? What was our first date? How long have we been together?"

"Hm, good point," Max rubs his jaw, then shoots me a sly smile. "Should we meet up for lunch, to go over our story?"

The way he's looking at me almost makes me forget this is all fake. I remind myself that we're just friends.

"Good idea. You're near Granville, right? There's a diner I like that should be midway between us." I at least know he hops a second bus down Granville after this one.

"Hmm, where is your cousin's shop?" Max asks.

"It's a few blocks down Granville from our bus stop. Are you far from there?" I reply.

"Hm, I can hop a bus and meet you there, the walk will wake me up after spending the morning updating spreadsheets that are more boring than drying paint."

"That's fair, we can walk together, more time to hash out our story of a whirlwind romance." I grin as I brush my fingers over his arm again. If we're pretending to date for his friends, I might as well give in to the urge to touch him as though we're together.

I want to make the most of whatever companionship Max is offering. Agreeing to all this might seem desperate, but I need friends more than a relationship. It makes the most sense to keep to the bounds of our deal. No matter how many second, third, and even fourth thoughts I'm already having about the arrangement.

"Yep." Max pats the back of my hand where I'm resting it on his forearm. The casual touch sends a zing of warmth through me. The bus brakes abruptly, jostling us together. I have to pull my hand away from him to brace against the seat back in front of us. Max flushes. "So, I'll text when I know what my day looks like as far as when I'll have time for lunch. We can get our stories straight. For veracity."

"Cool. It's a fake date," I wink at him.

Part of me wonders what an actual date with Max would be like, but the entire point of this charade is to make more friends. If I allow my emotions to complicate my friendship with Max, it will only end in disaster. If we blur the lines, then I might come out of this experiment without even Max's newfound friendship, let alone the big accepting social circle he wants to introduce me to tonight. That would defeat the entire purpose of playing along with this ruse.

CHAPTER 9

Max

I have to do a delivery run around noon. Errol needs me to pick up the signed contracts from an audio recording studio for Day Dreamer 2 today. The higher ups pulled a last-minute casting change on a couple of minor characters. So that's turning into a logistical pain in my ass. It means I'm heading toward Simone's part of downtown around noon, though.

I tell Errol I'm taking my lunch while I'm out. He gives me his distracted permission, suggesting I eat my lunch first, since the contracts contain confidential information. Poor guy looks exhausted these days, apparently his kid hasn't been sleeping well and getting him out the door to school has been a battle. I don't envy him that, though I'd love to have a few sleepless nights of my own, if for different reasons. Simone reasons.

Simone says it's okay to use Si to refer to her in the

general sense and as an occasional nickname. Or if I don't know what mode she's in and she isn't there to ask. Otherwise, she asked me to use the name and pronouns that match whichever gender mode she's operating in that day. Like, telling my friends that my new datemate, Si, enjoys dancing is fine, but tonight I should introduce her as Simone, since it's a girl day.

Seeing Simone for the first time jarred me this morning. She's pretty. That's no surprise, since she's pretty no matter how she's presenting. I just didn't know whether I'd still feel attracted to her as a girl. Except, seeing her made me realize that it's not just how she looks that I'm drawn to. It's the way she glowered so fiercely at the bus after getting splashed by it the first day we talked. The muttered affirmations that spilled from her lips, more like a curse than a mantra. The snarky texts we've been exchanging about work throughout our day cemented our friendship.

Then I saw her in boy mode, wearing snazzy bow ties, a new one each morning this week. That made my dick pay attention. Simone is hot. That doesn't change, no matter the packaging. Does finding her sexy in girl mode make me homoflexible or bi? Or am I still gay and she's my exception? I don't know if my attraction to Simone has to mean anything. She's hot, I like the way she moves in girl mode, the sway of her hips more pronounced. She doesn't hide behind boxy blazers or baggy hoodies and that confidence in her body is hot as fuck. That doesn't change who I am. She's not the first girl I've admired, only the first one I've actually wanted to bang. Simone's happiness matters more to me than my labels, so I don't dwell on the revelation.

The person I'm getting to know clicks with me on a level I haven't experienced since leaving Ontario for better job prospects out west over a year ago. It seems fortuitous that we met not long after my contract got extended, giving me breathing room to worry about stuff outside of work.

Eye-On is only the latest in a string of short-term contracts I've landed, hoping to gain a foothold in the video game industry. Making games is a dream come true. The fact Errol took me under his wing means I've had someone in my corner when I get tasks I don't know how to perform dumped in my lap.

Thanks to his help, my original six-month contract at Eye-On got extended for another year. He's even dropped hints I might work my way up the ladder to a production coordinator position, if I stick with it. So I keep following his tips for ways to make myself an invaluable part of the team, taking on extra tasks as needed. I've become the go-to guy for the rest of the production team on *Dreamer* and *Battle Fox* alike. It's a good gig, and the year contract extension I signed over the summer is a relief. It makes this all feel more permanent. Like I have space to put down roots and consider starting something real with someone like Simone.

Simone texts me the address where she works when I let her know I'm heading over to meet her for our pre first fake date meeting.

The tea shop is cute. It's smaller than Sin and Chocolate and more closely resembles a retail space than a place where you'd visit to get a warm drink on a chilly day. There are kettles and milk steamers behind the long counter. Simone's told me all about the barista side of the job.

When I walk through the door, Simone turns at the sound of the chime and beams at me. Her smile lights up her face, and I can't help returning it.

"Hey, Simone," I greet her, approaching the counter. "Think you can help me find the one mythical tea that will convince me to forsake my morning java?" I wink broadly. Vague tea requests are Simone's top complaint about the customers here, so I hope she realizes I don't actually mean the question.

Simone rolls her eyes at me. She blows her wispy bangs, which she somehow straightened out of their usual curls, out of her face and says, "I don't think I can convert you, mate. Based only on the evidence of your Insta coffee selfies, you're hooked beyond redemption."

"That's true," I agree sheepishly, though my heart gives a funny little lurch that she checked out my social media. "Have you been internet stalking me?" I ask, pitching my voice to make it a flirt and not an accusation.

"I plead the fifth," Simone says airily.

"You watch too much US television. We don't have the fifth amendment," I point out.

"Still don't have to incriminate myself," Simone retorts, sticking her tongue out at me.

"True enough." I chuckle and Simone snorts. "So are you ready for lunch?"

"I will be as soon as my coworker gets back. Should be any minute now. I can get you a latte or something while you wait?"

"Sure. I never refuse a caffeine fix, even if it is from an inferior plant source," I joke.

"You caffeine addicts are all the same. Any requests or shall I surprise your taste buds?"

"Surprise me."

Simone looks me over appraisingly, then turns to the latte setup at the end of the counter to fix my drink. "You look like you need a bit of sweet. One crème caramel mate latte, with extra caramel, coming right up." She flashes me a flirty smile over her shoulder and gets to work.

The finished drink she slides to me smells good. Earthy and sweet. It tastes different from what I'm used to, but the frothed milk and the sweet caramel drizzle on top make for a heavenly first sip. The strong earthy taste of the tea isn't half bad.

"Well?" Simone leans over the counter, watching me expectantly as I take my first sip.

"It's not bad," I answer, mirroring her posture and leaning against the counter to get closer. The move puts us scant inches apart and the impulse to close the distance tugs at me. Before I can act on it, the door chimes. Simone straightens to her full height and I back off, too.

"Sorry, the ramen place made me wait ages for a seat. You can take an extra five minutes too, Si," a breathless voice rambles from the doorway. Simone's smile deflates slightly at the nickname.

"Not a problem, Hob," Simone replies to her coworker. "I'll be back around one thirty, then. Ready, Max?"

"Sure," I agree.

"Here." Simone hands me a lid for my drink and I press the plastic into place before following her out of the tea shop. When the door closes behind us, she rolls her eyes. "He's a pain. More like an extra fifteen minutes," she grumbles. "Diner still sounds alright?"

"Sure, I'm always on board with tasty and cheap. What's your favorite thing on the menu?"

"They have great shakes. Or if you'd rather do something else we can grab burritos? There's a tasty little place near Gastown that makes the best fish ones. Although they don't have much seating; it's a literal hole in the wall."

"That might not be ideal. Fish burritos another day? Lead the way to the diner?" I say.

Simone takes my hand and heads along the busy sidewalks to our lunchtime destination. I almost trip over my own feet at the jolt of connection. She's touching me like we're on a real date. And I like it. A lot. Why the hell didn't I ask for a real date? I could open up my mouth and fix it, right now, just call off the whole fake thing and ask if we can do this for real. The words won't come. Saying them might screw this up, I'll seem indecisive. Fickle. Keeping silent guarantees I get four months of holding her hand and going on dates, even if they aren't real. I can pretend. I squeeze her hand a little tighter. In response, she shoots me a soft smile, brushing a stray lock of hair off her face.

When we get to the diner, we seat ourselves. I browse the laminated menu, but Simone already seems to know what she wants. When a server comes to greet us, Simone orders her entire meal, so I panic and order a burger and coffee. As though I knew what I wanted all along.

"You come here often?" I ask, amused that she didn't so much as glance at the options before ordering.

"Like I said, they make cheap, tasty food." Simone shrugs.

"No judgment. There's a great little diner near the studio where we go for lunch a lot. They do all day breakfast, classic diner food, and various Chinese dishes. It's way tastier than it sounds. No milkshakes, though."

"All the more reason to order one."

"Pro tip, I think when you ply someone with drinks, you're supposed to use the alcoholic kind," I joke. Since I chugged the latte that she made for me on the way here, I don't need any more beverages. Too bad I'm a sucker for unending diner coffee. "Also, I'm a fiend for bottomless coffee."

"Duly noted," Simone says with a coy smile.

The server returns with Simone's pink milkshake and a pot to fill my mug with coffee. I stir the accompanying packets of sugar and creamer into my cup. And freeze when I catch sight of Simone's lips wrapped around the straw as her cheeks hollow and her eyes flutter with delight at the taste of strawberries. I can't quite tell if she intends for her seductive expression to entice me or if she's just that into her milkshake. Then our eyes meet and she looks all flustered and I'm pretty sure it was pure enjoyment. I sip my coffee to cover for my overt ogling.

"So, we need to get our story straight, right?" Simone asks, swirling the straw through her thick drink.

"Right. The closer we stick to the truth, the easier. We should tell them we met at the bus stop, got to talking and hit it off."

"Sounds good. You saved me from the rain, then invited me out for drinks?"

"Sure. My buddies usually hit up The Taphouse, because we get a discount through work, but let's say we met Saturday night by the quay? We had a video game day at Gui's for most of the afternoon, but I left after pizza, so they'll believe I had a date afterward."

"Okay, cool. So we got drinks and walked along the waterfront?" Simone pokes her straw into the milkshake.

"Yeah. Sounds good," I agree.

"Right, so first date questions, go," Simone gestures at me.

"Cats or dogs?" I ask.

"Never had a pet before. I'd be clueless with a fuzzy friend. I'd say fish, but I'd forget to feed them. You?"

"Cats. We had the sweetest old tom when I was in high school, I loved when he'd sleep on my chest, purring like an engine. It was soothing."

"Nice, what's his name?"

"Ace, it was a joke between my grandfathers."

"Cool. Ace the kitty. Would you ever adopt a cat of your own?"

"I might, if I move somewhere that allows it. Then you can learn to make fuzzy friends."

"I'll hold you to that. Favorite color?" Simone asks.

"Blue," I reply.

"Yellow, like sunshine and happiness," Simone teases.

"Biggest pet peeve?" I ask. Simone quirks a brow at me and I roll my eyes. "Not work related. Crotchety customers who expect you to read their minds about their tea preferences don't count. What bugs you in daily life?"

"Still the same answer," Simone supplies, her nose wrinkled in distaste. "I despise having to guess what people are thinking. Especially if there's a non-zero chance they're thinking I'm a freak and they don't want me breathing their air."

I cringe at that answer, because there's a level where I can relate. There are times and places where I don't feel safe as a gay man. But the matter-of-fact way Simone talks about this reminds me of my chat with Pia and Theo. How real the threat of violence is for a trans woman, or someone perceived to be one.

I don't want to contemplate anyone hurting her. I reach for her hand and Simone gives me a sad smile. She lets me squeeze her fingers in a reassuring grip, I hope the touch conveys that I care about her. Our eyes meet, and I fancy that she can read how upset I am and that it's because the thought of her hurt claws at something vital in my guts. I could fall for her, and the steady way she holds my gaze gives me hope maybe she could feel something for me too. Underneath the silly game I've got us playing to protect my heart.

"Sorry, I took that to a sort of heavy place for a first date, huh? Do-over. I also get pissy about the great toilet seat debate. Pun intended. Like, at some point, everyone has to sit for number two, and no one wants to fall in, so just shut the flipping lid. Besides, leaving the seat up when you flush is gross, no one wants to bathe in your aerosolized effluvia."

I smile at her word choice, forcing myself not to dwell on her other answer. She's cute when she gets fired up about silly stuff like the toilet seat, or the rain. "Noted, if I have you over, I'll remember to leave the seat down on your throne, your ladyship."

"See that you do," Simone says haughtily, adding, "and that's when, not if. We're fake-dating, I'll be gracing your throne." She gives me a broad wink. "Speaking of which, we should check out each other's digs, so we know what color the sheets are."

"Blue. Favorite color and all," I offer with a wink of my own.

"Mine are white, and they're on the pullout couch in Celine's living room, so we're pretend fucking at yours, hope that works for you?"

"Sure, I've got a housemate, but we just share a crash pad. No issues with bringing someone home. Other than Errol seeing the dude in passing while dropping me off, my friends haven't even met him. On that note, let's say we've been on a second dinner date since that first one? Tuesday, say? And we text daily?"

"Sure. What else would a real datemate know about you, Max?"

"I'm a runner at work. They sometimes joke that I'm their coffee peon, fetching crap for people or going on coffee runs when they're too busy to get their own. Oh, right, most of the people you'll be meeting tonight work with me at Eye-On Games. The studio is pretty chill about dress code and junk, but I meet with vendors and stuff so I try not to go total loungewear."

"What about your friends?"

"I've told you about Errol, right?"

"Yeah, he's the one who got you the job and invited

you to the gaming group after you hit on him at a party, right?"

"More or less." Max nods. "He's my supervisor, and he's with Rene. They have a son named Mo. Rene used to play pro hockey for the Canadiennes. Now they coach kids. Then there's Theo and Jude, the guys who are getting married. Jude animates, and he's Gui's little brother. Theo does lighting, and he's our game master when we play VentureQuest. Gui is an animation supervisor, and his boyfriend is Paz. He's the baker at Sin and Chocolate I mentioned, he makes the best brownies. Pia does character design, she's an amazing artist. They're in a polycule with two guys, Emil and Gregor.

"The three of them trade off staying home with their baby when we go out like this, so you'll meet either Emil or Gregor tonight, probably Emil? The baby's name is Rain, and they're using they/them pronouns until the kid can pick their own. And last, but not least, Laura. She makes the 3D models for characters and game assets. She and Paz's cousin, Alice, have been flirting for ages. I'm pretty sure they're working toward getting together? The unresolved sexual tension between them has been off the charts since Al broke up with her girlfriend over the summer. They flirt at every opportunity, but Laura is being tight-lipped about whether there's more to it than that. Hm, what else?"

"That's quite a group. I've pretty much just got Celine, these days. My bestie from high school was Gina. We shared a crappy apartment while she was at university and I was working shitty retail jobs. We've drifted apart since she graduated and got married last spring. I paid the rent alone through most of the summer, but the lease ended in late July. My old landlord demanded more rent, forcing me to move. Celine offered to let me crash with her. But anyway, tell me more about you."

"Yeah, this might overstep, but Gina sounds like a jerk for dropping you like that."

Simone shrugs. "It is what it is. Can't make someone be your friend, right? Now, spill your secrets for me, all the juicy deets I should know about my boyfriend."

"Right. Well, you know me, I'm sort of trying to figure out my place here? I wanted to be a play tester or a pro-gamer, when I grew up. Turns out, I don't have the skills for that. So I figured the next best thing to playing video games for a living is making them."

"Sounds reasonable." Simone flips her hair.

"Yeah. Well, it's a hard industry to get started in, all about who you know. Like I said, I kind of got the job through Errol after I tried to buy him a drink."

"You mentioned he turned down a date. Did you fuck your way into your job?" Simone teases without a hint of judgment, eyes twinkling with delight at the scandalous implications.

"No!" I wave my hands in front of me in denial. That wasn't how the night progressed. Much to my chagrin at the time; Errol's a hottie. "He declined my offer of drinks, but we chatted. Errol laughed when I told him I wanted to make video games, but I had a gig with a TV studio as a production assistant. I got all huffy, thinking he was making fun. He apologized and said it was just a funny coincidence, since he worked at Eye-On.

He mentioned the studio was hiring a new production assistant. We talked games and the industry for hours and by the end of the night, he offered to put in a word for me. I figured he was just tipsy, or being polite. But he followed through on that offer. Worked out for me, I needed a friend way more than a one-night stand and I love the job. The studio is a fantastic workplace. My co-workers are entertaining. They come from all over the world. Gui and Jude are from the US. HR handles getting our new hires work visas, since artists and programmers are skilled workers. It's a chill vibe."

"So, you love your work?"

"Yeah. I do."

"What games do you folks make again?"

"*Battle Fox* and *Day Dreamer* are the most recent two. We've got *Dreamer 2* and *BF2* in the works now. I didn't work on any of the older titles and I signed an NDA not to discuss any of the newer projects they haven't announced to the public yet." I wink. That last bit is totally a line that I've used to pull at the clubs with solid success. Some guys are into the intrigue of me knowing something about my work that I can't share. Especially if they're gamers. Not that Simone is a guy. Or someone I want to pull for a one and done encounter.

Simone reaches across the table and her fingers brush the back of my hand. I turn the palm up to hold hands with her.

"Sounds way cooler than my crap job," she says ruefully.

"What's your dream job?" I ask.

"If it was just about picking something I enjoy doing, then something in the culinary field. Baking is my favorite. I love pleasing people's taste buds. My current job working for Celine is the best I've had in a while, so no complaints."

"For what it's worth, you make a hell of a latte, almost good enough to make me drink tea on the regular," I say.

"Aw, shucks, thanks, mate." Simone tilts her head demurely. "I had you pegged as one who likes it a little on the sweeter side. Coffee drinkers often prefer the stronger black teas." She winks at me.

Oh hell, I'd like her to peg me a different way. I bite back a flirty reply to that effect. That's overstepping if this is just a show for my friends. I lick my lips. Before I can work up to a more suitable reply, our server saves me from needing to respond by delivering our meals, then leaving us to our food.

Simone dips a fry into her milkshake and eats it in delicate bites. I can't tear my eyes away from her lips until she dabs self-consciously at her mouth with a napkin.

"Did I get something on my face?" she asks.

"No. It's nothing." I say.

"You sure?" She touches her lips, like there might be a stray bit of food on her face.

"Yeah." Reaching for a subject change, I ask, "So, what

else do we need to figure out for tonight?"

"Are we fucking or taking things slow?"

"Um, probably fucking?" I say, because I've yet to be in a relationship that didn't start with chemistry in bed. Or up against a wall. Or in the back of a car. Honestly, I can't imagine being with someone I'm as attracted to as Simone, and not fucking that person every chance I get, it's just not me.

Maybe that's part of my problem getting guys to stick around. Picking dates based on sexual chemistry leaves me bored if I have to spend time interacting with them about topics outside my areas of interest. Yet, sleeping with people I connect with requires risking those fragile early bonds of friendship. That's another reason I didn't pursue Jude once I realized we could be friends. Instead, I did what I could to nudge Theo into realizing he was being an idiot. Guess it's only fair they want to meddle in my love life right back.

"So, we should touch, then. It's still early days, but we're in that besotted, can't get enough of each other stage, right? You going to be alright grinding up on me all night long?" Simone asks. She doesn't meet my eyes, staring at the milkshake as she jabs another fry into it. Touching her sounds more than alright, but I wonder if it's something she wants?

"That sounds perfect," I blurt. Simone freezes, the fry halfway to her mouth. She starts to smile, until a glob of milkshake splats into her lap making her yelp instead. We both cringe.

"Fuck that's cold," she complains as she swabs at the

mess with a napkin. I hand her another, but she's scowling at her lap. "Damn, I'm going to have to change, don't need questionable stains on my lap when I meet your friends."

"It'll be fine," I say. The trip back to the North Shore is a pain. A round-trip to change after work during the evening rush will make her miss our dinner plans.

"No, it's alright, I'll see if Celine can bring me a different skirt from home when she comes in for the closing shift. Mind if I call her real quick to catch her before she leaves?"

"Go ahead."

"Thanks, I'll just be a minute." Simone smiles tightly at me. She sets her soiled napkin on the table and slides out of the booth to go place her phone call outside the diner.

I devour my burger, decent, and pick at my fries, cold, while I await her return. My phone buzzes with a text from Errol, reminding me I need to be back with the signed contracts before the two-thirty production meeting. I text him back that I'm just finishing my food then heading to the audio place. He sends back a thumbs up emoji. As I put away my phone, Simone slides back into the booth across from me.

"Sorry about that." She shoots me an apologetic smile and tucks a stray lock of hair behind her ear.

"All set?" I ask.

"Yeah." Simone waves away my concern. "She's going to bring me a change of clothes. I get out of work at five.

What about you?"

"Also five," I say. "We usually do dinner before dancing. I bet it'll be at The Taphouse. Like I said, we get a discount. I can cover your food, since I invited you, plus, discount card."

"That works. I can cover the first round at the club."

"Sounds good. Oh, what's your drink?"

"Anything with vodka." She swirls her straw through her shake. "Yours?"

"House beer," I say with a rueful smile. "Sort of on a budget. The entry level to living the dream doesn't exactly rake in the cash."

Simone rolls her eyes and presses her fingers to my forearm. The soft brush is oddly intimate, and her touch sends a thrill through my body. Her hand on mine offers more gentleness than I'm used to from a date. Or anyone really. "What's your favorite, if you weren't on a budget?"

"Whiskey?" I say after a moment to soak in the memories it evokes. "The kind you sip. All smoke and fire and earthy undertones. Reminds me of my gramps."

"Oh, yeah?" Simone asks, picking up that there's more to it than a simple drink preference.

"Yeah." I nod.

"You're still really close with them, huh?" Simone asks, sipping her drink.

"We are, yeah," I say, stirring up the familiar ache

of missing the men who raised me. They sent me out west with their blessings and enough of a cushion in my bank account to help me get established here. I should call them later this afternoon. We try to talk a few times a week, but it's been a few days. "When my mom dumped me off on them to go chase after the next man she thought could fix her life, they took me in, I was eleven. I was eighteen when we got the call she was dead. Gramps poured me and Grandad each a measure of his best whiskey and we toasted to her memory. The person she could have been in our lives. It was the first time I felt like I was their equal, like I was a man they were proud to have raised, if that makes sense?"

"Sure. A rite of passage. And a reminder of family and love."

"Yeah. Geez, I didn't mean to unload on you like that. Sorry. I don't talk about her much. All my friends know about my family is that Gramps and Grandad raised me."

"Still, good to know. Wouldn't want to ask about your mom in front of them and make things weird. Do you have any other close family?"

"Nope. Just them. Guess I had a step-father I never met, technically, but no actual family. What about you?"

"There's Celine, my cousin who I live with. Her folks are decent. We talk every so often. My folks figured parenting me was over the minute I graduated." Simone rolls her eyes. "I think they'd be equally disinterested in me regardless of the gender fluidity. They're not much more interested in my little sister's life than they were in mine. She's still a kid, though. Turns thirteen this year."

"I'm sorry."

"It is what it is." Simone shrugs off my concern. "Anyway, they call on my birthday and around Christmas to check in with me, but that's about it. They aren't the sort of awful that would kick me to the curb just because I wasn't the perfect cishet child they dreamed of having. But they aren't about to march beside me at a pride parade either. Mom begged me to keep my gender feels to myself, or just be Simone in private, but it came from a place of worry over my safety, I think. That, plus not understanding I can't take being Simone off like a dress. Sure, I can try to hide who I am, but it makes my skin crawl when I can't present in a way that matches who I am. Dysphoria is a real head fuck. It is what it is... We aren't close, but there's no real animosity, either."

"Sounds pretty shit to me," I grumble, defensive of Simone. She deserves better than indifference from her family.

"No sense being bitter about shit I can't change. I have Celine, and her parents are supportive, that's enough." Simone gives a gallic shrug, as if to say 'what can you do?'

"Well, you've got me now, too," I declare without thinking it through.

Simone chuckles. "You have a bit of a hero complex, huh? I don't need saving, Max."

I squirm in my seat because she's not wrong. Part of me does want to fix things for Simone. But a bigger part wants to be the one she talks to when she's feeling down or needs to vent about a crappy customer. "What are fake datemates for, if you can't vent about a crappy day or your crappy family to them?"

"Fair point." Simone concedes. She takes another long draw on her straw, which sends my mind right back to the gutter, imagining things we might do if we were really together. She interrupts my half-formed fantasies. "Sounds like we both got dealt a crap hand in the bio parent department. Good thing we found the family we needed elsewhere, right? I've got Celine and my aunt and uncle and you've got your grandfathers."

"Right," I say, wetting my lips and trying to string together a coherent sentence. Simone drinks the last of her shake with a loud slurp and winks at me. As if she knows exactly where her hollowed cheeks as she sucks are sending my thoughts.

"Does that cover everything?" she asks, all innocence.

"Yeah." I nod. "I think so. Family history, basic likes and dislikes, jobs, hopes and dreams, the usual getting to know you junk."

"We'll trick your buddies off your back. Don't you worry about a thing, Max," Simone waves to our server for the machine to pay our bill. She covers the meal before I can get out my card. I toss down cash for the tip.

"Thanks. This was nice. We should do it again," I say

as we stand to leave. Momentarily forgetting this is fake.

"For verisimilitude?" Simone asks, one sculpted brow arched.

"Um. Sure. Yeah. For veracity," I agree. Simone doesn't call me out, even though I'm pretty sure she sees right through my flimsy lies. We both have our reasons for pretending to have what I think we might both want. I walk her back to the tea shop before busting my ass to make it to pick up the contracts.

I get back to the studio barely in time for our production meeting. When I return to the studio out of breath, Errol frowns at me, rubbing his temples in that way he does when he's stressed. No one calls me out on my long lunch break, and I get all my work done just fine. Plus, I got to spend a glorious hour with Simone, so I count it as a win.

CHAPTER 10

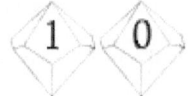

Simone

Celine brings me a couple of options to change into when she arrives at the shop to take over for Hob, since he opened this morning and she's closing. She talked me down from the ledge when I got upset about the stain ruining my after work plans. She'll be there to back me up during the end of the day rush.

My work apron covers the pale pink splotch from the milkshake. It's not as dire a stain as I'd feared. It just feels huge because I haven't had a date, fake or otherwise, in ages. Max is sweet. A tad prone to the stupid macho impulses that make me sort of wish I wasn't into dudes romantically. But I am, and he's not overbearing about it. Sure, he got all puffed up wanting to defend me from my parents, but I can sort of relate. If his mom wasn't dead, I'd have some choice words for her about abandoning her son. Even though she entrusted him to the care of people who loved him the way he deserves before she fucked off out of his life.

"What about tonight's big plans has you sighing all wistfully? You're like a regency romance heroine, girly," Celine asks during a lull between customers. It's not a leap to say she's happy I might have a date.

"Nothing," I squeak a reflexive denial.

"Mhm, does this nothing have a name?" she presses, watching me intently until I crack. She asked when she handed me the bag with my change of clothes earlier too.

"Ugh. You won't let this go, will you?" I whine, swiping at an imaginary mess on the counter by the milk frother.

"Nope," Celine agrees, hitching a hip against the counter as she settles in to wait out my reticence.

"His name is Max," I relent. "We're just friends, though. He asked me to come with him to a wedding, to get his friends off his back about finding a date."

"So you are dating him?"

"No!" I deny it with a little too much force, Celine gives me a knowing smile. "I guess it's like a fake date," I admit, hunching my shoulders at how pathetic that sounds. I'm sighing over a fake relationship.

"When's the wedding?" Celine pries.

"New Year's Eve?"

"So, you're not doing this fake date for a while, then?"

"Oh, well, we figured we'd just pretend until the wedding. For veracity."

"Veracity?" Celine repeats, tone dubious, arms crossed.

"Yeah. He's a good guy, everyone else in his clique is coupling off. I think he's lonely? I dunno, it'll get me out of the house. Might not be an actual date, but I'll get to dance, drink, and make merry. All with people who won't ditch me to fend for myself."

Celine looks at me, seeing through the bullshit and lies I'm telling myself about this plan. "You don't have to settle for pretending to be worth dating, Si." Celine says it without censure, but there's a mild rebuke in her words regardless of tone. I don't mind her calling me Si, no matter how I'm presenting because with Celine that nickname is always full of affection and acceptance. She was the first one to use that name for me, and I'll always welcome it from her. It's not the same as people who refuse to call me by name because they don't want to acknowledge the other parts of me.

"No, I know. It's fine. I'm in no position to pursue anything proper right now, anyway. I'm a mess."

"You don't give yourself enough credit." Celine clucks her tongue. "I promised not to mother-hen you, so I won't. But for the record, this Max would be lucky to nab a proper date with you, coz."

"I think he might agree with you," I grumble. Celine looks ready to pounce on that like a tiger with a bone, so I rush to forestall her. "But it's complicated, Celine."

"Only as complicated as you make it, girl." She glances at the clock and huffs out a breath. "It's dead in here. I can hold off the tea-seeking masses while you go get yourself ready for your fake date. While you're at it, consider how you might uncomplicate things with your Max, hmm?"

"I'll think about it," I agree in a tone that implies I'll do no such thing. I take her up on clocking out of work fifteen minutes early, though. Before I leave, I freshen up my makeup, layering on more eye shadow for an evening look. Then I dress in the slinky little black dress Celine brought for me to wear. Bless her, she remembered to grab my best gaffing underwear to stuff in the bag along with the dress. So I don't have to deal with tucking tonight, given the form-fitting dress is clingier than the soiled skirt I originally selected. My outfit looks fierce.

The sexy kitten heels my cousin jammed in the bag to go with it are snug, but the discomfort is worth it for the way they show off my assets. My feet are only a little bigger than hers. With a pair of nylons on, I can jam my foot into a women's size 10. My toes won't thank me for the abuse, but that's fine. I have a pair of flats in my handbag that I can switch to once we get to the club, that's a common enough trick not to raise suspicions. I'm excited to see Max's reaction to me all dolled up for a night on the town. Now that I know he isn't weird about me being Simone, I want to show off for my crush.

I take my time getting ready. With Celine's blessing, I leave the shop just before five. I won't have to wait long for Max's reaction. My nerves are roiling with anticipation. I hop a bus down Granville with no trouble, and it's a short walk to The Taphouse. A text from Max lets me know he's already inside, waiting on me and a couple of other folks to arrive.

I spot Max as soon as I walk in. He's surrounded by his friends, but as soon as our eyes lock, he stops talking and just stares at me. I raise my hand to give him a tentative wave, then I steel my nerves and approach the boisterous table.

"Simone! Hi, glad you made it. Shove over, Theo. Let Simone sit next to me," Max says as I reach the table. He's all but crawling over his friends to greet me.

Theo exchanges a look with the pretty twink who has to be Jude, judging from how close together they're sitting. The casual way they touch, and everything Max has said about them is a dead giveaway. Theo does a comical thing with his eyebrows that I can't quite interpret as he and Jude move to let me claim the seat next to Max.

I slide into the booth, feeling awkward. Max leans in to bus a kiss to my cheek. "You look hot as fuck," he says near my ear, low enough to be just for me to hear before he pulls back. His breath is a warm intimate tingle over my skin, sending shivers along my spine. So, there's my answer about his reaction. He likes what he sees. If it was all for show, he'd have said it for the table, not whispered the compliment into my ear.

So, I was right. He really likes me, the confirmation makes me giddy enough to almost overshadow my nerves at meeting the big boisterous group gathered around the table. Max likes me as Simone; he likes all of me. I grin at him, kissing him back on the side of his face. That flusters him. He turns back toward the table.

"So, these are the friends I've been telling you about." Max gestures toward his friends. "Everyone, this is my date, Simone."

We go around the table, everyone saying polite introductions and how nice it is to meet me. They all include their pronouns, but Max already told me they do that for everyone. I try not to tense up and take it as them all drawing attention to noticing I'm trans. No one comments on the fact that Max, who is out and proud as a gay man, is apparently dating a woman, trans or otherwise. I can't help wondering what he's told them about me, and hoping that easy acceptance bodes well. I fidget with my menu as they go off on tangents about work. The conversation spans their in game adventures, the kids Max mentioned, and whether the rest of our party will join us on time.

Theo mentions his friend Kevin had to cancel. There's bickering over which shared appetizers to order. Then Errol arrives with Emil and Rene, setting off another round of introductions. As they go around I can't help trying to figure out which of the others are the trans friends Max has mentioned. I have my guesses, not that I'd say anything unless they offer confirmation themselves. Pia, Rene and Emil stand out. Maybe Theo. There's a sense of connection that I get from those four in particular as we're introduced. Some kinship that makes me feel like I could be at home among them.

Gui gets a text from his boyfriend that Paz and Alice are running late and to eat without them, they'll meet us later for dancing. That makes Laura deflate, so I guess Max is right about there being something between them, though Alice didn't text her directly, so who knows what that something might be.

Not that I'm one to judge how other people conduct their relationships. Heck, the greeting peck on the cheek Max gave me is the most action I've had in an age. Sad, considering he likely only did it to convince his buddies we're an item.

I stay quiet while we eat. This group is a lot to take in, so I let their banter wash over me. I gulp my cocktail until I'm nicely floaty, and I try not to get too handsy with Max and make a bad first impression. Max's knuckles resting on the small of my back as we exit the booth to leave sends a full body zing down to my toes. Who knew a light brush of his fingers in such a PG spot could send a bolt of longing to my soul? It's not quite arousal. As a general rule, I'm not into sex when I'm in my Simone headspace. Not that I can't get turned on, it's just the idea of sex with the original factory parts sort of makes me queasy on girl days. I'm fine with it on Simon days and most of the time on Si days, though. That's stuff I'd tell Max, if we were really considering a relationship. I might tell him anyway, because he's easy to talk to and even if I don't push for more, I want to be his friend for real.

We leave The Taphouse in a big noisy crowd. We attract some looks, but that probably has to do with Theo's volume and not anyone looking to hassle us.

Strength in numbers, I suppose? It's nice to walk tall and confident in my slinky dress and sexy shoes without feeling like I've got a target on my back and no backup. That sense of comradery only grows when Pia loops an arm through mine on one side and Laura takes the other.

"Lovely to have another lady in the mix tonight," Pia declares. "I mean, I'm not entirely a lady, more lady-adjacent. But, the point stands—girl power. So, how did you and Max meet?"

"At the bus stop. He offered to share his umbrella with me." I appreciate having Pia and Laura pressed close on either side. For once, it's nice to be surrounded by people like me. And Pia just confirmed my earlier guess that they're some variation on nonbinary. So, she's one of Max's not cis friends for sure.

"Aw, how chivalrous," Laura coos.

"Max, I didn't know you were so gallant," Pia teases him.

"She looked cold," Max mutters defensively. "It was a blustery day."

"I appreciated not being completely soaked through that entire day at work," I say. I smile at Max, remembering the warm glow of getting to speak with a cute guy. It felt so nice to have Max take care of me, even that token amount. I still spent the day soaked, and the rain had forced me to remove my sodden compression tank because the damp material squeezed my ribs enough to make breathing ache. And without the comforting weight of the vest to ground me, dealing with customers was a nightmare. But the thought counted for something.

"So, you shared the umbrella, got to talking and one thing led to another?" Pia prompts.

"Yeah, that was a couple weeks ago. Afterward, we started talking every morning. Wasn't long before he asked me out," I tell the story we agreed to use.

"And she said yes," Max interjects.

"Good for you," Pia says.

"Hey, Max, a word?" Errol calls to Max from the vanguard of our group. He gives me a polite nod. "You don't mind if I steal him for a minute to discuss work, right, Simone?"

"Right," I agree, since I can't exactly protest without being the asshole. Max gives me an apologetic look, mouthing sorry at me, before he jogs to catch up to Errol. Laura and Pia are still flanking me, peppering me with getting to know you type questions. Do I like video games? What kind? Would I want to join them all for a video game day sometime? I answer and try not to act paranoid about whatever Errol and Max are discussing.

CHAPTER 11

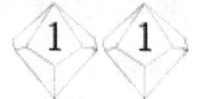

Max

Errol levels me with a steady gaze as soon as I join him toward the front of our group.

"What's up, Errol?" I ask, uncertain if that stern look on his face is disapproval.

"Nothing major. Did you get Richard's sign off on the new contracts?"

"Oh, yeah," I reply, relieved that this really is about work and not Errol grilling me about Simone. It had crossed my mind that my buddies might find it odd that I brought a woman as my date. None of them are hassling either of us. They just accepted Simone, no questions asked. Or at least, nothing they wouldn't have asked any other person I might have brought along tonight.

They're an accepting bunch. But I'm itching at the idea that they might perceive me differently for being attracted to a woman. Because I am attracted to Simone in her girl mode. I like the way she moves, the subtle changes in her mannerisms, and the way she touches me, delicate and soft. I can't help worrying that this might be another way I'm on the outside of the group looking in. Though actually, so many of them are either trans or partnered to trans people that Simone could actually help me fit in more. Not that I'm fake-dating her for any reason like that. God, now I'm overthinking everything. I guess that worry has more to do with this attraction challenging my own self-image than my friends' reactions. Gah, I need to focus on this conversation with Errol, not have some sort of identity crisis.

"I caught him the second time I went up to his office after our production meeting. Why?" I add hastily.

Errol grimaces. "We've got the sound studio booked for early next week. So, if the director wants any more last-minute changes, I'd like to know about it first thing Monday. That way I can follow up on any issues or at least try to smooth any ruffled feathers."

I make a sympathetic face, because, yeah, the eleventh hour changes in the character voices are a pain in my ass. It was the right call, though. The new actor fits the role better.

"I gave Richard the new contracts and the links to the online voice samples just before four. He had at least an hour to listen and pass along notes. I even checked his calendar, and he didn't have any other meetings or calls scheduled. So he should have had time."

Errol adjusts his glasses. "Good to know. I'll follow

up with him on Monday. Thanks, Max." He flashes a wry smile at me. "I won't tear you away from your date any longer. She seems a little overwhelmed by all of us, huh?"

"Yeah. I guess we're a lot to throw at a person," I agree, stealing a glance back at Simone

"I'm sure she'll settle in just fine. Rene and Paz held their own once they got used to us."

"I hope so. Seems like she's hitting it off with Pia and Laura, anyway," I observe, glancing back at the trio with their arms linked and their heads tipped close together. Simone is watching me, eyes intense and worried. I shoot her a smile, but her return grin looks sort of manic and fraying around the edges.

"Didn't realize you were bi or pan?" Errol adds, pulling me up short.

"I'm not," I deny it like an accusation, which seems to take Errol aback. He frowns, as well he might since he's panromantic. Half our group has professed attractions to multiple genders. I always do this, shove my foot in my mouth. It's not that I have an issue with bi people, it's just not how I've seen myself. I sigh, rubbing at my temples. "That came out wrong. I meant, I always figured I'm about a six on the Kinsey scale. But Simone does it for me, no matter how she's presenting, so I suppose I'm more of a five? Guess I'm not as rigid about my sexuality as I always assumed. Might take some getting used to."

"Ah." Errol gives me a knowing look and a warm pat on the back. Relief floods me. I didn't drive him away with my clumsy response. "Well, it's always good to be open to learning new things about yourself, huh?"

"Yeah. It is," I agree, meaning it more than I'd have thought.

"If you need to talk it out, I'm always around to listen," Errol adds.

I believe him. Mostly. But considering all the crap he's got on his plate with being thrown into parenthood and getting back together with his ex, I don't intend to burden him with my petty problems. Sure, I'm into Simone and that's a weird thing to realize about myself in my mid-twenties. I thought I had my sexuality figured out from the time I was a young teen, but it's not like we're dating for real. So it *shouldn't* matter, but it kind of does.

I might be pansexual. Alone in my thoughts, I wasn't ready to claim it earlier, but hearing the word from Errol forces me to confront this attraction. Well, considering Si isn't a dude either, I guess that's a giant and resounding duh, if my recent fantasies are anything to go by. I'm pan. I let that sink in.

This morning, my attraction to Simone took me off guard. But that's silly of me. She's still the same person I've been chatting with for the past couple weeks. I just didn't know until this morning that I'd still feel the same fluttery desire to kiss and touch her when she was wearing a flowery blouse and a skirt with those soft curves underneath and moving with that gentle, feminine body language. But watching her, being around her, still did it for me.

I'm still me. Still queer, no matter who I date. That's settled then. No need to bother Errol to talk about it more.

Rene nudges into Errol's side and murmurs to him. I catch something about taking full advantage of Gregor watching their kid for the night. I take that as my cue to drop back and rescue Simone from whatever interrogation Pia and Laura are subjecting her to.

"Max, good of you to join us." Pia grins at me when I drop back to walk next to them. She draws Laura aside so I can walk with my date. I offer Simone my hand and she takes it, seeming relieved to see me. She squeezes me hard. Pia and Laura drop back to walk with Emil, right behind us.

"We were just inviting Simone to our next LAN party," Pia says. "Can you hook her up with game codes or do you need us to track down an account for her?"

"Which game?" I ask, pleased that Simone seems more relaxed with me by her side. That sense of being someone she looks to as a protector strokes my ego and makes me swagger. I glance at her and she's smiling with her lip caught between her teeth, like she's holding back amusement. I grin, caught up in Simone.

"Pshaw," Laura scoffs, drawing me back to our conversation. "You even need to ask? Only the best RTS of all time."

"Starcraft?" I reply, knowing she means Age of Mythology.

"You've lost me," Simone says, looking confused.

"RTS means real-time strategy. Games where you have to manage and compete for resources to build your base. Then you strategically deploy your units to take out your enemies in real time," I supply a hasty explanation.

"I see," says Simone, in a tone that says she doesn't get the point. Not ideal that she isn't into the games I enjoy. Then again, if she hates the things I love, it will be easier to remember our relationship isn't real.

"Nope, not Starcraft, try again," Laura says.

"Company of Heroes?" I tease, glancing over my shoulder at Laura.

Pia chuckles as Laura crosses her arms and gives me a huffy look. "Thee, back me up, best RTS?"

"*AoM*," Theo calls back over his shoulder from in front of Simone and I. He and Jude were chatting about something unrelated with Gui. Theo turns and gives us an excited look. "Why? Are we playing this weekend?"

"Yes," Laura replies.

The rest of the gang gives a mixed response. Jude agrees with his usual good-natured cheer. Gui is on board, though he reminds us that Paz has work Sunday, so he'll probably bow out early. Laura says Alice might join us, which I assume will only be more likely with Laura planning to play. Errol and Rene decline the invite; they have other plans with Mo. Emil sounds excited. Pia, Gregor, and Emil will switch out who is playing between games depending on whether Rain is napping.

Local area network party is a bit of a misnomer, since we can play *AoM* remotely over a virtual private network. That's a mixed bag for me. On the one hand, I get to chill and play games with my friends this weekend. But using a VPN means I'll be playing alone from my lonely apartment. Voice chat helps, but it's not the same energy as hanging with my friends in person. All of them will be with their significant others. Well, maybe not Laura, but she and Alice have been hanging out on the weekend more and more, so I doubt she'll be alone.

Then it strikes me: I don't have to be alone either. "I've got my gaming rig and my old school laptop, if we've got an extra online account kicking around, you can come to my place to play, Simone?" I offer.

Simone gives me a tentative smile. "If you don't mind that I haven't played and will suck?"

"I'm sure Max has no objections to you sucking," Theo declares. Jude nudges him with an elbow. Theo winces, rubbing at his ribs with a put upon expression. "What did I say wrong, hun?"

"Save the innuendos for me, lover boy," Jude admonishes.

"Sorry, Theo's got a broken filter," I apologize to Simone.

"It's fine," she says, giving my hand a squeeze that I take to mean she appreciates my presence beside her. That fills me with warmth. When I look at her, Simone's expression seems more amused than upset by my friends. That's for the best, since Theo can't ever seem to help but voice his inappropriate comments.

Once we reach the club, it doesn't take long to get lost in the music. This time, I'm not stuck at the edges of our group getting the scraps of their attention. I'm not caught in the middle of Jude and Theo's fumbling flirtations, or getting a pity dance from Gui or Laura. Errol doesn't hover, making sure I'm okay.

This time, I've got Simone next to me. I skim my hands lightly over her hips as she moves to the beat. Her wrists loop around my neck and we dance close. The driving beat forms a hot and heavy pulse that moves us together. Our rhythm makes it impossible not to think about doing a whole hell of a lot more than dancing with the sexy person in my arms.

Hours fly past and before I know it, Errol is tapping my shoulder to offer Simone and me a ride home. I blink out of my reverie.

"Well?" Errol arches a brow at me as he adjusts his glasses.

"Nah, it's out of your way. And you won't have room for Laura if you take us." I wave him away. "Thanks for the offer, though."

"Laura and Alice already left with Gui and the others to crash at their place. You aren't far out of the way," Errol lies. Like he always does.

"You don't have to, we'll be fine," Simone says, though her tense posture says she might not fully believe that.

"Rene's got their appointment tomorrow, I don't want to keep you out late. We'll be fine," I insist. I glance at the time and consider our options. If we leave now, we can catch the SeaBus over to the North Shore and then it's not a long ride home from there.

It takes another minute to convince Errol we can

fend for ourselves, and he insists I text when we're both home safe. I promise to check in with him. That satisfies Errol's protective urges enough that he and Rene leave to collect their kid with Pia and Emil in tow.

"You ready to call it a night?" I ask, turning to Simone.

"Are you?" she fires back, leaning into my personal space. The move puts our mouths inches apart and I have a hell of a time tearing myself away and putting space between us.

"You could come to my place," I offer, not ready for the night to end.

"I shouldn't, but we can split a cab," she says. I wince, because a cab home from here will cost a pretty penny when we could just take transit.

"I was thinking the SeaBus?"

Simone worries her lip for a second, then nods, "Okay. That works, too. Last crossing is in twenty minutes; we better get our butts in gear if we're going to catch it."

"Yeah," I agree.

We leave, jogging down Granville to catch the bus to the SkyTrain. It's exhilarating to run through the chilly evening air after the heat of the club. I love the night breeze on my cheeks, but I don't miss that Simone seems vigilant about the people we pass. I scan the faces around us for signs of a threat. It's not like I've never had to be aware of my surroundings like that before. But not usually here and only when I'm holding hands with a guy or wearing Pride merch. This is different.

At the SeaBus terminal, Simone shies away from a guy who holds a door for her. He leers at her chest as he says, "you should smile more, sweetheart, might make you prettier."

Earlier she flinched at a drunken come on accompanied by a loud wolf-whistle from a passing car. And I kind of want to punch the assholes harassing her, but that wouldn't solve anything. The best I can do is to put my arm around her as we wait for the SeaBus. I glare at anyone who takes too much of an interest in us.

Simone rests her head on my shoulder. She seems content to relax against me. Her breath tickles my neck. I like the softness of her hair against my cheek, the warmth of her still pressed close even though we aren't putting on a show of dating for my friends anymore.

We're quiet on the boat and while we wait for the bus home from the quay. We're the only ones who get off at our stop. As we stand under the pale illumination of a streetlight, I offer her my hand. "Can I walk you home?" I ask.

Simone hesitates for the briefest moment, then slips her fingers into my hand and nods. "That would be nice, thanks."

"Lead the way," I grin at her and she does. "I had fun tonight. Thanks for coming with us."

"I had a delightful time. Your friends are something else."

"Is that bad?"

"No, not at all. I enjoyed getting to know them," she says.

"Does that mean you want to come over for video games tomorrow?" I ask. "No pressure."

"Are you sure you want me dragging down your team? I really am the pits at games. My buddies all used to laugh at me when I tried to play with them because I suck so bad. Gina's husband and his pals are into Halo and I was always the first to die, never could quite get the hang of the dual joystick controls."

"Don't worry about being the best. Theo might whine if you end up on his team because he has a thing about winning, but I don't care. I just like to play with people. Unless you'd rather not? No one will make fun of you if you need a while to figure out the controls and I'll do what I can to help you."

"What if I just come hang out while you play?" Simone suggests, worrying her lip with her teeth.

"That works too. I'll text you with details, but I'm a few blocks up the hill here, the basement unit on the corner of Skyline and Westview. Entrance is in the back."

"I bet Theo has a field day with that," Simone jokes with a chuckle.

"Theo hasn't been to my place, but yeah, he'd be all over the backdoor jokes. I usually go to the gang when we hang, since the North Shore is a bit out of the way," I say.

"Do you like it here?"

"Yeah, I've only been here since the end of January, after my first place in the city got sold and all the tenants got renovicted, but I like it. I've found some neat little places. Loads of great hiking trails. When the weather cooperates, Alice and Paz come to do the Grouse Grind. Sometimes Gui tags along to hang out, too, and we hike on other trails as a group. Theo was out of commission most of the summer recovering from a surgery, he's fine now, but he didn't make it out for any hiking. Anyway, I like the North Shore. Lonsdale has just about everything you could need, and Edgemont Village is adorable. Plus, we get free admission to the Capilano Bridge since we're in its area code. The long commute comes with its perks." I shrug, extolling the virtues of our part of the metro area.

I chatter to fill the walk because I'm too chickenshit to ask if she felt the same spark I did on the dance floor. If the same attraction is zinging through her body, like it is mine. From the way she was breathing me in on the ferry, I might not be the only one whose libido didn't get the message that this isn't a genuine relationship. I don't ask. All too soon, we're doing the awkward end of the first date shuffle in front of her place.

I kind of want to kiss her, at least a quick peck on the cheek, but I don't know how she'll receive the gesture. Should I stick to platonic hugging? A handshake? I stick out my hand like a dumbass just as she leans in to steal a quick kiss. My movement throws off her aim. I end up fondling her chest by accident as her mouth grazes the corner of mine. Simone dances back, laughing. "Oops, we should try that again. Only less fail."

"Yeah, good thing we didn't fuck up the casual affection in front of the gang, right?" I reply with a self-deprecating chuckle. The words sober Simone, almost as if the reminder this isn't real disappoints her as much as it does me.

"Yeah. Good thing," she says, voice strained. "Well, let me know about tomorrow. Good night, Max." She thrusts out her hand and we shake awkwardly.

"Good night, Simone. I had fun with you," I say. I'm itching to lean into her and give her a proper goodbye kiss. Instead, I let her go up the path to her door. I linger on the sidewalk to make sure she gets inside alright, then offer one last wave when she turns to glance my way. She smiles to see me waiting and blows me a kiss that makes my heart flutter. I pretend to catch it, give her a jaunty wink, and set off up the hill toward home. If it weren't so darn late, I'd be whistling to myself as I walk, but as it stands, I content myself with reliving the amazing night out with Simone.

CHAPTER 12

Si

I wake up on the couch with a terrible crick in my neck. The clingy dress that felt sexy when I put it on last night is less comfortable rucked up around my hips. It feels far too constrictive in a bad way, all twisted around me from sleeping in it. I didn't want to wake Celine by puttering around last night, so I just crashed on the couch without even bothering to pull out the mattress. My gaffing panties and the padded bra I wore yesterday to shape my chest lie heaped on the floor where I left them with the strappy heels and my handbag.

The makeup I didn't take off feels heavy and tacky on my face. My hair extensions ache from tugging at my scalp. My head hurts from drinking while we were out and my mouth tastes like ass. Everything feels off kilter and it creeps up on me that I'm not feeling like Simone at all right now. Not that the morning after look I'm sporting right now is my thing in girl mode either.

But I'm floating in the nebulous Si space where man and woman both seem like alien spheres that have nothing to do with me. I want the makeup off and to trade in the tight clothing for something loose and comfy, since I have no immediate plans to go out.

The only downside to changing is that Max's citrus and vanilla scent seems to linger around me. Must have transferred to my clothes where I pressed against him while we danced. I don't want to give up the reminder that a sexy guy spent most of the night pressed close to me. I like him. More than like. I want him.

I roll out of my blanket nest on the couch with a groan to pick up my undergarments and freshen up to face the day. I don't smell breakfast, so either Celine is still asleep, or she spent the night with her man again. She's spent most weekends with Harvey since I moved in here. It's like the final few months of living with Gina before her wedding all over again. Except Celine still talks to me and makes a point of spending time with me during the week. No matter the similarities, deep down I know I won't lose Celine to Harvey the way I lost Gina to her new life with her man.

In the spacious washroom, I remove my hair extensions, tidying them away. A few makeup wipes let me erase all traces of my smeared cosmetics. Then a hot shower washes the vestiges of Max's cologne down the drain along with the sheen of sweat we worked up together on the dancefloor. I dry off, dress, and wander into the kitchen in my lounge pants and a bulky sweatshirt to figure out breakfast.

I throw together a smoothie when nothing else sounds good, only to wince at the noise the blender makes aggravating my head. Tylenol and my blended breakfast take the edge off the dull throb and I feel more human by the time I get out my phone to surf social media. Gina posted a bunch of pictures from a dinner party she and her husband hosted. It's not like I would even want to attend a stuffy dinner with her husband's coworkers. I still feel left out, though. More evidence that Gina and all my old friends moved on without me.

I scroll some more and, oh, hell no. We might not be as close as we once were, but she seriously didn't tell me she's pregnant before telling the entire fucking internet? That stings. Like I'm someone she used to know.

I've sort of suspected we aren't friends anymore for a while. Even leading up to Gina and Cal's wedding, things had changed. But this feels like evidence that the best friend who stood by me through thick and thin isn't interested in having me in her life anymore. She moved on. Fine. So can I.

I give the announcement photo a heart reaction and type out the expected generic congratulations. I doubt she'll even notice amongst the same from her hundreds of other virtual friends. Then I close the app and stare at my phone's home screen, trying to figure out what to do with myself today. I'm not working this weekend, Celine hired a few part-timers from UBC to cover weekend shifts so I only have to work the occasional Saturday when someone calls out sick.

My phone startles me into dropping it with the buzz of an incoming message. For a wild moment I think it might be Gina, giving me her big news in a more personal format. It's not. The new message is from Max.

Max: Had a great time last night. ;) Still want to come hang out today? We're starting the games around four, but if you want to come to mine a bit early we can get the tech stuff sorted and maybe have a late lunch together?

My stomach swoops at the admission he enjoys spending time with me, even in the light of day. Is it sad that dancing with him and pretending we're an item is the most fun I've had on a Friday night in ages? I should play this cool, letting myself forget it's not real can only end in heartache.

Si: Yeah. I can come over. Gotta give your friends verisimilitude, right? ;)

Max doesn't reply right away. He must be making breakfast or he just has more important things to do than stay tethered to his phone, anxiously awaiting my responses.

Si: So, is three okay? Or I can do whatever time works for you.

I hit send, then regret how desperate the message sent on the heels of the first one makes me sound. Might as well tell him I've got nothing to do but wait on his convenience because I'm a loser with no friends and no life. Ugh, self pity is a crappy look. Before I can work up to a proper sulk, Max replies.

Max: Right. Got to keep up the ruse. Three is perfect. Can't wait. Um, what kind of day is it today? For you?

Si: Si.

Max: Cool. Nice.

Max: I mean, nice, no matter what kind of day it is. I like you in Simone mode, too. Or Simon. I enjoy hanging out regardless.

Max: Okay. Sorry if I'm being super awkward. I'll see you at three. Going to go pick up snacks when I get my groceries, any requests?

Si: I'm not picky.

Max: You sure?

Si: Yeah, surprise me.

Max: If you wanted to tag along to the store, I'm borrowing my roomie's car in exchange for picking up beer for him.

I consider the offer. I could use a grocery run and not having to ride the bus to the store or schlep things while walking is a win. And it means more time with Max. Downside, that's more time to feed my crush on the guy.

Si: You sure?

Max: Yeah, it's no trouble, you're on my way to the store. Give me half an hour to get dressed and crap.

Max: Stuff! I meant, do stuff. I did not just announce my literal toileting plans to you. That would be awkward.

Max: I'm shutting up now. See you in thirty? I'll text when I'm outside your place, if that's alright?

Si: ROFLMAO! It's fine. I didn't think you meant it literally. I can walk up the hill to meet you, if that's easier?

Max: That works too. See you soon.

I can't resist sending him one more text with just the poop emoji. Max sends back an embarrassed face. I reply with a string of laughing, ROFL faces. Then I put away my phone and go to make a grocery list while I putter around wasting time until I need to meet him. It occurs to me, belatedly, that ratty sweats aren't the best way to impress Max. This outfit fits my mood, though. I want to be comfy and cloaked in loose fabric over the compression tank that makes it easier to handle people's inevitable perceptions and judgments about who I am and my size.

It's nice out when I leave to hike the three blocks up the hill to Max's place after killing enough time not to rush Max through his morning routine. I find a path to the back of the house where he rents. The backyard is big and tree-shaded, typical of the mini mansions in this area. The screen of branches and the slats of a fence block my view of any details.

Most of the homes here are swanky, many have income units attached to make them affordable for their owners. That or they sit vacant as investments. That's not our neighborhood, yet. People still live here, for now. Even if no less than three of the lots I passed between our places are being gutted or torn down and rebuilt.

As I'm pulling out my phone to text Max that I've arrived, he opens the gate in the privacy fence set behind the trees.

"Hey, how are you, Si?" Max asks. His face lights up in a grin when our eyes meet and I return the smile.

"Good. Not too hungover, what about you?"

"I'm good. Figured we can grab brunch and then groceries? I like to snack when we play, and I'll fill up on junk if we don't eat first."

"I can do brunch."

"Cool, we're taking the white Camry. He said it's parked on the other side of the street?" Max clicks the key fob and the lights blink. We get in the car and Max drives toward Lonsdale. We find a place that does waffles and bubble tea. The milky drinks always remind me more of a melted smoothie than any tea we sell at the shop, but that's a plus in my book. I get a pretty purple taro tea with tapioca pearls and a waffle covered in berries.

"Never gained a taste for the pearls," Max says after we order. He got flavored jelly in his tea.

"They're not bad. I never can resist the chance to get balls in my mouth," I joke, slurping up a few through the wide straw.

Max laughs. "And you questioned why I thought you'd get along with the gang. That's something Theo would say."

I snort, because even after spending one night with his friend, I can't deny Theo would love my well-worn joke.

We don't have to wait long for the person working the counter to bring over our order. Max's waffle comes covered in sliced bananas and Nutella. There has to be a joke in there, but I can't seem to find it as I watch him take his first bite. A blissful expression covers his face.

"So, your buddies seemed cool with us dating, huh?"

I ask after eating a few bites.

"Yeah. They liked you." Max grins at me.

"Good. So, it seems like our plan is working out then, huh?" I poke at my waffle.

"Yep," Max says. We eat in silence for a while. The food isn't bad. A bit of a sugar rush, but I'm treating myself. It's also a treat to watch Max enjoy his food. Not that I'm perving on him or anything, but he's got really nice lips. And a very pink tongue that I am certainly not imagining having him use on various parts of my anatomy.

"So, about this game night," I say, clearing my throat and shifting uncomfortably. Unlike when I'm in Simone mode, I am very into fucking in Si mode. And I would love it if said fucking happened with the cute guy across from me. So I need a distraction before I say or do something stupid to fuck up our budding friendship.

"You said you aren't much of a gamer, do you want to play tonight or just hang with me?" Max offers.

I shrug, talking about our plans is safer ground than blurting out how hot he is. "I said I'm not good, doesn't mean I don't like to play. So long as you all don't fuss at me for sucking." I resist the impulse to tack on something flirty about sucking him or wink or anything. The dating is fake, but the friendship we're building could be real, if I don't fuck it up.

"Nah, it'll be fine, promise. If you don't have fun, we can bow out early," he offers.

"Yeah?" I arch a brow at him.

"Sure thing." He nods. "We're playing at being a new couple, running off early to do couple things will only add to our verisimilitude, like you said earlier."

Is it my imagination or does acknowledging this is all pretend upset him as much as it does me? Or more likely, he feels bad about lying to the people who care about him. "Cool. Still, I don't want to embarrass myself. After groceries, can we play a few practice rounds?"

"Yeah, that sounds fun," Max agrees. We finish our food and take our drinks to go.

Max picks up the promised beer for his housemate at the BC Liquor Store across from the grocery chain.

"It still weirds me out that I can't get beer at the market here," he comments as we put his purchase in the trunk before going into the Loblaws.

"Doesn't Ontario have government liquor stores?" I ask.

"Sure, we have the LCBO, but you can get beer and wine at some grocery stores, too. Makes it more convenient," Max gripes.

"Guess so," I say as I grab a shopping cart. "Want to share?"

"Sure," Max agrees with a smile. We stroll through the produce section. "Anyway, it's not like I'm a huge drinker or anything. I just sometimes like a beer with my dinner and it's a pain to go to another store to get it. First world problems, right?"

"Yep," I agree, snagging a leafy bunch of kale for my morning smoothies.

"I guess it's more the fact that it's different from home. Like the tangible reminder that I'm not home here bothers me? More than the actual inconvenience," Max says. He turns away from me to select some apples. Just as well he isn't watching me, since I'm sure my face is all mushy with emotions at him admitting to feeling displaced here. Despite his big accepting group of friends, I get the impression he might be as lonely as me under the cheerful facade.

I nudge my shoulder against his as I reach for a bag of grapes. "Well, I can't say it's the same as leaving my province, but I get the sense of being a stranger in a strange land after moving to the city."

We move to the next set of displays and I throw some squash in the cart. It keeps well, it's heavy when I have to walk for groceries. Besides, I've got some killer soup recipes to use it in for the cool fall days ahead of us. Maybe I can invite Max over to share. I add potatoes, onions, celery and carrots to the cart for the same reason. Heavy foods that keep well. We leave the produce behind and Max tosses a couple loaves of bread into the cart.

"Yeah. That. I'm getting used to it, at least. And I was lucky Errol took pity on me and brought me into the group. I just sometimes feel like I'm faking it, you know? I'm not an artist like the rest of them or anything."

"They care about you, though. They wouldn't pester you and try to set you up on dates if they didn't care," I say. The words are a little bitter because my friends didn't make any kind of effort to drag me along into the next phase of their lives. They just left me behind without a backward glance. Even Gina. I might not be as over our friendship as I thought I was if the news stings this much even hours later. I grimace and try to shove the thought away.

"What's wrong?" Max asks.

"Nothing. Just found out my best friend from high school is expecting her first kid, and it struck me funny that I didn't know until she posted it on social media. Even a few months ago she would have called to tell me. Or at least DM'd me before blasting the news to the world at large."

Max hums low in his throat, then says, "that sucks, I'm sorry."

I shrug. "That's life, mate. People move on. We have little in common these days. Still stings a bit to realize it's truly over, though."

"I bet."

We reach the butcher section and Max puts a couple of precooked entrees that just require reheating in the oven into the cart. I grab a package of turkey bacon to go in the squash soup I've got planned. The smokiness will complement the sweet squash and apple. I add some bone in chicken to the cart too, so I can make chicken noodle soup as well. I'm in the mood for comfort food. That should give me a nice variety of warm cheap meals for Celine and I for the week.

"What are you making with all this?" Max asks.

"Soup, well, most of it. Not the grapes or the kale." I wave my hand at the ingredients in question.

"Huh. Here I was thinking soup comes from a can," Max teases. He nudges his shoulder against mine.

"Blasphemy!" I stick out my tongue at him and he swallows hard, giving a nervous chuckle.

"So, do you just throw it in a pot with water?" he asks, rubbing at the back of his neck.

I snort, then realize he's serious, or at least, not entirely joking. "No. I mean, technically, yes, but there's more to it than just throwing food in water and boiling the shit out of it. Um, can you cook at all?"

"Not really? Gramps and Grandad are amazing in a lot of ways, but cooking is not their strong suit. Grandad learned the basics when he was raising mom, but nothing fancy and I never cared enough to learn, so I do a lot of packaged meals and takeout."

"Okay. Well, that settles it then, you're coming over to mine to learn a few recipes."

"Oh, I am, am I?" Max says, amused at my insistence.

"Yes. Do you want your first culinary triumph to be butternut squash soup or classic chicken noodle?" I ask.

"Tough call, squash soup sounds more fancy."

"It's not. But it tastes great. I'll teach you both tomorrow. Then, we'll have leftovers for most of the week."

"You don't have to teach me. I might be hopeless."

"No one is hopeless. If you can follow directions, you can cook."

"If you say so," Max's tone is so dubious it makes me

chuckle at him.

"I do, you'll see," I insist. "Come on, let's finish our shopping. If you like the lesson, we can make something you pick next week."

Max grins at me and we make our way around the store, getting the things we need for our lesson and the snacks he wants for our game night. Cheese puffs and soda feature prominently on his list, along with the sort of frozen meals you just throw in the microwave to reheat. I rag on him over those. He pushes back, citing the convenience and cost savings of bringing his own lunch to work a few days a week. I point out he can get the same benefit with actual food he makes himself, but it's all lighthearted and we're both smiling as we wait in the checkout line.

It's surreal to be shopping *with* him instead of next to him, selecting food for *us*. This is eerily similar to how my idle imaginings have cast a potential love interest at my side for these mundane moments. It's a pleasant fantasy. Nice enough that I allow myself to forget this isn't real for a while. I enjoy being with him, joking about dessert options with flirty glances and lingering touches. Who knew grocery shopping with my fake boyfriend could be more fun than the entirety of my last actual relationship?

CHAPTER 13

Max

When Si threatened me with cooking lessons, I sort of figured we wouldn't follow through on the offer. It seemed like a throwaway line to get me to stop asking questions about how to cook. So it surprises me to get a text the next morning asking when I want to come over for my lesson. I roll with it. Not as though I have other plans. The gang suggested more AoM might happen tonight, but I can skip it. Or play after we cook. It's not like they'll miss me if I'm not there.

Heck, since Si seemed to warm up to the game by the end of the night, maybe we can play together again. That would be #relationship goals right there. Sure, Si sort of sucked at the game, but the point doesn't always have to be winning, no matter what Theo thinks. I had a good time yesterday.

And after the stovetop kettle corn Si made for us to

snack on while we played late into the night, I'm convinced that I'll be learning actual kitchen skills. Here I was, thinking popcorn only came from a microwave or a movie theater. But Si's was better than the movie theater stuff. Doesn't hurt that in the kitchen, Si exudes a simple confidence I've rarely seen in my new friend.

When I knock on the door at the bottom of the hill, I'm pretty sure it's a Simone day. Si hides in thick layers and today's outfit is more form-fitting. Snug jeans and a blousy tee that hints at curves despite the outline of the compression vest under it. Si or Simone, I enjoy the view.

"Hey," I say with a brief wave. "What sort of day is it today?" I ask to be sure.

"Hey yourself, Max. It's a Si day," Si says, giving me an appreciative once-over. I'm glad I asked instead of guessing wrong. And glad I put on jeans that flatter my ass.

"Cool. So, cooking?" I ask.

"Yep, kitchen is through here, ignore the mess, there's only one bedroom, so my stuff is sort of taking over the living room," Si says apologetically.

"Not a problem," I say. As we walk through the living room, I can't say it's all that messy. Sure, there's a stack of folded bedding and a pillow on the couch. A couple of suitcases and a full laundry hamper stand stacked in the corner, but that's hardly a mess worth apologizing over.

"So, what are we making first?" Si asks, leaning on the kitchen counter. The kitchen is immaculate. Clean enough so that I'm retroactively embarrassed at the state of my kitchen yesterday.

No one cooks anything more involved than pasta with store-bought sauce in my kitchen. And yet we still had to load the dishwasher to clear counter space and hand wash the pot we used for the popcorn. I dug through every one of the disorganized cabinets before I found the lid. We didn't have a bowl big enough to fit the finished product, so we ended up eating it out of the stockpot.

If I'm learning to cook, I might need to start by staying more on top of the kitchen chores. Si said nothing about the mess, but it had to be irritating if this is the level of cleanliness my friend prefers.

"I don't have a strong preference. But, uh, sorry I tried to poison you with my health code violations yesterday," I say, rubbing at my neck sheepishly.

Si laughs. "Oh, god, don't feel bad. I'm not some kind of neat freak, I just try to keep things as nice as possible for Celine since I'm a guest in her home."

"Sure, but it was pretty nasty. We sometimes let things get away from us during the work week. Next time you come over, I'll do a better job cleaning."

"It's seriously fine, mate, no worries. We can start with getting the squash going. We're cheating a little by using the Instant Pot to pressure cook it, otherwise the squash takes a while to soften up. Once that's in the pot, we'll get the chicken soup simmering on the stove."

"Sure, sounds good."

"You good with using a veggie peeler?"

"Yeah. I think?" I agree. This is outside my comfort zone, but how hard can it be? Si hands me the tool in question.

"Great, so you get to work peeling the potatoes while I get out everything else we'll need. After that we'll cut the squash and apples in half and scoop out the seeds, those we don't need to peel. The flesh will slide right out of their skins once we cook them. Then chop up the potato along with the onions and bacon. That about covers the prep. To make the actual soup, first we cook the bacon, then we save it as a garnish and saute everything else in the fat."

"Apples?" I wrinkle my nose at the idea of fruit in a dinner dish.

"Yep." Si nods. "Trust me, they add a ton of flavor. Sweet and tart."

"Cool," I agree, still dubious, but willing to trust my teacher's expertise. Si guides my hands upon noticing that I'm still puzzling over how to hold the peeler.

After that, Si talks me through the recipe, showing me each task before letting me do the actual work. When I struggle with hacking through the firm flesh of the squash, Si lends a hand. And intervenes again when I panic over bacon grease splattering when I add the veggies to the pot to soften before we start the pressure cooker.

While the veggie soup pressure cooks, Si digs out everything to start the chicken soup. By the time we prep all the ingredients, I'm more confident with peeling and chopping the heaping piles of veggies. Again, we start with sauteing. Then we add stock and set the pot to boil over low heat.

"That's it?"

"For now. Once it's simmered a while, we'll season it again. And we'll need to remove the bones from the chicken, but yeah. Want to make fresh dumplings for the chicken soup? We can go with noodles or rice if you prefer, but dumplings are easy and tasty."

"Dumplings sound good."

"Cool. My gran used to cheat and use pancake mix for hers. It works in a pinch, but I prefer making the batter from scratch," Si explains, moving around the kitchen to gather ingredients.

"You really enjoy this, huh?"

"What? Cooking? Yeah. And baking. I love baking the most. It's relaxing to be in the kitchen, and I like how you can transform a pile of random ingredients into something amazing that brings people together. You know? Most of my best memories about my folks revolve around the kitchen. It was the one place we connected and talked about our days. Heck, Mom used to make cookies with me and it was probably the most emotional connection I ever felt with her. She'd let me make my own shapes with the dough or do designs with the chocolate chips. It was nice. Well. Until life got too busy and we stopped eating meals or baking together, but when I was a kid we ate around the dinner table every night."

"That's neat. I remember one year Gramps got a bee in his bonnet about making a full Christmas feast for us.

Like he remembered from growing up. It was a disaster. We ended up with a chicken that was a layer of char over a heap of raw meat. Crunchy mashed potatoes that tasted like raw garlic, scorched mushy bread that was supposed to be dressing, and a pumpkin pie that was jiggly raw filling in a charcoal crust. The only edible part was the canned cranberry jelly."

"Oh, wow, that sounds, uh, not great?"

"We went to a Chinese buffet instead of risking food poisoning by eating it. The buffet was great. The next year we all nuked a Hungry Man frozen turkey dinner instead of attempting another homemade feast."

"So, they set the bar low for me to help you impress your family by teaching you anything?" Si teases.

"Pretty much, yeah. I'll have to tell Gramps how you taught me to magic an edible meal out of vegetables."

"What do you have against vegetables?" Si teases.

"Nothing, if they taste as good as this kitchen smells right now," I enthuse.

"Good." Si flashes me a smile, then turns to get out more ingredients. "Because I use them a lot. More cost effective and nutritious than processed crap."

"That's what Jude says. He's conscientious about what he eats to help manage his diabetes. So, What's your favorite thing to cook?" I ask, perusing the various items in the tidy cabinets as Si selects what we need.

"Hmm," Si hums. "Tough call. It's more baking than cooking, but I might have to say bread. Nothing like the smell of it fresh out of the oven, and it feels like magic. The way the dough rises. Reminds me of the old story about getting something from nothing? These little tiny grains of yeast make a huge loaf rise. When Auntie taught me how to bake, she said the yeast was like a one-day pet. We feed and care for it while it lasts, and then in return, it will feed us a meal, too."

"That's poetic."

Si shrugs, self-conscious. "I guess. Celine's mom and mine are sisters. Their gran taught them to bake, and passed along all the family recipes. Auntie doesn't really get what it means that I'm genderfluid, but she said Simone should learn the family recipes. Like every girl in the family. So she taught me."

"Sounds cool."

"It was pretty special. But it sort of sucks that some parts of me get excluded from the tradition like that, you know? Like, why shouldn't Si or Simon have our family recipes passed along, too? If I wanted to learn? Or why should Celine have to sit through lessons she hates just because a musty old tradition dictates it? I don't know. It's just a bag of mixed emotions, I guess. Like, yeah, it was hella validating for my auntie to see me as Simone and pass along the recipes. But, I'm still me, and I'd enjoy being in the kitchen even if my girl mode never existed, you know? Same with my dad trying to get me into his home repair crap as some father-son bonding ritual. He never tried to teach my sister, even though she might enjoy playing with power tools. Becca was still little when I left home, but Dad had me help hand him parts and stuff at her age. She always hangs around watching, just begging him to include her, any time he gets out the tools or maintains the car. It's ridiculous not to teach her, too. Anyway. Sorry, I'll get off my soapbox now."

"Nah, it's cool, Si. I get what you mean about forcing kids into the roles you want for them. Before my mom noped out of my life, she used to sign me up for sports camps and peewee leagues. She never once let me register for the summer art camps I was interested in because she considered arts and crafts too girly. And now I'm working with a bunch of professional artists."

"So, do you enjoy making art, too?"

"Sure." I shrug. "I'm crap compared to my friends, though. Not much good at figure drawing. I do alright with sculpture and 3D media. Like painting miniature figures."

"Like that army of tiny trolls and goblins I saw on your shelves yesterday?" Si demands, sounding impressed.

"Yeah. I painted them all," I agree. "It's relaxing."

"Even that badass dragon looming over the battle?"

"Even Smaug," I confirm.

"You named the dragon Smaug?"

"Sure." I nod. "After my first favorite dragon."

"I didn't realize those were your work. I want a closer look next time I visit you."

"Sure, you can check them out any time," I agree. Then with a hint of teasing suggestion, I add, "I've got my favorites on display in my bedroom. If you want to see more, you can check out my mighty replica sword of smiting."

Si snorts. "Does that line ever get you laid?"

"Hey! Mind out of the gutter, Si. Can't friends invite each other into their bedrooms without it meaning anything sexual?" I play up my mock outrage, but Si sees right through me.

"Sure, but that was undeniably a line. So, does it work?"

"More often than you'd think," I admit with a wink. That gets Si laughing.

"I look forward to seeing your mighty oaken staff, I'm sure it's a very impressive rod," Si jokes.

"Whatever," I shove Si's shoulder. "Next time see if I let you fondle my wand of regeneration."

"Now who has a gutter mind?" Si shoots back at me.

"Guilty."

Our gazes lock. I lean in, thinking for a moment that Si might have leaned toward me, too. My lips part, I can feel Si's warm breath on my skin, imagine the way our lips will feel pressing together.

The timer on the Instant Pot beeps. We jerk apart. Si spins away to take care of our food, explaining the next steps of the recipe to me as if nothing had been about to happen. I try to gauge if Si is as flustered by our almost kiss as I am while I work the immersion blender.

We add in a can of coconut milk to make the soup creamy. It must have been my imagination running wild. I've fantasized about kissing Si often enough since we met that it's no wonder I read something into the moment that wasn't there. Si and I are just friends, no reason to complicate things.

We spend another few hours cooking. Si makes meals ahead for the week, so we start some yeast for a bread recipe. Then chop and portion ingredients for Si's morning smoothies while it proofs, getting all bubbly. We finish the dough and Si shows me how to knead it. While the bread rises, we roast veggies and various single servings of protein to fill sandwiches for packed lunches. Sitting near the warm oven, the dough doubles in just over an hour. I enjoy shaping it into rolls for sandwiches, though Si's turn out more even than mine. They have to rise again before we bake them, so Si shows me the dumpling recipe for the chicken soup while we wait. The finished product is totally worth all the effort.

It boggles my mind that I helped prepare the feast we end up producing and packing away into the fridge in neatly labeled tupperwares. Si packs up a bag of the re-usable containers for me to take home at the end of the evening. My bag goes into the fridge along with every-thing else, except the fresh bread.

"There, now all that's left is plating," Si announces. "You're staying to eat, right?"

"If you don't mind the company?" I agree.

"Not at all. Watch and learn, my young padawan," Si says.

By the time we're eating our bowls of squash soup, I'm exhausted from all the cooking. Pretty sure I'm going to dream about chopping neat little slices of vegetables. Si garnishes our bowls with crumbled up bacon, salty roasted squash seeds, and a swirl of additional coconut milk so it looks like something out of a cooking magazine. It tastes better than anything I've ever made before. I stifle a moan at the flavor.

"This is so good!" I rave, gesturing with my spoon.

"Thanks, mate," Si takes another bite to cover a pleased smile. "You did a good job helping."

"I mean it, you have true talent, Si. Why don't you do food stuff for a living? That's your dream job, right?" I wave my spoon around to encompass the tidy kitchen and all the food we made in it today.

"Yeah, well, culinary school is expensive, Max. And the restaurant business can be cutthroat. I barely lasted a couple weeks before all the pointed looks and barbed comments made me pack up my knives and apply for a refund on my loans."

"Oh. I'm sorry. I shouldn't have pried." I resist the impulse to reach for Si, to offer whatever physical comfort I may.

"It's okay." Si's tight, forced smile belies the words and I know I hit a sore spot. "Celine says I should try again. Or take part-time classes so I can supply pastries for the shop."

"Do you want to do that?" I ask.

"I'd like to bake for a living, sure. I guess I don't know where I'd even start since my attempt at cooking school was a massive failure." Si swirls the spoon through the soup in agitation.

"Maybe you could talk to Paz about how he got started baking for Sin and Chocolate?"

"I suppose that couldn't hurt."

"I'll text you his number later so you can chat, then. And in the meantime, I meant it when I said you are a phenomenal cook. Teach me more. Everything you know," I enthuse.

Si snorts out a laugh. "That might take a while."

"Then it's a standing date. You do your food prep every Sunday?" I ask, then realize I'm essentially inviting myself over to make Si cook for me and spend a ton of labor teaching me. All this food has to be expensive. This many frozen meals would add up fast, especially since we made enough of everything for Celine, too. "I mean, if you don't mind teaching me. I can chip in for the ingredients. Or pay for the lessons. God, I didn't mean to act like you owe me unlimited cooking lessons. I'm being a massive tool, sorry."

"There you go bragging about your tool again," Si clucks, eyes alight with a merry twinkle, the earlier pensiveness about my unsolicited career advice gone. "Don't freak out, mate. I had fun teaching you. You're good company. If you're serious about learning, you can join me for food prep. Just pay for your share of the ingredients."

"Are you sure? I'm happy to compensate you for your kitchen expertise," I offer.

Si bumps our knees together. "Don't worry about it. I'm happy to teach my fake boyfriend how to cook, it's only in my self-interest for you to learn." Si winks. "Besides, your friends will think it's cute. Adds to our credibility."

"Got to keep up the ruse," I agree, hating that I ever suggested fake dating. The past few days have convinced me I want a shot at something real with Si when this is over. Now that we've begun, I feel locked into the path we started down. I don't want to screw up our connection. Pretending lets me be a better version of myself. Someone confident who doesn't stumble face first into being an asshole.

CHAPTER 14

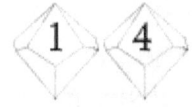

Si

The next week passes fast, I see Max most mornings on our commute, except on Tuesday when my shift starts later so I can close the shop for Celine. I don't have any issues with the additional duties, but I miss my Max time on the bus. We still text throughout the day, but it's not the same as seeing him in person. I chalk up missing him to our friendship being new. We're still in that exciting getting to know you stage.

Max has his game group on Friday, so we don't meet up after work like we did last week for dancing. He invites me along to an in person video game day at Errol and Rene's place on Saturday, since all his friends are bringing their partners.

He calls it official fake datemate duty. I go along with his plans, playing down just how much I've been enjoying spending time with him. I am a little nervous about seeing his friends again. They seem chill, so my vague fears of rejection are likely unfounded. Last week, during the online video game party Max roped me into, none of them batted an eye when I joined their group voice chat presenting as Si. Even though they met me as Simone.

Max showed me how to set my username to include my pronouns, or lack thereof, like the rest of them. He introduced me as Si, no pronouns, in the voice chat. They all rolled with that like it was no big deal. To them, it wasn't. No one had any trouble alternating Pia's pronouns or calling Rene they. For once, I'd found people who got me, no explanations required.

Gina and her friends tried, but it was rare to go an entire night with no name or pronoun slip ups when I used to go out with them. Most of them weren't malicious, just careless. Although, I'd overheard a few of the ladies griping. They said it would be more reasonable of me to pick one thing and stick with it instead of changing it around on them all the time. They never got it. That my identity isn't a choice or something I can control. Any more than I can control the color of my hair or how fast my nails grow or will myself taller. Sure, I can dye my hair, or trim my nails, but that's just esthetics. Underneath the mask, my nails didn't stop growing and my hair still sprouts from my head in an ashy shade of dark blond.

Max isn't like them. He tries to understand me, and when he doesn't get something, he asks. I like that about him. I've also noticed he alternates Pia's pronouns meticulously in every other sentence, even when they're not around to hear him. And that means a *lot* to me. It tells me he's getting my pronouns, or lack of pronouns, right when he talks with his friends, too.

When it's time to leave on Saturday, Max and I meet up at the bus stop. We're going the opposite way from our usual. So we can take the SeaBus to the SkyTrain, since that's the most straightforward route for us to get to Errol's place in Burnaby.

When it's not packed full of morning commuters or drunken revelers, I enjoy taking the ferry across the water. Max's presence at my side reassures me that I have backup. It's kind of fun to take a short boat ride to kick off our day.

Max buys a coffee at a cafe on the quay, and he sips it leisurely as we watch the waves through the window.

"Have you ever played *Battle Fox* before?" Max asks me.

"Nope. Don't have a game console."

"That's alright. The controls are pretty intuitive. The people who made the game kind of rock." Max winks and I take a second to realize he means that the place he works made the video game we're playing today. The one I've seen gracing ads around town. His job is pretty cool.

"Oh yeah? I take it that Eye-On made the game?"

"Yep. Errol's kid about shit a brick when he realized his dad made Ollie Owl. Pia painted him a life-sized mural on his wall."

"Errol's kid is Mo, right?"

"Yep. Pia, Emil and Gregor's baby should be there

too, Rain."

"Okay. Any other children?" I check.

"Nah, not yet, anyway." Max purses his lips, then gives a minute shake of his head. "And it's a sore spot for Emil. The three of them want another kid. I guess there's also Theo's nephew Sky. He comes to town with Theo's mom and sister sometimes, but they won't be there today. Some of the others have niblings too, but I haven't met any of them."

"Is it alright to ask why it's a sore spot for Emil?"

Max shrugs. "Yeah, he's been open about it, so I don't see why not. Pia carried Rain, but I guess Emil tried to get pregnant for years before that. It was before I met the gang, so I don't know exactly how it all went down. Just that it was rough on him and now he's going through IVF."

"So, he's trans?" I ask, knowing he is. What I really mean is that I want these people to be *my* people. The way they're already Max's. He was right that I could fit in with them. It's not so much that they all accept that a man, or nonbinary papa like Rene, might want to carry his or their baby. It's that it means they see the world outside the binary I'm so used to bending over backwards to accommodate with everyone else.

"Yeah. I told you I have a lot of not cis friends. They're cool, right?" Max asks, looking at me like my approval means the world to him.

"Yeah, Max. They're cool." I pat his hand and he beams at me.

"Glad you think so." Max's smile turns shy and he gets

that awkward look, like he's second-guessing every-thing he wants to say until he blurts out a change of subject to a more benign topic. "Anyway. We do other games, too. Ever play Spectral?"

"Never heard of it," I reply. Between people bringing young children and all the games I don't know how to play, I'm having second thoughts about agreeing to this outing. It sounds too much like the last few times I went along to luncheons with Gina's new friends. How they all talked about babies and brands I'd never heard of for products I'd never need to care about since I have no interest in parenting.

My mom press-ganged me and Celine into babysit-ting Becca as an infant. That was more than enough of dealing with diapers, bottles, and wailing babies for me. Mom always guilted me into compliance. If I com-plained, Dad would half-heartedly agree I shouldn't have to watch the baby because, 'that's more of a girl thing, isn't it, dear?' Ugh. I shove away those memories to pay attention to Max again.

"It's a collectable trading card game. Like Pokemon? Or Magic. The rules are simple enough to learn. We usu-ally do pairs. Theo and Errol always have extra decks, so I can show you how to play, if you want to learn?"

"Sure," I agree with a shrug that I hope hides how out of my depth I'm feeling. "Why not?"

"Cool," Max beams at me. And just like that, I'm glad I agreed to tag along and learn about his hobbies. Last weekend's game turned out entertaining. The friendly commentary over the voice chat kept me engaged with the game and the group. Today might prove fun, too. Or it might suck, but it's worth giving it a shot to make Max smile at me the way he is now.

We're the last guests to arrive at the gathering. Errol's place is a bit of a hike from the SkyTrain station. But it's a nice day, so we walk across the park hand-in-hand rather than wait for a bus. It's one of those moments that make me wish this was real, but I don't want to rock the boat when things are going so well between us and I'm starting to feel at home with Max's friends.

The other guests have already crowded around Errol's coffee table with their consoles set up and a tournament in the works when Errol greets us at the door. "Hey, glad you could both make it. Come on in. Don't mind the mess, we're looking at samples to get the ball rolling on the renovations, now that my tenants have officially moved out from upstairs."

He must mean the bits of tile and wood in various colors and finishes stacked atop the table in the entry-way. It's where I'd have left a stack of mail and loose change if this was my place.

"So, before you ask," Errol adds, "Pia and her family had to cancel. Emil's taking last week's bad news pretty hard."

"Oh, shit, is he okay?" Max asks. I assume they're referring to what Max mentioned on the way here about Emil trying for another kid. I know better than to pry into something so personal, so I keep my mouth shut as

Errol steps aside to let Max and me enter. We kick off our shoes to join the other pairs heaped by the door.

"Yeah, I mean, he will be. Pia said he's starting another round of hormones, so he wasn't up for visiting today."

"That stinks." Max says. "Poor guy deserves a break after everything the three of them have tried."

"That's too bad," I echo Max. I was looking forward to getting to know Pia and Emil better, but I can understand why they opted not to come. It's still surreal in the best possible way to be surrounded by people who don't find this conversation strange. Who take for granted that of course Emil could be a pregnant man. This is what I've been missing, people who make me feel like I belong.

"Yeah," Errol agrees. "Fingers crossed this next cycle will be the lucky charm. We're organizing meal deliveries for the four of them for the next week, since Emil has a rough time with the hormones."

"I'm in," Max volunteers. "Just tell me how much my share comes to. I hope this next cycle works out for him."

No wonder Max loves these people so much he can't bear to risk disappointing them. They're a family. His family, whether he sees it or not. Dare I hope they could be mine too? Even if Max and I are never more than friends and pretend exes at the end of this, I'd be content with having this community around me.

"Same, I'll keep you posted. On a lighter note, we're starting the games off with *Battle Fox*," Errol sweeps his arm toward the living room where the games have already begun.

"Nice! Can you believe Si hasn't played *Battle Fox,* yet?" Max says, clapping Errol on the shoulder. I like how Max's greeting provided his friend with what to call me today.

"Well, you're in for some fun then, Si," Errol says, picking up on the cue about my name. "Make yourselves at home, snacks are on the counter, games are in the living room."

"Max! Come get your nails touched up, I was just telling Mo here how chipped they're getting," Theo waves Max into the living room. I trail behind him and get introduced to a school kid in a *Battle Fox* crew t-shirt.

Max does introductions, claiming me as his datemate, which the kid takes in stride along with my lack of pronouns.

"Let me see?" Mo holds out his palm, wiggling his fingers in a gesture for Max to offer his hands. Max places his fingertips in the boy's outstretched palm, and Mo clucks over the chipped paint. "You're supposed to touch it up or take it off before it gets this bad," Mo chides, he hands Max a little tub of acetone. "Here, take off the rainbows and I'll fix you up. Can I do your nails too, Si?" he asks, turning his focus to me. "I've got all the colors."

"He does a fantastic job using them, too," Theo interjects, showing off gold and pink stripes on his nails. The pink matches the new dye job in Theo's hair since I last saw him.

"It's 'cause I practice a lot," Mo says solemnly. "So, what color do you want? I have sparkles, too," Mo gestures to the bottles of polish covering the coffee table in front of him. Rene clears their throat meaningfully and Mo rolls his eyes. "You can say, no. Papa told me not to be pushy."

I can't help but smile at the matter-of-fact way this kid refers to his birth-parent as Papa. It's another little reminder that I'm among my own.

There's a midnight blue bottle near the edge of the table, it has a glittery shimmer to it that reminds me of the night sky out in the country. I reach for it and hand the bottle to the kid. "How about this color?"

"Sure, good pick. Daddy got me that one, so it's new. Go like this." Mo spreads his fingers on the edge of the table. I mimic the gesture, and Mo gets to work brushing the polish onto my nails.

By the time I'm done, Max is ready to present the kid with a clean slate and Mo paints his nails a cheery yellow with a golden luster like sunshine. The way Max glances at me, like he's seeking approval after making his selection tells me he didn't pick my favorite color by chance. I can't help thinking it would complement my nails. Intertwined, our fingers would form a pretty contrast, day and night.

Mo moves on to the animated fighting game on the television after he finishes with our nails. He takes up heckling Theo like it's a favorite pastime. If his frequent glances at his parents are anything to go by, the kid pushes the boundaries of what he's allowed to say. He swaps out actual curses for goofy child-friendly equivalents, following the adults' leads.

Listening to the adults swapping in poop-talk for shit-talk is hilarious. I don't play, pleading that I need to let my nails dry long after that ceases to be true, but I enjoy watching Max interact with his buddies.

"Oh, he-" Theo starts, then changes course when Jude elbows him and Errol clears his throat, "-eck, yeah! Take that, losers!" he fist pumps as his character pops up with a victory pose after the latest match.

"Carp," Mo complains, "I almost had him!"

"We'll get them next time," Max ruffles the kid's hair affectionately.

I doubt that, since they've just lost their third match in a row.

"Good game. I think it's time to switch up the teams," Errol suggests, "Si, do you want to play?" He offers me his controller, which would put me on Theo's team. Good strategy, if he wants his kid to win the next match.

"Sure," I agree, taking the controller and expecting to lose miserably. To my surprise, I kind of enjoy the game. True to Max's words, I find the controls intuitive. Less dizzying than the last time I tried to play Halo with Gina's husband. I don't win, but I have fun losing. Theo grumbles, but avoids blaming me for dragging his team down, despite my frequent deaths. He even comes to my defense around the third time in a row I get knocked out of the fight right after my character respawns.

"Come on, people! Stop beating up my poor newb. How are we going to get Si hooked on *Battle Fox* if you all gang up like that?" he grouses. The others let up a bit, voicing half-hearted apologies. When I get a lucky hit in on Max's character, Theo laughs in triumph and fist bumps me. "Nice one!"

That's probably why I'm enjoying myself. They're all nice about my suckitude. Yeah, they trash talk each other, but no one attacks anyone else over a lack of in-game skills. It's friendly banter, not hidden barbs.

My team still loses by a wide margin, but I'm grinning when we put away the controllers in favor of the card game Max told me about. That's a bit more complicated than the video game, but I enjoy being on Max's team. He explains the various strategies the others are using to me after we lose in the first round of their tournament.

We hang out and eat snacks after getting knocked out of the game. Max draws Paz into talking about my interest in baking. We swap favorite kitchen disaster stories and compare notes on blondie recipes, since Paz brought a pan of them. I relax, chatting with a fellow baker while the others finish their game. The entire day is more fun than I expected.

CHAPTER 15

Max

I trek down the hill to Si's place on the second Sunday in November with a spring in my step. It's become routine after eight weeks of lessons. A routine I love. I'm excited to spend the day with Si. We stopped at the store for groceries on the way home from Gui's place after our latest game day last night.

Si seems more comfortable with my buddies, swapping recipes with Paz and shit-talking Theo like a pro. I assumed Emil and Rene bonded so fast because of their shared love of kids, but they both took to Si fast, too. We've gone out dancing a few more times and had several group video game days, both online and in person. All without arousing suspicions that Si and I are anything but the real deal.

Laura and Alice even suggested everyone come out to the North Shore. They're planning an outing to check out the Capilano Suspension Bridge, all lit up for the season, to mix up our usual routine. The glimpses I've seen of the holiday display driving by on the bus each evening are enough to convince me it would be fun.

Ever since Si agreed to pretend to date me, it's been nice to have the pressure to settle down off my shoulders. It's freeing to just feel like a part of the group again. Instead of being everyone's pet project or an object of pity because no one wants me.

I mean, I realize that my broke ass is no great catch, but it's not something I want constant reminders of. Everyone thinking I'm with Si means I don't have to think about it at all. Sure, I'm not getting laid, but a hookup would feel too much like cheating on Si. And really, I'm so hung up on my new friend, I don't want anyone else.

The biggest downside to this arrangement is that lying to everyone sucks. Putting Gramps and Grandad off the trail has been hard. They've commented on how much more naturally I'm smiling when we video chat and that I keep talking their ears off about my new friend, Si. Recently, they've started asking if they get to meet my special person soon. I hate lying to them, so I've been cutting our calls shorter than usual.

Simple enough, considering the time difference and my work schedule. Life makes it difficult to squeeze in our regular chats to begin with. Now that my weekends are busier, what with Si's cooking lessons and the two of us hanging out more, my family time is mostly sporadic texts. I also trade voicemail messages with my grandfathers when we miss catching each other on the phone.

Si and I planned the meals we'll be making today on our bus ride home last night. A few of the ingredients are for a surprise dish Celine apparently requested that has me antsy to get to today's lesson so I can learn what we're making. Having meals in my fridge, ready to reheat all week, has been a welcome treat since Si offered to teach me to fend for myself in the kitchen. It doesn't hurt that Si's food tastes way better than anything in the freezer aisle. The cookies tucked into my share of the food last week were divine.

When I knock on the door to Celine's apartment, I'm once again greeted by Si in a flowy blouse, loose joggers, and just a touch of subtle eye makeup. Hot. And huh, Si's curves are more pronounced today. Like the compression vest is missing in action. Interesting. I don't call attention to it.

"What sort of day is it?" I ask, to be sure. I trail my host toward the kitchen, and I can't help admiring the view. It's getting harder to tamp down on my attraction to my fake datemate.

"Si," Si replies, with an over-the-shoulder grin. "More often than not, I'm in Si mode. I like that you check in with me, though."

"I'll keep asking, in that case," I say. It's become a habit by now.

Si lays out our ingredients and tools, just like every week. "With my old friends, I used to wear pronoun pins, but I lost the last set and I didn't bother to replace them. People either don't see them, or they ignore them, or they make stupid attack helicopter jokes. So I switched to doing colored bracelets to help Gina and the others remember. Pink for Simone, blue for Simon, and green for Si. It helped, since some of them disliked having to ask. Or they'd just assume based on my presentation, even though I sometimes switch it up with more femme or masc styles in Si mode. And I don't always have the time or feel safe to femme it up as Simone."

"So, you don't do the colors anymore?" I ask, curious why, if the color system resulted in less grief.

"Nope. Don't like the bracelets. Any sort of jewelry, really. It chafes. Can't seem to forget it's on my skin." Si rubs a thumb over the spot where a wristband would rest. As if even talking about wearing wrist adornments is uncomfortable. "The most I can handle is a lightweight necklace in girl mode. Colorful ribbons or a lace choker, stuff like that. Or my bow ties when I'm in boy mode. I prefer for gender not to matter, and if it does, for the person to ask. It doesn't matter at all in most of my daily interactions. Strangers don't need more than my name to refer to me. The people who matter know to ask."

"Makes sense." I nod. "Like, how you can't assume someone is happy just because they smile, right?"

"Explain?" Si gives me an assessing look.

"Right. So, like how you can't know what's going on inside someone else's head unless you ask them."

Si smiles, "Yeah. Something like that."

I nod again; it feels momentous, being on the same wavelength about this. Like this is something that matters to Si and I'm not completely clueless. "Yeah. When my mom took off, my friends all commented on what a good mood I was in, all smiley and joking. It was only a facade; I thought if I let myself crack, even a little, I'd crumble. I was miserable and depressed for the better part of that school year. Yet all the pictures of me from that year, I've got this stupid cheesy grin like I didn't have a care in the world. I get it's not the same as being genderfluid, like, at all, but I understand what it's like to just wish someone would ask instead of assuming they knew me from the face I presented to the world."

"That's, yeah, pretty similar in some ways. Sorry no one asked. How are you, Max?"

"I'm great. These cooking lessons are life changing. Seriously, I don't think I've ever eaten as well as I have since you started teaching me. I've been sending pics to Gramps and Grandad, and they don't believe I cooked the food. They keep asking what brand it is and telling me taking it out of the package to nuke it doesn't count as 'from scratch'."

Si laughs at my story, which gets me laughing too. "We can take a video of the process this week, give them irrefutable proof," Si suggests.

"Good idea," I agree. "So, what's first?"

"First, you wash up. Then get to chopping." Si points me toward the knives. "Knife work is a key skill for any chef. The more you practice, the better you'll become. Then your prep will take less time and result in more uniform results, which means more even cooking."

"You just want me to handle your zucchini," I tease, hefting the thick green rod from the counter.

"Nah, I want you to handle my aubergine," Si counters, lifting the veggie in question to eye level. We both crack up at that one.

I reach for the eggplant. Si makes a lewd noise as my fingers touch the smooth end of the deep purple vegetable. I laugh and run my fingers along the length of the eggplant. Si continues with over the top porny moaning, like I'm touching the actual organ the vegetable has somehow become synonymous with.

Honestly, the large oblong veggie really isn't that phallic compared to the others we've cooked during these lessons. Too girthy for most people's comfort as a stand-in dildo. It's more rounded and bulbous than long. I guess if you squint hard enough, the fat end sort of looks like balls? Not that I'd ever actually stick any veggie up my ass. There might have been a time I considered it, before I discovered sex toys were a thing. Lucky for horny, curious, fourteen-year-old Max, the closest thing our veggie crisper back home ever held to a carrot or zucchini was leftover fries.

I continue to fool around, pretending to give Si's eggplant a showy hand job with big, exaggerated strokes. Si's moans of feigned pleasure amp up in volume and intensity. It's hot, and funny. We're both cracking up, when a throat clearing interrupts our hilarity. Si whirls around with a guilty expression.

"Celine, sorry!"

Celine, the cousin who is letting Si crash here. I've spent almost every Sunday in her apartment for almost two months, saving the two times Si came to cook with me at my place. All things considered, it's surprising we haven't crossed paths before now. Then again, she spends most weekends with her boyfriend, Harvey. Si seems convinced it's a matter of time before she moves in with him. That's a source of anxiety for my new friend, so it has come up in our chats several times.

I get why. Housing isn't exactly affordable in the city. When I was searching for my current place, the only listings I found without a lengthy commute for under a grand a month came with several pre-existing house-mates. And a lenient interpretation of what makes for a legal bedroom.

Celine saunters into the kitchen and leans against the counter at her cousin's side. She sounds more amused than anything. "Si, my dear, is this a Si day?" She pauses until Si nods. "You're only supposed to use the eggplant as code for sex, not the actual sex act. I can see why it might seem confusing. Pro tip: don't shove your literal eggplant up this lovely boy's ass, because you'll probably hurt him. I'm sure the ER nurses would love the story of digging it back out again, though. Bet it would be a memorable x-ray film. Great for parties."

"Thanks, coz, I'll keep that in mind. Sadly, peaches aren't in season, so I don't have anywhere else to stick this lovely aubergine."

"That's a pity. Guess you'll have to turn it into egg-plant parm to feed me in recompense for being such a fount of wisdom," Celine says, gesturing airily.

"Rude! What wisdom is that?" Si retorts.

"Sex tips, duh. Since you've got a new beau in here, making you moan loud enough to wake me before noon. Here's some free bonus advice: you don't actually sprinkle your partner with water when you're done." Celine winks. I glance at the clock, but it's only a few minutes before noon, so it's not like we were being unreasonable with our noise levels.

Si snorts, unconcerned at the jibes. "Thanks, I better dump out that cup of water I had at the ready then. Why have the emojis lied to me? Such a brutal betrayal."

"Hey, judging from how happy Si just sounded, I was doing pretty darn good with the hand job!" I complain.

"I think I might like you, new beau," Celine says, giving me a once-over.

"This is Max, he's my new friend and fake boyfriend. The one I told you needed a plus one for his buddies' wedding," Si introduces me. "Max, my irrepressible cousin, Celine."

"Nice to meet you, Max. I'm sure Si would love to have you demonstrate your stroking technique again later, in private." Celine teases with a suggestive wink. She grabs a handful of snap peas from the veggies Si has arranged on the counter and crunches one between her teeth.

"Celine!" Si complains, "Seriously, Max is a friend, that's all."

"Sure, all your friends want to touch your eggplant and make you moan, Si."

"Uh, yeah? Isn't that what friends are for?" I jump in to defend our actions. Maybe it was a bit sexually charged for casual friends? Theo would make a joke like that. If he cooked. Heck, he might buy an eggplant just to make the joke. We aren't being that weird, right? "Have I been doing this friendship thing all wrong?"

"This is the first time I'm hearing that you're not supposed to fondle your friends' produce," Si jokes back. "I guess I owe you an apology, Max. Apparently vegetable humor among friends is too sexually charged, time to get this lesson back on track. Let's chop up the veggies and cook them, nothing sexy."

"The horror. But seriously, are we making eggplant parm? That sounds fancy."

"I don't know about fancy, but it's certainly tasty. We'll do two pans, so there's enough for everyone tonight. Plus leftovers for the week. Then you can just reheat it and serve it with spaghetti."

"Ah, so you're giving cooking lessons with the weekly meal prep now, Si? I won't get in your hair. Just letting you know Harvey is coming by for dinner tonight," Celine says, still looking between the two of us with interest.

"Oh. Cool. Do you want me to clear out after we eat?" Si offers.

Celine looks guilty as she says, "Would you mind terribly? Sorry, coz, I hate to waltz in and sexile you after disappearing most weekends for the past little while. It's just that I've got a doctor appointment first thing tomorrow over on Lonsdale. So it would be a hassle to stay at Harvey's place tonight, hence he's coming to me."

"You can come hang at my place, Si. If you need a place to crash tonight," I offer without thinking the words through. It's not as if I've got a spare bed hidden somewhere. Still, if Si needs somewhere to be, I want to help.

"That would be cool, if I won't be a bother?"

"Nah, I've got room. We might have to cuddle a bit, since my bed is only a full-size futon, but we can make it work, right?"

"Sure, right," Si agrees, rubbing sweaty palms on the soft fabric of the joggers I've spent the morning admiring. I wish my hands could follow the same path. But that's crossing even more lines than inviting Si to share my bed tonight. Celine looks between us again, like we're a puzzle for her to solve, then she shakes her head, throws up her hands and leans in to kiss Si's temple. "Thanks, coz. I'll let you two get back to the cooking lesson. Nice to meet you, Max. Don't be a stranger."

Celine leaves with a smile and a wave. Si huffs out a breath.

"Sorry, she can be intense. I hope it's alright that I told her the truth? About us just being friends, I mean."

"Oh, yeah, no problem. I doubt she'll meet my buddies. It's not like we ever hang out on the North Shore much, Al and Laura's light watching tour aside," I say. I get it too. Keeping this a secret from Gramps and Grandad is hard, but it would defeat the entire purpose if they blurt the secret to my friends, who they occasionally see when I video chat with my family at group get-togethers.

"Hm, good. Now, let's start this eggplant. It takes some extra prep to sweat out all its bitterness before we bread it, fry it, layer it into a casserole, and bake it."

"That sounds complicated," I complain.

Si chuckles. "I promise not to overwhelm you."

Si guides me through the meal prep, and once again, makes everything seem simple. We finish boxing up all the prepared meals and Si has a bag stuffed with neat tupperwares full of food ready for me, directions for reheating taped to each lid. I'm again amazed that I did this. I made all this food. Or, at least helped. Si makes the kitchen so much less daunting.

When we're done with the food, Si slips into the washroom to change into the compression vest that I've noticed always goes on before Si leaves the house. While Si is indisposed, I send Gramps the video we took, but don't get an immediate reply. I tuck away my phone when Celine's boyfriend arrives for dinner. Si plates up the eggplant parm and a salad that we cut up veggies for earlier. Harvey greets Si and I with warmth. He smiles and checks in with Si about what kind of day it is, so that endears him to me.

The four of us have a pleasant meal before Si grabs an overnight bag to spend the night at my place. We get my share of the food from the fridge and leave Celine and Harvey to their evening. As we walk up the hill, I try not to obsess over the fact that I'm going to be sleeping next to Si.

I wish I dared suggest dropping the fake part of our deal. But other than that barrier to sexual intimacy, everything about our relationship is too perfect to risk rocking the boat before the wedding. It's only another month and a half.

I'll just have to suck up my attraction and platonically share the bed with my crush. Good thing I put away my laundry and tidied my room yesterday, or else Si might have gotten an eyeful of the panties I sometimes wear. That might get awkward, but not for the reasons it usually does when I bring someone new home.

CHAPTER 16

Si

Max's place isn't as messy as it looked on my last visit. His housemate has friends over watching a ball game in the living room. Max exchanges a curt greeting with him, introduces me as his partner, Si, and leads me straight to his room.

I set down my stuff and take in the shelves full of painted miniature figures lining the wall across from his bed. He wasn't kidding when he said he was into this stuff; there are a lot of them. The bigger creatures are badass, their paint jobs exquisitely detailed. I can't even guess how many hours he must spend laboring over each tiny piece. The shading and level of detail make them seem almost lifelike. A host of tiny monsters and various fantasy folks wielding weapons stare down at us.

"Wow," I say, taking in the enormous beast perched atop the middle of his shelf. "This is epic."

"Thanks," Max says, he seems pleased at my attention to his art.

"Which one is your favorite?" I ask. Last time we talked about his hobby, he never gave me a reply. Just a bunch of teasing innuendo and an aborted kiss. Cockblocked by the kitchen timer. Then again, that beep might have saved me from throwing away the friendship we're building over a reckless impulse, if Max doesn't reciprocate my feelings. A couple months into pretending, and I'm pretty sure he's the best friend I've made in a long time. Maybe ever.

"Not sure. The chimera is among my best work," Max replies. He shuffles closer, so that I can feel his body heat behind me. He gestures at the creature I'm admiring.

The chimera is an impressive mishmash of animal parts. Three heads snake out of a shaggy solid body with ragged scaly wings spread wide and a stinger for a tail arched over the creature's back in a threat. The beast stands reared up on two powerful shaggy lion legs, two forelimbs flail at the air. One matches the goat-head on the left, and the right one matches the reptilian dragon head. It appears poised to leap into the air, or launch an attack. All three heads, goat, lion, and lizard alike, sport rictus growls, a threat to the heros arrayed at the beast's feet. It towers over them, massive in comparison. Max's shading makes it appear as though it might spring from the shelf and alight on his shoulder at any moment.

"Huh, this is stunning. Can't believe you painted these," I say, stepping closer to examine the shelves.

He's arrayed most of them into posed groupings. There are other fantasy monsters, a jewel-toned griffon, a hulking skeletal knight astride a warhorse festooned in improbable looking armor. Most of the figures are martial, or kitted out for adventuring, reminiscent of LOTR extras or something similar. A lower shelf features a series of figures, ranging from masc to femme to variations in between, dressed more for seduction than battle. Strategic folds of cloth draped alluringly over postures designed to show off curves. Those he painted with a lifelike glow. They have me reaching out to prod a very round buttock that's poking out of one of the youthful masc looking figure's scant clothing. Above the jeweled belt holding up some sort of flimsy undergarment, he's got well defined abs, flexed to show off his physique.

"I didn't know they made pornographic figures like that," I say with a chuckle.

"They're art," Max says, defensive. "Pinups. Bodies are beautiful." He reaches past me to pluck up the curvy figure behind the one I just caressed.

"Some are, sure," I agree. The gorgeous, literally painted-on muscles on the tiny lewds are making me self-conscious. Is that what Max likes?

"No, all of them. Everybody. Every body. Just because that one's pretty muscles are nice to look at doesn't mean this one is any less gorgeous, or worthy of being admired." He presses the figure he just picked up into my hands. I hold it up and see a bearded masculine face with come-hither eyes and a round, curvy body. The figure is barrel-chested with a bit of a potbelly. Max painted in a spattering of coarse dark hair over his bare torso and thick limbs. Not bear levels of hairy, but enough to show he's not clean shaven. Nothing cut or defined here. This pinup is big, bulky, and soft. And beautiful. Painted with the same loving care as the more stereotypically sexy figures.

"Wow," I say, unable to help the comparison to my own larger frame. It's hard not to see this as Max admitting he appreciates my body, too. How I look naked without my compression vest, or the padded curves I dress to accentuate on my Simone days. I'm not muscular, or a hairy bear. I'm pudgy, like the figurine Max just handed me. And when I examine all the loving attention to detail he put into this bit of plastic, I can't help thinking it might mean something.

"They're beautiful, all of them," Max says, voice soft as he gestures to the shelf. "You have no idea how hard it was to scrounge parts for some of them. I had to put that dude together with parts from like four or five different sprues. He's a bit of an amalgam. But totally worth it to have the curves I appreciate for my little pinup collection."

"Sprues?" I repeat the unfamiliar term, focusing on the trivial since the implication Max finds my body attractive is too fantastical to be true.

"Yeah, the figures come in pieces you have to assemble, on little plastic sprues you have to clip them out of, sort of like a frame?"

"So you build them and then paint them?"

"Yep. It makes them fun to customize, too. The torso for that guy came from a set meant for bedecking in some badass obsidian armor that I repurposed for one of my skeleton lords, over there." Max points out the skeleton directing a pack of hounds near the big guy on the warhorse I'd admired earlier.

"So, how did you get into this?" I set the sexy big dude back on his shelf with care.

Max chuckles. "Gramps bought me model airplanes. A new one every time he visited. It always made me feel special. I'd build them with Grandad, before I realized who they were to each other, and he'd tell me stories about the two of them in the old days. Mom hated it. Said it was a waste of time and that Grandad shouldn't fill my head with war stories and give me ideas about serving like he did. In the end, she threatened not to let me see Grandad over it. Looking back, I think she feared losing me. The way she lost her mom, and maybe my dad? She never talked about him, always told me different stories any time I asked. It got to where I figured either she didn't know who he was or he wasn't a great person, so I stopped asking."

"I'm sorry. That must have been difficult."

"Yeah. She had a hard time taking care of me more often than not. Grandad did the best he could to give me stability when she couldn't. Anyway, looking back, she wasn't well. She framed everything as us against the world. She made me promise to never leave her, and I think she was afraid that if I was close to Grandad, I'd have a reason to go. I guess she ran away before I could leave her."

"That's sad."

"Yeah. I hated her for leaving for a long time, but I was lucky to have Gramps and Grandad. I wouldn't trade them for anything. They love me. So, yeah, every-thing about my mom is complicated. But anyway, I en-joyed building the models, and painting them. When Mom put her foot down with Grandad about the planes, I still liked to hang out around the local game shop. It was between school and home, and it was where I bought all the paints and glues and stuff to make them. The owner let me hang around and watch her work on her Warhammer minis, so long as I didn't bother the paying customers. I got my first job working there as a cashier for a bit in high school. But she got me into the hobby. I was sort of her gaming group's unofficial mascot at the shop. Painting fantasy creatures or bat-tle bots was even more fun than replica planes. So, long story long, I dove right into it. Even though I didn't play much table top before moving here."

"Are they for gaming?" I ask.

"Some of them. There are loads of different brands and games that use specific miniatures. And some gam-ing groups go all out with using appropriate figures to mark their characters and the monsters they're facing. If I ran a game, I'd use them. I have them anyway, and it would be cool to show them all off to everyone. But we usually just use spare dice, or desk toys from work when we play. Theo has some crappy generic ad-venturer figures he brings sometimes if we're in a dun-geon or for battles where character placements matter. And pretty much everyone at work has collections of little toys and action figures and stuff at their desks. I brought in a few of these guys for my desk. Paz got Gui this fully articulated dino figure at a con a couple months ago that we take turns posing in improbable ways for him."

"Ah, that sounds fun."

"Yeah, have I mentioned I love my job?" Max grins.

"Once or twice," I joke, wishing I loved my job half as much as he does his. "What else can you do with them?"

"Play?" Max shrugs, looking self-conscious. "I like to pose out epic battles, as you can see. Or you could make stop motion videos with them. But I just like to display them."

"They're art," I say, remembering him telling me he isn't much of an artist. Clearly he was being too humble. "You're talented, Max."

"Yeah?" He sounds way more hopeful than that scrap of praise merits, so I double down on it.

"Yeah. You're a great artist."

"Thanks." Max smiles at me, his cheeks dimpling. And yeah, he's swoon worthy. Our gazes lock for a long, heated moment. I'm tempted to kiss him, but then he drops his eyes to the ground and shuffles toward his closet.

"So, I've got a sleeping bag, if you want me to take the floor?" he offers.

"No, we can share the bed," I insist. My back won't thank me for a night on the hard floor of what amounts to a basement. Even if there is a faux-wood laminate over what I assume must be concrete. And I don't want to be the reason Max screws up his back.

"You sure?" he checks.

"Yeah. I like to cuddle. Totally platonic, right?" I ask.

"Sure." Max nods, overeager. Then he wanders toward his computer and changes the subject. "Let's see if anyone wants to play *AoM* or *Starcraft*."

"Sure, I'm down for some creeping Zerg action," I agree, since those are both games I enjoy playing with him and his friends. I like the sense of comradery from playing on a team with him, and the Zerg are badass little bug-beasts.

Max logs onto his desktop to see if any of his friends want to play. "Looks like Theo is online and ready to construct additional pylons." Max quotes a line from the game and we share a smile.

He gets me set up on his laptop. We play a few rounds against Theo and Jude, exchanging good natured trash-talk via voice chat. Between games, Max leaves the room to grab drinks. Theo and Jude continue to chatter with me in his absence. It's sort of like a stay at home double-date. Or like we're all becoming friends in our own right, and I enjoy it.

Max and I keep playing even after Theo and Jude call it a night. From the number of suggestive jokes flying by the end of our last match, I suspect they're not headed straight to sleep. The thought makes me wish I could do the same with Max when we retire to his bed. But I don't want to risk the easy companionship that's developed between us over the last couple of months. To forestall the awkwardness of sleeping together as friends with the guy I'm getting more and more besotted with, I suggest playing against each other. He jumps on the offer. So we play again.

By the time we notice it is well past midnight, we're both too exhausted to be self-conscious about lying side-by-side on Max's too small futon. We fall asleep curled up facing away from each other, but I'm not even a little upset to wake up with Max spooning me. My only regret is that the thing that woke me up is his alarm clock. He springs out of bed, cursing about being late for his morning meeting before I can enjoy any dozy morning snuggles. That's just as well. The last thing I need is more fantasy fodder to fuel my growing feelings for Max.

CHAPTER 17

Max

There's a message from Jude on my workstation when I get to my desk after our morning production meeting. There's an issue with the rig for a new playable character, and animation is reporting broken facial controls on the same character. Too bad the person responsible for the issues is on vacation. Production ended up as the go between to make sure the fix gets reassigned without compromising other ongoing work. It's a mess. Since I have zero pull to get things done, I sit there while Errol and half our team figure out a solution. They need to get the fixes done before we waste more animation hours on work that will need redone once they fix the rig.

Jude: Lunch today?

Max: Sure.

I figure he means the entire group of us. That's not unusual, but I've been bringing my food since Si started teaching me to cook. Fewer meals eating out have made my bank balance less dire over the past couple months. That helps lower my general stress. All the more reason to accept Jude's offer.

Jude: Great, what do you feel like?

Max: Soup?

There's an inexpensive ramen place in walking distance, and I've got a reward punch card for a free side. Plus, their menu works with Jude's dietary needs. Jude agrees and we hash out the details between working.

Today, I'm updating tracking spreadsheets and sending out gentle reminders to artists and programmers who are behind on their quotas. Fun times. Most of them don't take out their frustration on me about the reminders. Some do. I pass their concerns along to Errol, per his instructions.

By the time I'm done with my reminders, it's time to meet Jude for lunch. He gets done first and comes to my desk.

"You ready?"

"Yeah, are we waiting on Theo?"

"Nope," Jude shakes his head. "He's eating with Gui today. They wanted crappy fast food, so I bailed. Figured I haven't seen much of you this week so I'd take advantage of being abandoned to my own devices to catch up, if that's okay?"

"Yeah. Of course," I agree.

"Cool. I mean, I was planning on eating with you regardless, but like, this way we get one-on-one time."

Jude grins.

I shut down my work station and we head for the restaurant we agreed on earlier, chatting about our work days. Jude vents about the broken rig issue. I fill him in on the details from our morning meeting to address the problem.

"How's the wedding planning coming along?" I ask when the work talk has run its course and our food has arrived. I wait patiently for Jude to test his blood sugar and dose himself with insulin before he slips his supplies back into his bag and answers.

"Great. Do you want me to gush about it for the next hour?"

I can't hide my grimace and Jude laughs.

"It's fine," Jude assures me. "I get that not everyone wants to hear me obsess over the color palette and making sure the ties match the flowers. Let alone Theo's hair."

"He's going to dye his hair to match the wedding colors?" I ask, surprised, since Jude seems particular about his vision for the perfect day.

"Sure." He nods. "His loud hair choices are part of him, I want our wedding to reflect us, you know? It's going to be a rainbow explosion, but I still want it to look nice, not like a rainbow unicorn broke into the venue and had explosive glittery diarrhea everywhere. It's a fine balance. Speaking of which, did you have a preference on which color your tie and shirt are? Pia called purple, Laura is doing red, and I think Gui will want green, but the rest are fair game."

"Yellow," I say without hesitation. It's Si's favorite. It might not flatter me the most, but I know it will make Si smile.

"Great. I'm excited. And nervous."

"Why are you nervous?" I ask, surprised.

Jude stirs his soup and ducks his head. "It's just, planning a wedding is a ton of work. And it's all expensive. His mom is super excited. She offered to pay for a sizeable chunk of the costs as a wedding present. Theo's the baby and she didn't get to throw a big party for either of his siblings, so she wants it to be special. But it means we're driving out to his home town every other weekend to peruse vendors and make plans. And I'm afraid it might all scare him into changing his mind."

"Have you asked Theo how he feels about it?" I suggest.

Jude sighs. "He just tells me he wants to do whatever will make me happy. But I want him to be happy with our plans too, you know? It's not just my day, it's ours."

"That's valid, but Theo doesn't strike me as the sort to keep his mouth shut if he doesn't like something."

Jude snorts, amused. "Yeah, he's good at making his opinion known, most of the time. Unless it comes to real emotions. Then he has a hard time admitting things upset him. We'll figure it out. It's been easier since I convinced him to go with Whistler as the venue. We booked an inclusive package with some vendors included rather than having to decide every tiny detail on our own. Plus, it saves his folks from hosting everyone, and footing the bill, and helping coordinate everything. I just want everything to be perfect. I know Thee has concerns about making the day reflect us and not just some commercialized stereotype, with the package deal and all."

"You'll sort everything out so the pair of you can add your own creative touches. Theo will love whatever you decide on," I say, hoping to soothe Jude's nerves as he plucks at his napkin. Then with a teasing wink, I add, "If not, you can bring him around with your wily wiles."

"You know it." Jude winks, unconsciously flirty and sweet. He resettles in his seat, steeples his fingers and asks, "So, last wedding thing, promise. I've been meaning to ask if you and Errol would be up to helping Gui plan the bachelor party? We want to include all the industry folks we know so they can celebrate with us without having to schlep out to the boonies for the ceremony. I know it's supposed to be the best man's domain, but he's doing double duty for the two of us with wedding planning stuff. You and Errol have a handle on all the deets for local event planning stuff from work anyway, right?"

"Yeah, of course, I'd love to help plan your party," I agree. The fact he asked touches me more than I'd have expected. It feels like he's not just including me as part of his gaming group, but as an actual close friend.

"Awesome! Anyway, enough about me and Theo, what about you and Si? And is that right, they go by Si?"

"Yep. Si prefers Si over Simon or Simone for general reference," I say, then correct the pronouns, "but no pronouns in Si mode. What about us?"

"Oh, right, thanks for reminding me. So, is it serious between you two? You're cute together."

"I mean, it's still early days." I fidget with my spoon. Lying to my friends roils my insides with guilt. But gossiping about work and our respective significant others is a welcome reprieve from the constant matchmaking efforts of the past summer and fall.

"Hmm," Jude hums, giving me an odd look. "Not that early. Either way, should we put Si down as your official plus one for the wedding? Or wait and see what sort of day it is, presentation-wise?"

"You're assuming I'm bringing Si as my date?" I ask.

"Aren't you?" Jude arches a brow. "You've been dating for around two months, haven't you?"

"Yeah, I guess we have. Weird." I grin at the realization before it hits me like a gut punch that we don't qualify for that two-month milestone because we aren't together. It's felt like an actual relationship. We talk every day, share the highs and lows of our lives, and I've had Si's company at almost all of our group events since we agreed to our ruse. Si's warmed up to my friends since our first awkward club outing and the LAN party the following day. The whole point of this is to have a date for the wedding, so I stop playing coy. "And I am bringing Si. If that's okay?"

"More than," Jude agrees, nodding. "We'll have to rearrange the singles tables a little, but that's not a bad problem to have. Theo is kind of scarily into helping everyone find their match. It's cute, watching him try to plot out real-life scenarios like one of his campaigns.

I'm glad you met someone you click with, though."

"Well, first, you think everything Theo does is cute, because you're besotted. More to the point, you're to blame for corrupting him to the romance side. You know that, right?" I joke, ignoring the comment about me and Si. No sense lying about my relationship status more than necessary. The problem is, it's getting to where I'm not so sure this is actually fake anymore. Si and I click. Sure, I meant the outings with Si and my buddies to get them to shut up about setting me up on dates. The night out dancing with Simone was about not having to endure Theo and Jude trying to wingman me into a relationship. Not with Jacob, Paul, Kevin, or anyone else with a pulse at the club. But with Simone there, it ended up being the most fun I've had with the gang outside of our game nights in ages. Si eases that lonely ache I used to get from standing on the edges of the group, watching everyone else find the love I didn't dare admit I wanted.

Our weekly cooking lessons feel like spending time with a real partner, not faking it to fool my friends into getting off my back. So I don't have a real response to whether Si and I are serious or if our relationship makes me happy. All I know is, the sight of Si at the bus stop every morning makes me grin. Our message thread has displaced the group chat at the top of my phone's message history. It's become the thread I check anytime I have a second to myself or see a meme I want to share.

"Dude, that's awesome!" Jude laughs. "Here was Gui, all protective of me, and then I was the one who went and corrupted Theo with romance." He seems to find this hilarious. I chuckle along with him. It's hard not to join in, when he's so amused.

"Is that better or worse than blinding him with science?" I joke.

Jude blinks at me.

"You know, like the song?" I clarify. "Poetry in motion?"

"Nope. Never heard that one." Jude shrugs. "Probably less bad? I'm telling Theo you think I corrupted him, FYI. He'll love it."

"Go for it, you know it's true. Also, I'm sending you a link to the song after we eat."

"Sure," Jude agrees. We finish our meals and head back to the studio. As we're walking, Jude nudges me. "So, did Si blind you with culinary science?"

"Huh?"

"You've been bringing in your lunches, you never did that before."

"Oh. Yeah. I'm hopeless in the kitchen, so Si offered to give me lessons on the weekends. You know, like those meal prep influencers on YouTube who pre-cook a bunch of meal components? Where you just reassemble stuff in various combinations to make a bunch of different healthy cheap meals?"

"I'm familiar with healthy cheap meals," Jude agrees dryly. Of course, he knows all about not eating a diet of junk food.

"You know what I meant," I shove his shoulder, exasperated. "Gramps and Grandad are amazing, but neither of them cooks, so I never learned much beyond the barest basics."

"So, you found yourself a personal chef to date?" Jude shoves me back.

"Sort of. Si bakes a lot, too, is that still a chef thing? I've got an extra meal, since we ate out today. If you want to hang with me again tomorrow, I can bring enough for two. It's got kale and roasted chicken and peppers with brown rice, so you can eat it. Si made peanut butter cookies for me, too, if you wanted something sweet. They're more protein than carbs, right?"

"Eh, I'll pass on the cookies, but the rest sounds tasty. We've missed having you eat lunches with us with this new, healthier Max. Maybe with both of us teaming up against junk food, we can convince the others to bring in lunch a few times a week instead of eating out so much."

"I'm game for that."

"Cool, well, back to the grind, see you later, Max."

"Later, Jude."

CHAPTER 18

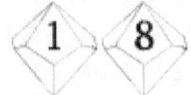

Simon

I close the tea shop by myself on Friday. The weather is turning cold and there isn't much foot traffic, so I convince Celine to head to her weekend with Harvey a few hours early. She agrees with the caveat that Harvey's place isn't far from the shop so I can call her back if we get slammed with customers. That's not likely. We do brisk business most days, but the late afternoon latte crowd has already thinned away to nothing. Celine goes, leaving me alone in the shop for the last few hours before closing. I text with Max, monitoring the door in case I get any late shoppers, or the occasional early evening latte seeker.

Simon: Whatcha doing?

Max: Fighting with a toner cartridge so I can photocopy flyers reminding people to log out of their workstations when they leave for the night. Errol asked me to post them around the studio, even though I already sent three studio-wide emails this week alone. *eye roll*

Simon: Who is winning the fight? Toner is pretty wily. Watch your back, mate.

Max: Nah, it's cool. I've got a pretty high touch AC. It's the actual copier that will really get you. It gave me a nasty paper cut with a sneak attack bonus earlier after luring me into loading in more paper and staples.

Simon: Nerd. You have your game tonight, right?

Max: Yeah. Why?

Simon: I'm closing in another couple hours. I could, like, swing by and bring you a latte or something?

Max: It's out of your way.

My heart sinks at the rebuff. I'm not invested in whether Max wants tea or not. It's just a convenient excuse to visit him. Maybe kiss his cheek in front of his friends. Use the fake relationship thing as an excuse to touch him more than I would otherwise. Might as well take advantage of them thinking we're together while I can. But it looks like the only action I'm getting tonight is going to be solo.

I desire more than this platonic friendship with Max. I want to kiss him and touch him without it being awkward. Or just for show. I don't want to pretend or second-guess how much of what he's doing is an act. Even when it's just the two of us with no one to fool but ourselves, sometimes I wonder.

I wish I could bridge the gap. How do you tell your fake boyfriend you're catching real feelings for him? The obvious solution is to lay my cards on the table.

What do I have to lose? Just the best friends I've made since Gina. I don't want to risk what will happen if he doesn't return my feelings. Better to go on pretending. Cling to the illusion of everything I want with Max for as long as possible rather than to risk losing him entirely from my life.

Simon: Yeah, sorry. Didn't mean to overstep. Forget it.

Max: Wait, sorry. That came out wrong, I'd love to see you. Just letting you know I can't visit for long. Theo gets grumpy about delaying the game, and I can't bring you up to the conference room after hours. Company policy about visitors is sort of strict to prevent details about our projects leaking. If you ever visit during work hours to see the place, you'd have to sign an NDA and junk.

Simon: Oh. Right. I can forget it, if it'll be a hassle.

Max: No hassle, I just don't want to disappoint you after you go out of your way.

Simon: No worries, it was close enough for you to visit on your lunch break the other day, right? So the distance can't be that bad. Give me your order and the studio address. Verisimilitude, remember? Boyfriends do this sort of thing.

Max: They do. I guess. I'll see you in a few hours then? Game starts at six, but if you text me when you arrive, I'll come down to see you. Is it okay if I ask the others if they want anything? We can pay.

Simon: Sure, the more the merrier, my treat. I close at eight, so I'll be there after that.

Max sends me a thumbs up along with his work address and drink order. I grin at my phone like a total sap until I get a customer stopping in on their way home. That leads to a steady trickle of business until the streets become less busy again.

The hours drag after the evening commuters clear the streets. I enjoy the lull. Without my coworkers or any customers, the shop is cozy. I tidy up the displays from the day's idle browsers moving things. That still leaves over an hour to kill before I lock up.

The last hour passes as slow as molasses. It's like the clock knows I'm going to see Max soon and wants to stretch out the time until that happens, just to screw with me. I make Max's latte just before closing. He texted me an order for Jude too, asking for something herbal, whatever is popular, and fits his listed dietary restrictions. So I brew him one of our more popular lavender lattes and send Max the deets to be sure Jude can drink it. No added sweetener or caffeine, as per the order.

Of course, making a drink seems to summon a last-minute customer who hems and haws about which tea to get until it's five minutes past closing. I make the sale, locking up after the customer. Then I give the milk frother and the rest of the drinks to order gear a proper wipe down so it's clean for the morning shift.

Once I grab my stuff, I take a bus to Max's studio. The building isn't what I'd expected. It's dingy and industrial looking. The studio has all the ground-floor windows papered over, so I can't see inside. I can't imagine working here, with the windows covered and no natural light. It would make me feel too boxed in and antsy. The big glass display window at the front of Celine's shop is one of my favorite features. I can gaze out on the busy sidewalk and people watch when we're not busy.

I text Max from the locked glass door that leads to a nondescript lobby. When I peer through the door, the wall boasts a plaque that reads 'Eye-On Games' in stylized letters. The logo beneath the name is a fiery eyeball. *Nice.* My phone buzzes with Max's reply stating he'll be right down. I surf social media while I wait, but it's not long before Max opens the door.

"Hey! Glad you made it." Max takes the drink tray with his and Jude's lattes from me and grins.

"Hey," I greet him back, feeling awkward. If we were really dating, I'd lean in and kiss him, but we're not. It's not like his friends tagged along for me to put on a show for their benefit. They must all be upstairs. We stand there shuffling our feet.

"So," Max says, "are we on for grocery shopping tomorrow? I'm not borrowing the car, but I figure with two of us to carry stuff walking won't be too terrible?"

"Sure. Do you have preferences for this week's meals? Celine wanted chili, since the weather is getting cold. I'm thinking of making cornbread as a side. And I figure if we're getting ground beef for that, we can do a couple big pans of shepherd's pie to pop in the oven too."

"That sounds tasty to me." Max nods.

"Cool. Well, I won't keep you from your game, I just wanted to stop by and see you."

"Thanks," Max lifts his cup toward me, "I appreciate the drink delivery."

"No problem."

"Um, so, see you tomorrow?"

"Yeah. Tomorrow. Text when you want to go shopping."

"I will."

I turn and walk back to the bus stop, vaguely disappointed with how that went. At least I got to see Max tonight.

CHAPTER 19

Max

Every pair of eyes seems fixed on me as I slip back into the conference room with the drinks Simon delivered. I ignore their pointed stares and hand Jude his lavender latte. It smells pretty good, from the whiff I got carrying it up the stairs.

"What? Here, you go, Jude, he said it's a lavender dream latte, in case you want to get it again. Caffeine-free and sugar-free, and he used unsweetened almond milk."

"Mm," Jude hums his approval as he takes a sip of the drink.

"Max is in lurv," Theo teases me with a wink.

"Leave him be, this is tasty." Jude elbows his fiancé. "Don't get me cut off from hand-delivered fancy beverages I can indulge in without fucking with my sugars."

"Paz would bring you fancy tea lattes too," Gui

points out, sounding a tad defensive.

"Yeah, but Sin and Chocolate doesn't do tea," Jude says. "No shade, but they've got like three flavors, all of them bagged teas, and two of them are full caffeine and the third is chamomile." His nose wrinkles in an obvious show of what he thinks of the flavor. "I'd rather have the break room berry bliss herbal stuff, but this tastes more like the flavor advertised."

"They've got loads of flavors at Simon's cousin's shop," I put in helpfully and sip my drink. "This one is a decaf London Fog. The other day Simone made me a maple latte thing that tasted pretty good, too."

"Luuuurv," Theo repeats, but he's grinning at me, not teasing in a mean way. "Back me up here, Laura?"

"Yep, never thought I'd see the day our Max opted for tea over coffee. Must be love," Laura agrees, poking me in the ribs.

"More coffee for the rest of us," Pia says with a broad wink.

"Are we playing or dissecting my love life?" I grumble, not because I mind them noticing I like Simon. No, the hollow feeling in the pit of my stomach is because they might just be right and I can't tell him how I feel without risking our arrangement.

Theo takes the cue to launch back into our game session.

"So, where were we before Max's love life interrupted us?" Theo asks, tapping a finger against his chin, like he just can't resist one last barb about me dating. I roll my eyes and flip him the bird. They didn't need to stop on my account, and I'd said as much when I went down to grab the drinks from Simon.

My role as recurring villain is less involved, now that the heroes have gotten free of my evil clutches. Not that I'm complaining. It's not like there's much for Maximus Powers, my evil sorcerer bent on destroying all dragon-kind, to do now that the party has escaped from the mercenary camp. They left my precious research nothing but ashes and destroyed the rare spell components I need to replicate the xenomorph spell I used on the dragon prince.

The party's daring escape took a few game sessions. They had no easy route to freedom and got fixated on trying to gather intel before fleeing. Gui and Errol decided the mercenary leader's schemes were part of a broader attempt to disrupt the peace between Ethar and Laud. So they wanted proof of the conspiracy before leaving.

In the end, they overpowered a guard. Right after Laura failed her persuasion check to keep them from discovering Jude's character is a dragon in disguise. The mercs took the magical charm that let Lyran pass as human. Jude got in a lucky attack that knocked the guard prone, leaving the door to the cell open. From there, they attempted stealth while they searched for a reversal spell for Sythern.

A lucky merc caught them at it. Their discovery led to several game sessions worth of battling their way clear of the camp. Pebbles, Laura's dragon companion, whom she had convinced to fly away during the group's initial capture, returned in the middle of the fighting to help. I threw some spells at the party during the fighting. That was fun. But now my remaining mercenary allies have scattered with their leader dead, and all my research got reduced to ash, sidelining my sorcerer for the foreseeable future.

Theo says he might bring Maximus back after suitable time to regroup, or he might not. He suggested I can either roll up a new character or take over one of the NPCs so I can play with the party in the meantime. Tonight, I'm watching the others play, but I think I'll take him up on the NPC offer, at least for a few sessions. Watching isn't as much fun as playing.

Our heroes' quest now is to restore Sythern to their true dragon form. Before anyone in Ethar learns of the spell. Earlier, Errol gave me a rather pointed look when he reminded everyone that if only the party had a sorcerer, we could undo the evil magic, no sweat. I laughed when Theo made him roll a knowledge arcana check. And he gave Errol a negative modifier for getting too meta about which spell he thought Maximus could have used to undo the xenomorph. I just stuck out my tongue and reminded him that Maximus hated dragons, so he would prefer Sythern to remain in their human form permanently.

"We were deciding where to go to restore Sythern to their true form," Laura supplies.

The group escaped from the mercenaries at the end of our last session. Now they're arguing about how best to get the information they need to advance their quest. They salvaged some of Maximus's partially burned research notes. That, and a vial of a strange smelling potion that Jude's character recognized as the scent of the fire-phlox flowers Maximus stole from the citadel gardens before their escape. Maximus wrote his notes in a cipher. Theo made prop pages for the group to analyze. He put in a bunch of effort to make them appear like something an old-timey magic-user might have written. He stained the paper to seem aged and singed away parts of it for real.

When Theo hands them over, Errol scowls over the strange scrawl of script. Laura's dragon-singer identifies the language they're written in, not one any of our brave adventurers are fluent in reading. So, they tuck away the notes and potion for safekeeping while everyone argues about the best course of action. In the end, they opt for heading to Pia's mentor's tower in the hopes the powerful necromancer might help. Or at least point them toward sources of arcane knowledge that might hold the key to Sythern's plight.

CHAPTER 20

Max

When Jude asked me to plan his and Theo's bachelor party, the warm glow of acceptance and trust sort of overshadowed just how big of an ask it was. It's not like that was the first time Jude and I hung out together alone, but his request made our friendship seem more real. Less like a default byproduct of sharing a peer group. I don't always read social situations well where it concerns my acceptance in a group. Jude singling me out for inclusion drove home the point that he considers me a close friend.

As far as the actual party, Jude and Theo must not realize the difficulty of booking a downtown venue in December on short notice. Or, as Si keeps pointing out when I send near daily stressed out texts, they might just have expected Errol, Gui and I to throw together a bar hop. Something simple. Tickets to an event, a typical night on the town. With the holiday season in full swing, it limits our options.

Errol and Gui agree with Si that we're just supposed to be giving the guys a night to celebrate their impending nuptials with all their industry acquaintances who can't make it for the actual ceremony. Except Jude entrusted the task to me. Other than providing a guest list and the missive that it's a joint party for both grooms, he gave me free rein. And I want to prove myself worthy of that trust, not make him regret giving it to me. Deep down, I know that's silly. Jude's a total romantic. He'd be the first to tell me I don't have to earn his friendship by jumping through arbitrary hoops. But he's one of the best friends I've had in a long time. I'd hate to let him down. So, I'm taking my charge as party planner seriously.

It's gotten to where Si jokingly reminds me almost daily that the party isn't some sort of loyalty test. It's not. But I still want to impress Jude. Show him I merit his trust in my skills. Part of that drive for perfection might be the guilt that I've been lying to my friends for months.

It's weird that being part of the happy relationship club has made me feel closer to my friends while also feeling alienated by the lie festering between us. Sure, now I'm in on the griping about our partners' foibles and gentle teasing about having someone to get intimate with after a night on the town. But it also means I can't confess to Jude that I want to ask Si on an actual date once all this is over. I can't ask Errol for his insights on what it's like to fall for someone without sex being a part of the picture. I've never had feelings this intense about someone I've only shared a handful of chaste kisses with. If I ask for advice navigating these uncharted waters, then my friends will know I've been lying to them. It might drive a wedge into our friendship. So I'm stressed about that too. It's almost over, though. The need to lie, the fake arrangement between Si and I, the bachelor party I've been throwing myself into planning. My obsession with Jude and Theo's celebration is partly a distraction and partly a penance.

If not for the cupcake crisis the week of the party, I might have kept it to myself. But then Gramps calls while I'm scrambling for solutions to a party centerpiece one guest of honor can't touch. Sin and Chocolate doesn't do catering, so I ordered from another bakery. The person I spoke to assured me they could do diabetes friendly cupcakes, except they were confusing those with gluten-free. We discovered the discrepancy when I called to confirm delivery. The owner canceled the order without a hassle, but it was too late to find another bakery for a custom order.

In hindsight, it was probably a huge over-reaction to decide that if Jude can't have cupcakes, nobody can. I mean, considering that Jude barely even *likes* cupcakes and Theo lives for chocolate, it was definitely not a proportional response. But somehow making this party perfect for my friends has gotten all twisted around in my head. I can't banish the fear that if they don't love the party, they might stop loving me. If this is even close to how Jude felt about finding me a date, maybe I get why he was so insistent. So now I'm waiting on a call back from Paz to see if he can help. When my phone rings, I don't bother checking who is calling, just answer.

"Hello?" I say, distracted by all the tasks I've still got

to accomplish.

"Well, there he is! We've been trying to get hold of you, Max," Grandad's chiding rings with relief at hearing my voice. That hits me with a pang of guilt.

"You had us worried," Gramps adds. "You've stopped answering our calls. Has your new paramour kept you too busy to talk to a couple of old men?"

"No. Of course not! I always have time for my two favorite old fogies. I've missed you both. A lot." My voice catches with just how much I've missed them and how much I hate keeping secrets from them. "I've just been busy with work and planning the bachelor party I told you about."

"For Jude and Theo?" Grandad checks.

"How go the wedding plans?" Gramps asks.

"Yep, for their party. The wedding plans have them stressed. I get why, considering the amount of effort I put into organizing this party. It's overwhelming enough to plan a single night, and they've got the better part of a week of festivities to arrange."

"I'm sure the party you're throwing will be perfect," Grandad says, ever a fount of encouragement. It's nice, but I know I can do no wrong in his eyes. That makes it harder to trust I'm genuinely good enough, no matter what he says.

Gramps makes a low tsking sound before saying, "You always were such a perfectionist, don't stress yourself out, Max. I'm certain your friends will appreciate all the effort you're going to, and if not, they don't deserve you."

"Thanks, you two," I say, achingly homesick at hearing their familiar voices. Once this is all over and the end of my deal with Si breaks my heart, I should swing a visit home to visit them.

"Now, enough about this party. Tell us how you've been," Gramps says, changing the subject.

"Are you still seeing young Si?" Grandad asks. The last time I spoke with the two of them in real time was when they video-called me during one of our cooking lessons a few weeks ago.

Simon was gracious about having a 'meet the parents' moment sprung on him out of the blue. He told my grandfathers what we were making and raved that I'm an excellent pupil. He even fielded their pointed, 'are you good enough to date our son,' type questions with good humor. They liked him. And Si seems to return their regard.

I've been too guilty about deceiving them like that to answer their calls since, opting to return voicemails long after I know they're asleep or exchanging perfunctory texts. I know that isn't a long-term solution, but I'm all twisted up about the entire situation. If I could go back and ask Si for a date instead of this fake nonsense, I'd do it in a heartbeat. Even if it meant going to the wedding alone in a couple weeks. But that ship has sailed.

"Max?" Gramps prompts, and I realize I still haven't answered what should have been a simple question.

"It's fake. I'm a lying liar who lies," I blurt out the truth, unable to bear lying to them a moment longer.

"What did you lie about?" Gramps asks.

"What's fake?" Grandad asks at the same time.

"Everything. Si and I aren't together. We're just friends. We met on the bus, like I said, but I was too chickenshit to ask for an actual date. So I suggested we pretend to be together to get Jude and the others to stop setting me up on surprise dates. And I was afraid you two wouldn't understand, or you'd let something slip to the others, so I lied to you, and everyone else who cares about me. And I'm lying to myself and Si most of all because I'd give anything to make it real."

"Oh, Max, you've backed yourself into a corner, haven't you, my boy?" Grandad asks, fondly exasperated with me. "What were you thinking?"

"I don't know," I say, miserable. "Guess I didn't want to be alone anymore, on the outside looking in. So when the idea hit me, it seemed workable."

"Why not tell Si and your friends the truth?" Gramps suggests. "If they truly care about you, they'll understand."

"Because. If I tell them now, it will just make them hate me. Si and I went through months of pretending only to end up alone at the wedding? No. Besides, I don't want them to blame Si for my poor judgment. Even if I can't have more, I don't want to screw up the connections Si's made with my friends, you know? It's better to stick to the plan for now. I'll just have to come clean after the wedding and hope everyone can forgive me."

"Or, you could tell Si that it's become real for you,"

Gramps says.

"What?! Why would I do that?" It comes out squeaky and defensive.

"Because it's the truth," Grandad says. "You've seen where lies get you, so why not come clean, my boy?"

I sigh, not even questioning his certainty that he knows my heart. He's right. "I'll think about it. Don't tell any of my friends for now? I promise I'll sort everything out after the wedding. There's too much on everyone's plate to give Theo and Jude their perfect day. I don't want to fuck it all up with needless drama right now."

"Your secrets are always safe with us, but I don't think you're giving your friends enough credit," Grandad says.

"Your Grandad's right, any friends worth keeping would have listened if you told them you were uncomfortable with the matchmaking. And they'll listen to why you took such drastic measures to get them to stop," Gramps agrees. "Tell them in your own time. And remember we love you, no matter what shenanigans you get up to."

"You'll sort it all out, I'm sure," Grandad says. "Tell your dear Si, we say hello."

"I will. Thanks for understanding."

Gramps harrumphs. "All is forgiven. Next time don't go so long without calling, you hear?"

"I won't. Love you both," I say.

We chat a while longer, but then Paz calls to sort out

the dessert debacle. I wrap things up fast, but not before another hasty exchange of 'I love yous' with my family. Paz and I figure out a plan for providing enough diabetes friendly desserts for the party. He even suggests enlisting Si's help. The two of them have been sharing recipes and discussing options, traditional and otherwise, to help Si become a professional baker like Paz. If my dessert dilemma in any way helps achieve that goal, I'm on board with that.

CHAPTER 21

Simon

When Max tells me Jude asked him to help with the bachelor party, he's stoked about being included. It's obvious to me that his friends all care about Max. If they didn't, he'd never have needed me as his fake date in the first place. His friends wouldn't have noticed or cared that Max was so obviously lonely and starved for affection if they didn't care. There's no reasoning with him when he's stressed out and desperate to prove himself. I do the best I can to support him, helping him assemble dozens of balloon centerpieces in the days leading up to the event and assisting Paz with the desserts.

Max found the venue he booked through an event manager he's dealt with through his job. They had very few available dates. The two husbands-to-be have plans to be in Squamish with Theo's family for the entire week between Christmas and New Year's Day, further limiting the options for dates. So the party is several weeks before the wedding. It's not conventional, but it works.

The defensive part of me that's falling for Max wants to resent his friends for stressing him out with putting this entire party on his shoulders. Gui's the best man. As Theo's best friend and Jude's big brother, he should be the one doing this stuff—not Max. Now Max seems convinced that if tonight's party doesn't go perfectly, Jude and Theo will somehow hate him.

I know that's not true. A few minutes chatting with the others makes it clear they're just as concerned about Max throwing himself into this task with so much fervor. In the weeks leading up to the party, all I can do is remind him that his plans sound great. I know for a fact his friends are telling him the same, that even if the party flops, he still matters to them. Errol even added me to his party planning chat with Max and Gui, so I have the messages to prove it. If not for those messages, I might've resented them both more for putting that kind of pressure on my poor guy. Or not *my* guy. The guy I'd very much like to be mine.

Instead, their concern tells me his stress is internally motivated. A product of Max's ingrained need to please everyone around him to earn their friendship. It makes me sad for him. Regardless of what he can do for them, it's obvious to me that his friends care about Max. It stinks that he has such a hard time realizing he's as much one of them as any of his other friends.

I wish I had the unwavering support and love I've seen among his friends. From all of them banding together to help Pia's family through their fertility struggles to the way they trade off childcare help. They're all pitching in with Jude and Theo's wedding, too. Max's friends help each other, more like a family than most families I know.

Heck, Gui's partner, Paz, is baking the wedding cake because Theo loves his baked goods. Pia and Errol's respective kids are being included in the ceremony, along with Theo's nephew as flower folks. Everyone volunteered to help with whatever wedding tasks they need during the wedding week. If I had friends like Max's, I wouldn't be so screwed with Celine's impending good news that's liable to leave me scrambling for housing. The more time I spend with everyone, the more I regret that this whole situation is a lie.

Max puts together an amazing party, with Gui and Errol's help. I guess it doesn't hurt that all of this is something Max already does as part of his work duties. He arranges peoples' schedules, makes sure reservations are made, and ensures vendors get booked and paid on time. He grumbles about it a little, but as things come together, his anxiety about the mile-long to-do list turns to pride at a job well done.

Amid all the party planning, Max insists on paying my share of the costs for the wedding week. Otherwise, I'm not sure how I'd swing staying at the ski resort for five days. He claims my cooking lessons saved him enough money on food to cover the cost, anyway. I doubt that, but it's a kind gesture.

It's not ideal timing for me, but it might be a welcome distraction from packing up the life I've been building in Vancouver. Celine's lease renews in mid-January, so I expect that's when my cushy housing situation will end. My cousin has spent less than a handful of weekends at home all fall. It will shock me if Harvey doesn't ask her to move in with him on Christmas. It's just the sort of gooey romantic overture she deserves. She'll love that he's making a grand gesture. I think the only reason they've held off on making her move official, is that they both know I have no other viable housing options in the metro area.

I don't begrudge Celine her happiness at all, it just sucks that I'm holding her back. An albatross around her neck when she's otherwise doing well for herself. With the tea shop thriving and her relationship with Harvey getting more serious, Celine is living her best life.

Her moving will leave me scrambling for housing when I get back to the city after the weekend of wedding festivities. I've resolved not to borrow trouble, but I can't afford Vancouver rents on my own. I don't think I can stomach the risk of searching for a random housemate who will be okay with me on my Simone days. Or the dysphoria of hiding that part of me from a housemate.

Max is so busy during the weeks leading up to the party that I don't bring up my petty issues. Despite the last minute setbacks with the desserts that result in Paz roping me into a day of frantic baking, it all comes together. But Max seems more pensive than ever after dealing with the cupcake conundrum for some reason.

It's a relief when the big day arrives. The event space Max rented for the evening looks great when we arrive. It feels weird to be there with Max as a couple. Not because it feels like we're faking, but because it doesn't. Walking into the decorated venue with Gui's slideshow of the happy couple playing on a projector, it hits me that this could be real. My concern for Max is as real as anything I've felt for anyone I've dated. I can't focus on that now. Not when I'm supposed to be pretending that we're an item instead of pining over him, so I turn my focus to admiring his labor of love. Even if we aren't really together, what's the harm in letting myself have the illusion that he's mine while this lasts? My heart isn't going to get any more broken for enjoying the next few weeks to the fullest. My emotions are already invested.

Bouquets of rainbow balloons and colorful streamers decorate the walls and tables. The catered nibbles are all laid out on tables, and complimentary drink tickets are ready to hand out as the guests arrive. A DJ is setting up near the dancefloor.

Taking in the feat of organizing, I'm filled with pride for Max that he put all this together. The sort of pride I'd have for Celine or a proper boyfriend. Max put all of this together for his friends. On an impulse, I kiss his cheek.

"It looks perfect," I say.

Max flashes me an anxious grin, his face lighting up at the praise and hopefully the kiss. He certainly didn't push me away, although no one was around to notice it. But I can tell he's too distracted for anything I do to banish his worries. "You think? I wasn't certain about the balloons..."

"For sure." I nod. "It looks perfect. You said you based the balloon bouquets on their dating tradition with the flowers, right? It's meaningful without spending a fortune on fresh flowers for tonight. They couldn't have asked for more. You did good."

"Thanks. I hope they agree," Max is still fretting, but he squeezes my hand and smiles at me as Errol approaches. Max has been holding my hand a lot recently.

Errol claps Max on the back. "The place looks amazing, Max," Errol praises him. "You outdid yourself."

"I try. You think they'll like it?" he asks.

"They'll love it," Errol insists. Then he turns toward me, taking in my fitted shirt and bow tie, stuff I don't typically wear unless it was a Simon day. "Glad you could make it tonight. Is it a Simon day?"

"Yeah," I agree. "Wouldn't miss Max's party event of the season," I add with a flirty wink at Max.

He tugs me against his side and brushes his lips over my temple. "You're obligated to say you like it," he grumbles. Then he adds in an undertone, "I'm pretty sure it's part of the whole datemate deal."

Errol chuckles. "Don't let Rene in on that little rule, they have a hard enough time accepting compliments as it is. Next thing I know you'll get them thinking I'm blowing smoke up their ass about how well their suit fits for the wedding."

"What's that about my suit?" Rene asks, joining Errol.

I'm still hung up on Max's word choice, calling us dating a deal. Was the comment just a joke? Or was it a subtly coded reminder not to think his arm around my waist and lips on my skin mean anything? I'm going to work myself into a tizzy if I fixate on every little thing and try to read deeper meanings.

No more overthinking. I just decided to enjoy having Max in whatever capacity I can, and I intend to do just that. Nothing is stopping me from availing myself of my free drink ticket and dancing the night away with Max and his friends. That's what I wanted out of our deal, right? People I could be myself around. Max has spent the entire fall delivering on that promise, so I can do the same. Keep the others from trying to set him up on more dates he doesn't enjoy. Once the wedding is over and Celine moves in with Harvey, I'll probably have to give up all this. Max. His friends. The city. Paz's overtures about making baking a career. I'll need to find cheaper housing and start anew.

It will hurt, but for now I can live in the moment and dance with the guy I've spent the last few months falling for. Tonight will be fun. The next few weeks will be one last hurrah. Where I can enjoy the crap out of these new friends and having a pretend boyfriend. Someone to cook with, go out with, kvetch to about terrible customers and the pitfalls of living on my cousin's couch. Then when it all falls apart, at least I can remember this brief interlude with Max fondly.

I tune out their chatter about suits for the wedding and Errol's home renovations. I can't relate to contractors going over time and over budget, and I'm still not sure what I'm wearing. Celine said I could borrow a dress from her closet to bring in case I'm feeling more Simone on the day of the ceremony. Otherwise, I've got a suit I bought cheap at a second-hand store when Gina's friends all ended up engaged around the same time. It's already gotten plenty of mileage since none of them wanted me presenting femme on their big days. I don't want to dwell on those so-called friends. Gina didn't even invite me to the baby shower she plastered her social media with last week. I had to unfollow her after that.

We've drifted too far apart to bridge the gap, and I'm not even sure I want to anymore. The ease with which Max's buddies accept me drives home the difference between people who tolerate my existence and friends who like the real me. They understand what it's like to fall outside of society's norms, and to embrace it.

I tune back into the conversation between Max, Errol and Rene in time to catch Rene eyeing me.

"We've got the first shift handing out drink tickets," Rene says.

"Why don't you two go relax and have a drink before everyone shows up?" Errol suggests. "Gui ought to bring the men of the hour anytime now."

"Sounds like a plan, I'll relieve you in an hour. Come on, Simon, let's take advantage of the perks of hosting." Max winks as he peels a few drink tickets off the roll and leads me to the open bar.

CHAPTER 22

Max

Three hours in, and Theo and Jude's bachelor party is a tremendous success. The guys seem to have a blast partying with everyone they know in the city. I've met dozens of new folks from other animation studios ranging from television shows to visual effects for feature films. Not a shocker, our industry isn't huge. People move around among the studios here, hopping from contract to contract. Errol knows almost everyone, and he introduces me to so many folks in production that I'm not sure I can keep them all straight.

Now, most of the guests have arrived. The music is pumping, the food all but gone. That leaves little for me to do aside from enjoying the party with Simon. At least until it's time to clean up and make sure any lingering guests get poured into cabs. My date's a little tipsy and leaning heavily on my arm as I survey the crowded dance floor.

"Dance with me?" Simon asks, his gaze full of longing, so I take his hand and lead him onto the floor and we dance. Simon stumbles, so I hold him close, bodies swaying. He grinds against me, heedless of the music's rhythm, and it sends sparks of need and desire through me. I shift to get a better look at him, see if he means to press himself against me like this. The move brings our mouths inches apart and I'm caught staring into his wide guileless eyes. Simon's lips part, his tongue darting out to wet them. Without thinking it through, I close the distance, pressing our mouths together.

Simon sighs against my lips, then opens to me, his tongue slipping along mine. His grip on me tightens. His hand fists in my shirt to hold me close as he grinds our groins together with a growing urgency. I moan as he rubs his dick against mine through our pants. It's been a long time since I got this hot and heavy with anyone, let alone a person I'm developing feelings for. It takes all my willpower to pull back, break the kiss, and put some space between us.

Simon blinks at me, his eyes darting around, unable to meet my gaze.

"Sorry," he blurts. "Shit, I'm sorry." He swipes a hand over his mouth, then drops it to his side. As he retreats another step. He seems as unsteady on his feet as I feel. I don't know if he's experiencing the same dazed lust-haze as me or if he's just drunk, but I want him. So much. I reach out to stop him from fleeing. Simon doesn't wrench free from my gentle grip on his wrist, but there's a wariness in the way he's watching me that tells me it's a near thing.

"No, don't go. And don't apologize. You did nothing I didn't want. I just don't want to be cleaning up the aftermath of the party with jizz soaking my pants."

Simon's tension eases. "Yeah?" he asks on a shaky exhale.

"Yeah," I echo in a firmer tone.

Simon still looks dubious. "You're not just saying that for verisimilitude, are you?" he slurs, stumbling over the word that's become the bane of my existence. It's a too frequent reminder this isn't as real to him as it has become to me.

"Not even a little," I assure him. "Dance with me some more?"

Simon nods, he steps closer to me again, placing a tentative hand on my shoulder. I grip his hips and tug him closer, moving to the music again. We don't grind the way we were when I let myself get carried away, but we dance together again. Our movements are stiffer, a touch awkward from overthinking every point of contact between us. That could just be me, but the concentration furrowing Simon's brow belies that theory. We're both going out of our way not to overstep some imaginary line between our fake relationship and the real lust we almost succumbed to here on the dancefloor.

We make it through the rest of the party without another kiss. My dick is unimpressed with the need to keep my distance and not fuck things up with Simon by making out with him. No way am I losing out on my wedding date at the eleventh hour for the sake of an orgasm. Not even the best sex of my life is worth enduring Theo and Jude's wedding weekend solo if I ruin everything by crossing that line and Simon backs out of coming with me. That's what I tell myself as I help my buddies clean up the decorations after the guests have all left. Simon downs several shots along the way, until he's unsteady on his feet by the time the music stops. He still helps gather up trash anyway.

The overhead lights dispel the magic of the evening. Absent the mood lighting and flashing neon strobes from the dance floor, everything appears shabbier. The harsh overhead fluorescents reveal flaws, and I'm glad not to be shining any light on whatever it is I feel for Simon right now. I want to preserve the illusion of the unattainable. The rosy blush of the fantasy of a relationship we're constructing to show my friends. All the little touches for verisimilitude, as Si likes to call it.

Simon sticks around to help with the clean up. With all of us pitching in, we soon erase all traces of our party and get everything we brought loaded into the back of Errol's car and Alice's SUV. Errol and Rene offer Simon and me a ride home, which we accept. It's late and I'm too exhausted to turn down the kind offer. Simon and I squish together in the back with Pia and Gregor for the drive to their place. Rene and Errol need to pick up their son, who Emil is watching along with Rain. He can't drink, what with being pregnant and sick as a dog with it, from what Pia's said. He gets cranky if he has to be on his feet too long, so he volunteered to be the kid wrangler for the evening.

The four of us squeeze tight in the backseat and Simon ends up riding half in my lap for the few blocks to Pia's place. That does nothing for the aching erection tenting my pants, but we both ignore it as best we can. Once we park, Errol goes inside to get Mo while Rene reinstalls the booster seat that we had to take out to fit everyone.

"Great party, Max," Rene says.

"Thanks," I smile at them. At first, I couldn't comprehend why Errol got back together with them. Rene running off with their kid and abandoning Errol reminded me too much of my mom for me to trust they wouldn't run again. I have issues about people bailing the minute a better offer comes along or life gets too complicated. But Errol isn't me, and Rene's situation is nothing like what my mom did when she abandoned me.

Rene had their reasons for what they did, and Errol forgave them. My trepidations are irrelevant. Besides, Rene's good for Errol. They push him in ways the rest of us don't. We exasperate him with our antics, in and out of game, but he's different with Rene. Softer. The two of them are in love, so I've accepted that Rene is part of our group now. If not the gaming group, then the wider circle we hang out with on the regular.

"Thanks for the extra drink tickets," Simon says. He's a bit wasted.

I don't comment on Rene not drinking, it's rare for them to have much alcohol when we go out. Maybe one cocktail along with food, if that. It's none of my business why they seem to have abstained tonight.

"You enjoyed yourself, huh, Simon?" Rene teases as they tug on the seatbelt to make sure the booster is snug against the seat.

"Uh-huh. Max let me borrow a whole buncha tickets and got me drunk."

"He did?" Rene glances between us.

"Yes," Simon slurs with a drunken tilt into my side.

"You feeling okay?" Rene asks, holding a parental hand up to check Simon's forehead, like he might have a fever.

"Mhm, that's nice," Simon says, leaning into the touch. "You're nice. I like all you folks. Max said I would, and I do." As drunken declarations go, Simon's is pretty tame.

"Did he?" Rene asks, sounding bemused as they pull back their hand.

Simon nods, then winces at the motion, and presses his face into my neck. The unexpected intimacy sends a thrill straight to my dick, making me squirm in my seat. "The car is spinning. Why is it spinning? Make it stop."

"Here, drink some water," Rene grabs a spare re-usable bottle from the front seat and hands it to Simon. "Barely any cooties. You should probably drink most of that and take a couple Advil before you hit the hay. You staying with Max tonight?"

"Yeah, but we don't sleep together..." he gulps down the water greedily. I don't have it in me to lie and cover for that little truth nugget. It's not like we have to sleep together to be a couple or anything. However, we've also done nothing to dissuade any of my friends from their assumptions that we're fucking. So the blanket statement that we're not sort of throws doubt on our story. Too late to fix it now.

"None of my business either way," Rene says, eyeing me appraisingly for a moment.

"No one's business," Simon agrees earnestly. He snuggles into my side and he's snoring on my shoulder by the time Errol returns with Mo dozing in his arms.

Errol buckles the groggy kid into the booster seat before heading toward the Lion's Gate Bridge to bring me and Simon home. We talk about the party in hushed tones. Errol congratulates my mad organizational skills and I ask how the renovations are progressing at Errol and Rene's place and when they're planning to list their rental unit, since it's almost ready for occupancy again. Errol makes vague noises about listing the unit after the holidays since he's been busy. I snort at that bit of understatement. Errol is ridiculously busy with all the hats he's been juggling. Rene jokes that Simon and I should consider moving in. It sends a pang of regret through me that I can't correct their assumption Si and I might want to live together soon.

The thought of renting from Errol has crossed my mind several times since he first mentioned his old tenants moving out. Too bad my lies about being with Si complicate the matter. But, friend or datemate, I enjoy living so close to Si. Moving might fuck up our easy friendship.

I have Errol drop us off at my place. Celine is opening the tea shop in the morning, so Simon asked to crash at my place tonight. With how much he indulged at the party, it's just as well that I can monitor him, in case he gets sick. I help my very drunk and half-asleep pretend datemate get inside and tucked into my bed on his side. After more water and a dose of pain meds for his inevitable hangover, he looks cozy. He mumbles something about a goodnight kiss; I pat his flushed cheek instead. It's not my style to kiss him when he looks ready to pass out any second.

I let myself out of the bedroom and settle into my sleeping bag on the couch. We've only shared my bed once before. It was far too pleasant an experience to chance repeating when the goal of this entire ruse is in sight. I don't want to risk falling any harder by waking tangled together with him again.

CHAPTER 23

Simon

Christmas proves anticlimactic. I can't say I'm at all surprised when Harvey presents Celine with the key to his place and an engagement ring on Christmas morning. He asks her to move into his place and share the rest of his life with him. I've seen it coming for months. Sure, figuring out a new living arrangement sucks, but that's life. Celine deserves every happiness, and she shouldn't make her life choices around my convenience. So I plaster on a big smile and congratulate the happy couple.

I always intended sleeping on my cousin's couch to be temporary. Once I started paying a share of the rent, I let it drag on too long. In part because looking at options got exhausting, considering I can't afford anything. And in part because I didn't want to disrupt the status quo with Max. I enjoy being so close to him and sharing our morning commute most days. Unless I'm opening the shop and have to go in earlier, I've been heading into the city at the same time as Max regardless of my schedule. It's not weird if he knows about it, right? Rearranging my day to spend time with a friend, even if it means wandering around downtown to kill time before my later work shifts, is reasonable.

Still, now that Theo and Jude's wedding is less than a week away, there's a rapidly approaching expiry date on this thing between us. What if Max ditches me after the wedding? Once the newlyweds settle into blissful matrimony, I'm sure they'll tone down the matchmaking. Max will still have to go to their US reception slash family reunion in the spring, with all Jude's relatives. But I can't swing airfare, so this ceremony is it for us. Our last hurrah as a fake couple. Then, if his buddies bug him again, Max can use the fake breakup as an excuse to say he's not ready to date again, yet. That should get him some mileage. It might hurt less to be the one to leave. Like ripping off the bandage. I won't have to see Max every day when this ends.

My heart squeezes tight at the thought of not seeing him anymore. I want to text him, but I don't. He's spending the holiday with those of his friends who are still in town. Theo, Jude, Gui, Paz and Alice are all spending the week with Theo's family by Squamish. Jude's folks and some of his closer relatives are flying in early to join them there. The rest of us are driving to Whistler in a few days.

Pia, Emil, Gregor and Rain invited Max and Laura to join their family observance of the holiday. They told Max I'm invited too, but I already told Celine I'd be home. Errol's family, including his parents who are visiting from out of town, are joining everyone at Pia's place for a big holiday dinner. Max texts me pictures of a large Christmas tree bedecked in colorful lights next to a smaller one decorated in blue and white that Emil calls his Hanukkah shrub. When I ask what that is, he says it's a thing Emil's parents did for him and his brothers when they were little. To help them fit in as the only kids in their class who didn't observe Christmas.

The mention of a family tradition reminds me of the traditions Celine and I grew up with. My folks might not have been the most invested in parenting, but they always took me, and later my baby sister, to visit my gran for the holidays. All the aunts and uncles and cousins gathered together.

Until Becca came along when I was eleven, Celine and I were the youngest. Born eighteen months apart, we were always close. Celine and I would play with whatever amazing toys she got from Santa until Gran called the entire family to the table for an epic holiday feast. I brought my gifts too, but they tended toward the sort of things my dad wished I would ask for rather than anything I actually wanted.

One year I asked Santa for dress-up clothes, like the ones Celine got for her birthday. Dresses with sparkling accessories, full flowy skirts that puffed up when you spun in them, and stubby high heels that clicked when you walked. My mom got me a bunch of superhero costumes from the Halloween clearance bin instead.

She knew it wasn't what I'd meant. She also knew I'd make a scene in front of the family, if I went into the day hoping that Santa would come through for me. After the debacle of the previous year when I'd asked for a baby doll and got a football instead, she was ready for damage control. So, she and Dad sat me down on Christmas Eve and explained that those things weren't for boys. When I'd told her Santa would bring them anyway, because he knew I wasn't a boy, she snapped at me. It was time for me to grow up and realize that Santa wasn't real. The sooner I realized that, the better. Thinking I could change the way I was born was as much a fantasy as he was. Her words burned. If only she realized how right she was about defying my nature; no amount of willing myself *normal* could change who I was then. I refuse to deny any part of myself now.

After that year, I stopped trying to tell them who I was. Celine and her parents were the only ones who listened. All of my early explorations of Simone, and later Si, were with her. Playing at makeovers with Celine at our gran's house was the first time I got to try makeup. No matter how hard it was to live with my parents denying who I was, those memories with Celine remain suffused with that warm holiday glow. The idea that magic could be real and someone like Santa was out there, capable of accepting and loving me, had sustained me through the nightmare that was puberty. Not to mention a new baby under our roof.

My sister and I were never close. She was a loud baby, and I got roped into babysitting duty when I just wanted to go out with Celine and Gina and be a teenager. I resented having to play the responsible big brother when just the word 'brother' made my stomach flip most days. If they'd have just called us siblings, I'd have coped better, I think. It didn't help that mom showered Becca in the sort of pretty sparkly things I was drawn to and denied. Becca got to be the girly-girl I could only dream of being.

The irony of it is that now that I have the freedom to indulge my Simone days, they aren't anywhere near as frequent as they were when I was a kid. Simone is still a huge part of me, but my girl days are easier on me now that they're no longer some shameful, dirty secret my folks pressure me to hide. Back then, the need to be Simone was like having an aching tooth. No matter how much it hurt to wiggle it and press on the sore spot, I kept coming back to that burning ache, unable to just leave the raw exposed nerves alone. As long as I couldn't embrace that part of myself openly, being Simone consumed my thoughts. Now, girl mode is just a part of me.

It's been years since I went home for the holidays. I spent last year celebrating with Gina, Cal and some of their friends. Celine joined us for a sumptuous meal too. That was just before she met Harvey, so she and I spent the holiday sipping wine while Gina and her friends compared engagement rings and browsed bridal magazines.

This year, Max invited me to join him with his friends. He claimed they wanted me to join in the festivities, but I don't have the heart to make holiday memories with him when this is all going to end soon. I'm not strong enough for that. That doesn't keep me from feeling like a total heel for crashing Celine and Harvey's holiday and their celebratory mood.

Celine and I call our gran and get put on speaker phone to say Merry Christmas to everyone at once. Otherwise, I don't talk to my parents. I have a quick chat with Celine's folks about how they want us to visit more. They drop hints I'd be welcome to rent the studio apartment over their garage, if I ever decide I've had enough of city life. I wonder if they offered because they realize how limited my options are now that Celine is for sure moving.

Becca babbles that she got a phone for Christmas so I have to text her now. She gives me the number and I send her a Happy Holidays GIF. She replies in kind, but that's where the conversation stalls. We have little in common, Becca and I. Maybe that can change if I move back home to live with my aunt and uncle, silver linings and all that. I'd have to give up the seed of hope that Paz has been nurturing about getting me a baking apprenticeship, and I'd be giving up Max.

Restless, I end up lying to Celine about spending the evening with Max so I can bundle up and go for a long walk along Lonsdale. I wander until I find a warmly lit Chinese restaurant that's open. I eat my holiday meal by myself at a table for one. At least I'm not the only lonely one sitting here.

Max sends me goofy texts while I eat. We exchange selfies and food pics. He says he wishes I was there. I don't tell him I do too, just send a flirty emoji and a vague excuse about family time with Celine.

CHAPTER 24

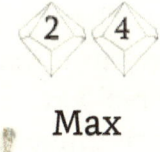

Max

The big wedding weekend with its attendant festivities creeps up on me faster than I'd expected. It's hard to believe Si and I have been pretending to date for the better part of four months. Si's been sort of standoffish and weird since our kiss at the bachelor party. It wasn't exactly our first kiss.

We'd done the obligatory chaste peck on the lips in front of my friends on other occasions. Mostly when the other couples in the group acted affectionate. It shouldn't mean anything. Just another way of selling our connection.

Except it meant something to me. It meant examining what I'm doing with Si and acknowledging that I don't want this to remain fake. Gramps and Grandad told me to tell the truth, and I think they're right. After the wedding, I need to lay my cards on the table.

I've never had this sort of connection with anyone

I've dated. Heck, Si makes me enjoy going grocery shopping and look forward to cooking our meals together on Sundays. Our chat thread always makes a crappy day brighter. It feels like we can discuss anything with no judgment.

I love my friends, but we tease each other a lot and sometimes it's nice to have someone who won't turn everything into a joke. That's my Si. We fit together. It's just weird that Si seems to have pulled away since Christmas. Slower to reply to my texts and pensive when we got together for dinner the night before driving out to Whistler with Errol and his family.

Si's being weird about the holidays, too. I asked how the day with Celine and Harvey went, but Si only replied with vague platitudes about enjoying family time and the spirit of the season. The noncommittal texts on Christmas made me want to go over there and check whether everything was alright. That would have overstepped my role in Si's life though, so I refrained. Part of that might be cowardice. Not wanting to rock the boat so close to the big day. But Jude and Theo put so much effort into planning their wedding, I won't cause drama with only days to go. This week is about them, not me.

The morning we leave for the five-day trip, Errol and Rene pick us up early. They bring extra donuts from their Tim's run to share with us. Mo is already zonked out in his booster seat beside Si.

The ride out to Whistler with Errol and his family is hours of breathtaking vistas and phenomenal views. I can see why they call it the Sea-to-Sky Highway. It feels like we're in untouched wilderness on a road that runs along the boundary between the ocean and the snow-capped mountains. It's like something out of a Venture-Quest campaign.

I've always thought the city had some spectacular views, and it does. North Van looking down on the bright city lights of the skyline all spread below me is gorgeous. Like someone upended thousands of twinkling jewels and scattered them across the Burrard Inlet, but this is next-level pristine nature at its finest.

I could almost fall in love with this province that's so far from my home. And speaking of love, there's Si sitting beside me, craning to catch the passing scenery out my window, despite having lived in the province since birth.

"Ever been out this way before?" I ask.

Si shrugs. "Nope. Don't ski, or do heights, so I didn't see the point of driving out of my way for snowy mountains. Why bother when I can just look north of the city to see my fill?"

"That's fair. The view is worth the drive, though, eh?" I ask.

"Yeah," Si agrees, flashing me a sweet smile.

"It's pretty, huh?" Rene asks, turning to smile at us as they echo our conversation. We agree, still looking out the window together, but now Si's head rests on my shoulder. It should be a casual touch. I've sat with my head on a friend's shoulder during a long car trip before. It's not a big deal. Purely a gesture for verisimilitude with Rene watching us? Or, dare I hope, a sign that Si wants something more, too? The rest of the drive with

Si pressed against my side is strange. I'm caught somewhere between an agony of wanting things I don't dare to ask for and the bliss of pretending I have them already.

CHAPTER 25

Si

There's more snow the further north we drive. Last night North Van got a dusting that I'm sure turned to freezing rain further into the city. As Errol pulls up to the place where our group has reservations, there's a decent accumulation on the ground.

The wedding party and their plus ones and kids are all staying together in a rented condo. Theo, Jude, and their families are staying a few doors down. Our place is a cute townhome style lodging in a row of similar dark wood buildings with five bedrooms. It boasts all the amenities, including a two-car garage and a hot tub.

Pia, Emil, and Gregor drove down last night with Rain. They claimed the ground floor main suite. It's the one with the most space for the three of them to share a bed and still set up a travel crib for Rain. Laura rode with them and she and Alice are sharing the other ground floor room with its two twin beds.

We're on the second floor. The first bedroom has a full bed, and a spare cot folded in the corner for Mo. So, that's Errol and Rene's room. The second has all Gui and Paz's stuff piled at the foot of the bed and no cot, but is otherwise identical to the first. By the time we open our door, I already know what to expect. It's a carbon copy of the other two bedrooms on this floor. One bed for Max and I to share.

Max shoots me an apologetic look and squeezes my hand as we dump our stuff on the floor. He mouths an apology, but the others are all hovering around chattering about all the events planned for the next few days. There's no privacy for us to address the bed issue without giving up our ruse. I set my bag down and give Max a peck on the cheek, whispering that we can figure it out later into his ear. It should look like I'm sharing sweet nothings with him, if any of his friends are paying attention.

We get roped into a board game, *Settlers of Catan*, in the living room along with half the group. The other half changes into swimwear to try out the hot tub on the back patio.

Theo and Jude are among those cavorting in the water, loud and splashing. I kind of envy how unselfconscious Theo is with his top surgery scars on display like that. I hate being exposed, hate the crawling sensation of eyes on my skin. As though they're all trying to sort me into a tidy little box and label me.

I don't know the rules for the game, but it seems less intimidating than being half naked with the others.

Plus, it occurs to me that Max and I haven't seen much of each other's bare skin before. I don't want the first or only time we're together topless to be in a group setting.

Mo is helping Emil set up a baby swing in the corner. Max gets us each a drink and I listen to the game rules. The group from the hot tub joins us for our second round of the game. I end up on a team with Max since the game maxes out at six players.

Max murmuring strategy in my ear feels intimate. We're tucked close together on a couch, next to Gui and Paz. The latter seems more focused on distracting Gui than the game. At least I'm not the only one who lacks any investment in winning. Pia's team has their attention divided between the game and their cranky toddler, who eschewed the swing in favor of trying to pull themself up on every available stationary object. Rain has threatened to upend the game board multiple times.

The poor mite cries like their little heart has broken when their parents foil their efforts and take away their stolen game pieces before they can slobber all over them. Or choke on the various little bits and bobs. Rain's wobbling, sad lower lip reminds me of when Becca was little. I've been texting my sister more since Christmas, and she seems interested in connecting for real. Sure, we mostly exchange silly GIFs, but it's a start.

Laura and Alice are giving the others a run for their money. Theo and Jude are in second place. Errol, Mo, and Rene also seem to be in the running. Part of the game involves trading resources and Theo and Gui exchange way too many jokes about having wood for sheep.

It's nice to be here. Surrounded by friends. Despite my lack of investment in the game's outcome, I enjoy the sense of being included. The game ends, Alice and Laura high-fiving and celebrating their victory. Theo pouts theatrically about it, demanding a rematch. Errol puts paid to that, pointing out our dinner reservation is in less than an hour and we all still have to get ready and drive to the restaurant. Everyone is in high spirits as we pack away the pieces and sort the cards into their place in the box.

Tonight's dinner is just the wedding party and family who have already arrived. We meet Theo and Jude's loved ones at the restaurant in a reserved event room. Max points out Jude and Gui's folks. They're standing with a couple of guys who share Gui's solid build and facial features. Jude introduces the pair as his cousins Julian and Mat.

Max mentioned Jude and Theo throwing Julian at him as a potential date. I'm surprised Max would rather be here with me than the handsome, muscular guy with a smile out of a toothpaste ad. We sit near the cousins while we eat. Julian seems nice enough, but hearing him wax on about how excited he is for a morning run gives me a clue. My Max would do anything to avoid waking up early for a sunrise run, no matter how gorgeous the scenery is.

Theo's family has assembled, too. His parents sit with Jude's folks. His sister, Erin, jokes around with his brother Ty and Ty's husband, Fred, about the last-minute preparations that remain to do. Skyler and Mo sit together, chattering happily. It sort of reminds me of when Celine and I were little at big family gatherings. Mo is a fair bit older than Sky, but he's patient with the younger boy. Both older kids tolerate Rain toddling over and slobbering on Sky's action figures while they're waiting for the adults to finish eating.

After food, we separate again. The two sets of parents of the grooms retire back to their shared lodgings. Theo's mom offers to watch all three of the kids while the rest of us go check out the nightlife around the base of the mountain.

Before I know it, we're hitting a bar with strobing lights, dance music and a boisterous crowd of friends and cousins encouraging the two grooms-to-be to get shit-faced.

Max and I dance together, and it's like the first night I went out with him. Or the bachelor party. Only now I've got nothing to lose. We've only got days of our deal left. I desperately want to wring every bit of enjoyment out of our time together.

So I don't hold back, reveling in Max's hands on me, his dick hard against my ass as we grind together among the moving bodies on the dancefloor. I turn in his arms and let him feel that I'm as hard as he is. And when he tips his head toward me, I seal our lips together in a breath-stealing kiss. His friends—our friends?—catcall as Max devours my kisses, neither of us holding back. And then we're crowded together in the back of an SUV, stumbling into the rental and up the stairs. Behind closed doors in our room.

Distantly, I recall there was a problem with the full-sized bed we're sharing, but for the life of me, I can't summon up what that problem might be. It looks perfectly inviting from the doorway with Max's arm around me. I tug him down onto the mattress with me, kissing him. Max rolls away and I pout.

"You're wasted, Si," Max chides me gently. "Sleep it off, we can pick this back up if it still sounds like a good idea when you're sober." Then he tucks me under the covers and it's so cozy, I don't have the energy to argue with him. There's a warm furnace at my back and a comforting weight beside me in the soft bed as I drift off to sleep.

CHAPTER 26

Max

Wednesday morning, I wake up disoriented. There's light streaming into my eyes from the wrong direction, and another person's arm is flung across my chest, a leg pinning my hips in place. For a half a second, I think I must still be dreaming. But no, the soft huff of another's breathing nearby is real.

"Si?" I groan, my mouth is dry and my head aches from overindulging last night. It's not as late as I initially feared. We aren't in my basement room at home, where the sunlight doesn't slide across my bed until late afternoon. Last night comes back to me in fits and starts.

Board games with my friends. Dinner with Theo and Jude's families. Cousin Julian with his chiseled physique and affable smile that didn't hold a candle to Si's bright grins and the soft presence snuggled against my body.

I recall dancing together in the strobing lights of a bar. The others in our party dancing all around us. Errol and Rene driving us home, Si snuggled against me on one side and a tipsy Laura lolling against my other side, not at all unfamiliar from countless other times Errol took us both home. I recall running my fingers through her long dark hair, combing it out of her face and telling her how silky and pretty it is. Cringeworthy, except she'd been equally complimentary about my hair, patting my cheeks and telling me we should be friends forever. BFFs. Promise. And then she'd demanded similar promises from Si, Rene, and Errol.

When we got back to the house, Alice took Laura's arm and helped her drink some water in the kitchen. Si and I stumbled up the stairs together. Errol and Rene followed us. Neither of them had imbibed, but they seemed amused at our stumbling efforts to best the stairs. Gui and Paz got home before us, and I could hear them fucking through the door when we made it upstairs.

Our closed door muffled the sounds, and then Si shocked me with amorous advances I couldn't in good conscience go along with. Not when we were both drunk off our asses and our relationship was still a ruse. I kept enough sense not to want our first time to happen while we were both drunk. So we fell asleep in the shared bed and now I'm feeling more rested than I have any right to, after partying into the wee hours.

"Mhm? Morning," Si greets me with a shy smile.

"Sleep okay?"

"Uh-huh, more than ok. You?"

"Yeah, I'm good. You're warm," Si says, sliding cool feet along my calves. I twitch away, but my bedmate seems unabashed.

"Last night was fun."

"Yep. Think the rest of the weekend will be quite so boisterous?"

"Might be. Tomorrow's the rehearsal dinner, so another fancy meal, but we might be on our own tonight if you wanted to make something with me? I think my buddies rented out the rock-climbing wall and booked an escape room for this afternoon, and after food we're all hanging out here."

"I've been meaning to try one of those escape rooms. Never could get a group together," Si says.

"We've done a couple. They can be fun. Fair warning, Errol gets bossy and Theo will get sidetracked by irrelevant details."

"I would have expected nothing less."

"Yep, you know us too well." We exchange smiles. "Tomorrow is all the final wedding prep stuff, skiing for those who are into that, and VentureQuest in the evening. Then Friday is the wedding, but since they're doing the ceremony later, we've got brunch and the arcade in the morning. Then getting all set up for the ceremony and reception. There are fireworks and a ton of parties, it being New Year's Eve and all."

"So, we're ringing in the new year with a champagne toast, fireworks, and the whole nine yards?"

"Yep. That okay?"

"Can't think of anyone I'd rather spend the day with," Si teases me, stretching along the bed. The motion has my dick taking notice of the warm body next to me. It occurs to me that if I want to prevent our arrangement from becoming too real, I need to get up now. Before either of us does anything we'll regret later. I want to talk before we get any more physical. That way we can walk away from this weekend as friends, if nothing else. If we fool around, I don't know if I can manage friendship.

"I think I smell coffee," I say through a yawn. "Let's see what's on offer for breakfast."

Si mirrors my yawn and throws in an exaggerated stretch that has last night's shirt riding up to reveal a stripe of alluring torso. Si scratches at the bare skin I'm longing to touch.

It's going to be a wretchedly long weekend at this rate, if I'm going to keep my hands off of my date. I can do this though. Of course I can.

CHAPTER 27

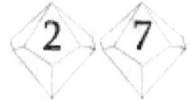

Max

It's so completely Theo to spend the night before his wedding running our game. We've spent the past two days enjoying all the mountain's amenities, and the rehearsal and dinner went off without a hitch earlier. The entire group is here and Theo's been dying to spring this one-off side quest dungeon on the others.

After Sythern's escape, my sorcerer hunkered down to lick his wounds. Theo and I had tossed around ideas for his return, but that wouldn't happen for a while. None too exciting when I've been sitting on the sidelines for the last few game sessions. So, after several conversations with Theo on the matter, I've got a new character to play and he'll take over Maximus as an NPC to use in future shenanigans.

The party is still trying to undo the magic that turned Sythern into a human and learn how to stop the remaining mercenaries from unleashing their spell on all dragonkind. Theo offered to let me play the dragon prince rather than leaving them as an NPC.

Theo and I got off to a bumpy start at my first session with the group, mostly because I had my doubts about getting into the roleplay. Now, after the better part of a year playing with my group, it's nowhere near as daunting. They all get into character, and I found Maximus's villainy quite entertaining. Especially with the over the top monolog Theo encouraged me to lean into a few sessions back when it looked like all hope was lost for the young dragon prince.

I'm having fun delving into Sythern's character for this side quest. Their current state of being is interesting. A dragon trapped in a human body and unsure if they will ever resume their natural form. The poor dragon prince is out of sorts after Maximus subjected them to a forcible xenomorph spell.

The prince often moves to flex the tail or wings that are no longer there. Their facial expressions have odd incongruities in this form. While they have acclimated to reading their mate's facial cues, their own muscles are unused to having a human face. The wider emotional range conveyed through subtle brow wrinkles, nose twitches, and mouth shapes available to this form are still alien. Overwhelming when compared to their own more rigid feathered and scaled features. And Sythern losing their ornamental tuft of crest feathers has the prince drawn to any bright baubles the party comes across. They're used to moving a much larger bulk. Plus, having a human libido is a novelty for the prince, much to their horror.

Theo and I had a few long chats about how the dragon character might respond to the xenomorph spell. How it compares to Theo's dysphoria in some aspects, and differs in others, and what that might be like for my character to experience. It's given me a better appreciation of both the character I'm playing and insight into my friend.

Sythern's change in body didn't change how they see themself. They're still a dragon youngling, the lesser wyrm and heir to their domain. Their lack of sexual attraction and disinterest in sex for recreation also remained unchanged. But now their human body responds in ways it wouldn't have in their dragon form. Not that those details are super relevant. Except that the dragon is unused to the occasional tightness in their pants, clothing being another strange human thing. That problem only worsens when their mate, Tamsin, does something heroic. Like breaking them out of their cell and fighting off evil mercenaries to free them.

Basically, Sythern was all swoony over Tamsin before the xenomorph spell. Now they are all swoony over their mate while in a strange new form. So, I'm getting into character and preening like a very awkward newly human dragon when Si comes in from hitting the hot tub, wearing an oversized t-shirt that clings from being soaking wet. My mouth goes dry at the sight of Si framed in wet fabric. Want fills me.

Alice, Paz, Theo's siblings, Jude's cousins, and Gregor also crowd inside, letting in an icy blast of cold air. Si slips up to our room to change before I can make things awkward by staring. Once the hot tubbers have dried off and changed, they join Emil and Rene watching a movie with the three kids. Si seems amused by my efforts at roleplay. My datemate sits close to our game, blatantly listening in after the others all join Rene and Emil watching a movie with a fresh round of colorful cocktails.

No one gave it a second thought, when Rene opted to keep Emil company inside with a mocktail. It was unremarkable. Emil can't do hot tubs or booze, given his pregnancy, and Rene never drinks much, anyway. Plus, they've become good friends. When Rene also turned down the drinks Laura and Alice mixed, Laura made a cajoling comment about not needing a designated driver, since we're all staying in tonight. Errol shot her down fast, sounding defensive on his partner's behalf. Rene diffused the tension by pointing out that Mo, Rain, and Sky still needed supervision.

After that exchange, I caught Erin giving Rene an assessing look that made me wonder if there might be some subtext I'd missed. But Erin doesn't know about Rene's father, so I figure Errol's protectiveness stems from that history. It makes sense given what little I know about Rene's childhood from our more personal chats when they've offered me rides home.

I tear my eyes off Si watching me play at being an out of sorts young dragon and turn my attention back to the game. We're still puzzling out how we're supposed to get inside the ancient ruins. Pia's necromantic mentor implied this pile of stone might hold the secrets to undoing Sythern's dilemma.

Turns out that kicking off the session with celebratory drinks might not have been our brightest move. At least, not if we wanted to solve Theo's puzzles or make any progress tonight. The warm buzz of Laura's electric blue 'manna martini', which I think is just blue curacao, triple sec, and vodka, makes it easier to dive into character. In between bemoaning my odds of ever being restored to my true form, I suggest ways to open the ancient tomb we're here to raid. We've discovered what might be an entry among the rubble.

"If I had my tail, I'd just sweep away all this pointless debris," I declare huffily, pouting and crossing my arms awkwardly. I figure a dragon might have a frustrated wing gesture type thing, so I shift my shoulders a bit to portray that.

"I could give that a go, since I've still got my tail," Jude says, so earnest there's not even a hint that he might intend to rub in Sythern's loss. He's also playing a dragon character, Lyran. Except Lyran avoided getting xenomorphed into human flesh, so it's not a terrible idea. Still, Sythern is Lyran's prince and the smaller dragon ought to show some deference, right?

"You're still a juvenile, Lyran. Hardly big enough to knock down human walls," I say snootily. I'm the dragon equivalent of nobility, after all. Whereas Jude's character is a wee baby novice from the dragon temple. They ought to defer to me, right?

"We want to recover ancient research materials," Errol points out. "It might be more prudent to find the actual entrance, since we don't want to ruin the ruins further. Carl, do you see anything useful? Perhaps signs others might have passed this way before us?" he calls upon Gui's skills as a ranger. Typical Errol, bossing us around when we're acting too thick for him to handle our antics.

"Sure, Zelphod, let me take a better look," Gui agrees in his goofy in-character voice. Then he announces in his usual tones, "I examine the area around what we think is the entrance to the tomb."

He pauses, holding up his d20 in silent question. Theo nods. Gui rolls low. Theo cackles and Gui groans. Still, Gui has a decent modifier for tracking, so it might be enough to give us a much needed hint on how to proceed.

"I still get my proficiency bonus. Besides, we've got all day, so I can just take ten."

"Fair," Theo concedes. "Too bad the rest of your party trampled everything exploring. You see scuff marks in the dirt outside the tomb, but it's hard to make out details since the party's footprints obscure most of the surrounding dirt. The moldering mound of rocks that is crumbling under its own weight looks like the sketches from Pia's necro-tower. So you can be pretty sure you've at least found the correct spot to look."

"I examine the rocks, are there any distinct markings?" Pia asks.

"Carvings, they match the images in your mentor's books about the tomb," Theo agrees. He slides a rough sketch to Pia to look at.

The glyphs have little meaning to me, but if Theo took the time to draw them out, then they are probably relevant. Then again, it would be a totally Theo thing to supply us with a bunch of elaborate false leads.

Theo seems amused by our floundering attempts to read meaning into the strange markings and explore the exterior of the tomb. He said this little jaunt to the ruins should be a one-shot. Except we spend over an hour working out the cryptic cipher that unseals the ancient magical locks on the tomb entrance. So I'm pretty sure it's going to take multiple sessions.

Out of the corner of my eye, I keep catching Si watching us with a sappy smile. I ham up my roleplay to entertain our impromptu audience. Si has the best laugh, so no one can fault me for wanting to hear more of it. Especially since every one of my friends insisted on trying to set me up for this weekend, so they're to blame for Si being here with me. I might owe them one for that.

CHAPTER 28

Max

We get through the wedding ceremony with no issues. It's all lovely, very Theo and Jude. Everything is sweet, over the top romantic, and loud. They wrote their own vows and both of them get all teary reciting them, which has most of their assembled loved ones reaching for the tissues.

I even catch Si trying hard not to smudge the eye makeup that took ages to get just right before the ceremony. My date is smoking hot in Celine's borrowed floral dress and heels paired with the charcoal gray vest from Si's threadbare suit. It's a good look. Somewhere between the nerdy twist on classic masculinity Simon would have sported, complete with bow tie and professorial elbow patches on the suit jacket, and the full femme esthetic Simone favors on girl days.

Jude and Theo look elegant in their suits. Mo, Skyler, and Rain are killing it in the miniature formal wear they're all rocking. Sky has on a puffy rainbow skirt, paired with a suit jacket. Mo's suit more closely resembles the ones his dads are wearing. Sky asked for the puffy princess clothes. So that's what he got. Rain toddles along at Sky's side in a matching suit jacket and flouncy skirt.

The entire wedding party is pretty spiffy, if I say so myself. The rainbow spectrum of dress shirts under our matching waistcoats and suit jackets gets the idea across without the effect seeming too garish. Pia, Erin, and Laura have dresses in matching jewel tones. All of us stand lined up in rainbow order around the grooms for the photos after the ceremony. It's fun, goofing around and mugging for the camera with my friends and their family.

We take dozens of photos, some serious, others silly. We all horse around between shots. At one point, while the photographer is posing the three kids from the wedding party, Jude catches me grinning out at Si. He flashes me a knowing smile and says, "I'm glad you found your person."

"Huh?" I turn toward Jude.

Jude nods toward my date. "You look as sappy as me right now when Si's around." Jude slings an arm around me and pulls me into a fierce hug. "It means a lot that all of you are here to celebrate with us. You made me feel more at home when I moved here. Heck, if you hadn't kissed me, who knows how long it would have taken Theo to get his head out of his ass."

"You're welcome?" I say with a startled laugh, I'd all

but forgotten our bet. The chaste press of our lips to make Theo jealous hardly counts as a kiss.

Theo sidles up to us and hugs Jude from behind, kissing his new husband on the cheek. "Don't you worry, I'd have figured it out. You're as irresistible as Paz's brownies, hun."

Jude snorts. "Oh, I see how it is. Only *as* irresistible as baked goods?"

Theo wobbles his hand in a so-so gesture. "I mean, it's a close call."

"Is the honeymoon over already?" I tease.

"Right?" Jude chuckles, nudging me with his elbow.

"Nah, Jude knows my favorite thing to devour will always be him. We're just getting started, right, hun?" Theo asks.

"Yeah," Jude agrees, gazing into Theo's eyes with nothing but love. The photographer sneaks up on us and snaps a candid of the pair of them totally wrapped up in each other. Gooey sweet. We pose for a few more group shots. Standing there with my best friends, I feel like I'm truly part of the group, not the newbie standing on the fringes.

The photographer sends us away to get photos with the grooms and their family members. The rest of us head over to the reception venue to ensure everything is ready. Si walks with me, hand-in-hand. It's nice to have someone waiting for me after my obligations as a groomsman are complete. More than that, I'm glad my person is Si, in particular. Glad that radiant smile is just for me. I get to be the one twirling Si around the dance-floor later. We'll get to share our midnight toast, the champagne fizzing on our tongues.

It's the end of the year. The final hours of the ruse we agreed to carry out months ago. If I'm honest, though, I'd like nothing more than for this new year to mark a beginning between us. I can only hope Si agrees.

CHAPTER 29

Si

The reception reminds me of a last meal. Not just the end of the year. The last dregs of this bright spot of happiness I stumbled upon when Max offered me shelter under his umbrella what seems like ages ago. This is it. The beginning of our end.

My life feels like it's unraveling around me. After tonight, I have to confront not knowing where I'm going to be living in a few short weeks. The bottom line is, I either need to move to a cheaper city, which means giving up my job at Celine's shop. Or I need to take a leap by chancing a housemate I don't know.

Paz made my choices harder last night. While we were drinking in the hot tub, he let slip that he convinced his boss to offer me an apprenticeship at his bakery. The hours start early enough that I could still take shifts part-time at Celine's shop to make ends meet. The pay is minimal, so I'll still need a housemate.

If it comes down to my housing depending on it, I can hide behind the facade of presenting as Simon full time for a while. The thought of having to go into the closet for my physical wellbeing is a lead weight in my gut. My traitorous brain throws Simone to the forefront when I can't present femme. Like that part of me is desperately clawing to the surface, refusing to be denied, and I don't want to deny myself. I am Simone as much as I am Si and Simon.

Simon is the safest way for me to present. I might get razzed for being a fat femme gay boy nerd as Simon. But that's nothing compared to the hateful slurs and threats of violence I've had slung my way as Simone. It might be easier if wanted to pursue medical transition and live full time as a woman. In some ways. Harder in others. But that path isn't for me. Presenting as Simone when the urge strikes me is the right thing for me. Except if I'm living with someone who isn't okay with me. I wouldn't be able to manage that.

Max says we can stay friends after this. He swears his friends accept me into their group. I don't feel unwelcome with them. But I'm not as into their games and their interests. I enjoy playing with them, but if we stopped hanging out, I wouldn't seek other people to game with. And if I'm honest with myself, fake or not, this breakup is going to hurt.

I don't want to be around Max when I can't have him. Can't touch him, or listen to him whispering explanations of his friends' in-jokes and obscure game rules into my ear. It will be purest torture. I need a clean break after tonight, if my heart is going to survive this.

Celine promised to hold on to my stuff for me until I figure out my shit. Maybe I'll give in and take my aunt and uncle up on renting the spare room over their garage. There are always people hiring back home, if I'm not too picky about my job. There I can be Simone within the confines of my home, at least. Even if I'm not sure if I dare to wear full face makeup to a customer service job in the tiny town where I grew up. Everyone there knows about me. People know everything, but if I'm quiet and keep to myself, they'll probably leave me alone. They'll still talk, though. People always do.

"Hey, what's got you looking like someone kicked your puppy?" Max nudges me.

"Nothing. Who would kick a puppy? Asshole!" I grumble.

"Just an expression. Are you alright?" Max's hand on my shoulder steadies my nerves.

"Yeah." I force a half-hearted smile. "Fine. Why?"

"You look sad."

I shrug it off. "Nah, mate, just weddings are emotional, right?"

"Sure," Max says, tone dubious.

"What Jude said, about always wanting this and not being sure his home country would acknowledge it? This day is huge for them, right?" I say, hoping to distract him.

"Yeah. I guess it is. I'm happy for them, truly, and relieved I had you at my side to get them off my back.

Can't thank you enough."

"No thanks needed, we had a good run, yeah?"

"Yeah. About that, we should ta—" Max says the dreaded words that never lead to anything good, but he's interrupted by the sound of myriad glasses clinking.

The emcee announces that it's ten seconds to midnight and we should all grab our champagne to toast the happy couple and the new year. I snatch up the excuse, snagging two flutes of champagne from a passing server. I press one on Max. He flashes me huge, beseeching puppy eyes.

I wish I could offer him more than this goodbye, but I don't have the strength to fight. So when he kisses me at the stroke of midnight, I give myself over to it. Tasting the bubbly traces of sweetness and chocolate cake on his lips and tongue. It's not a chaste kiss, and I'm turned on out of my mind with Max pressed against me in his suit. If this is my last night with him, I don't want to walk away without knowing his taste. What he feels like pressed skin to skin. Buried inside me.

"Let's go back to our room," I plead into his ear when the kiss ends. Others are leaving, I already saw Laura and Alice slipping away earlier. No one should miss us.

Max twines our fingers together and leads the way across a snowy lot to a hired car that takes us back to our rented lodgings. We keep our hands to ourselves in the car. I fondle Max on the front step as he fumbles with the keys. He returns the favor, pawing at my ass as we make our clumsy way up the stairs, both of us laughing and high on lust. We get inside our room, Max kicking the door shut behind us. Then we collapse together onto the bed.

Max's mouth on mine is a world of sensation I want to lose myself in, to the exclusion of all else. Nothing else matters. Not my imminent undesired move back home, and certainly not that our relationship isn't real. Our chemistry is real, and that's what counts as I work my hands into Max's waistband to paw at his plump ass cheeks.

The familiar rasp of lace under my fingertips comes as no great shock. Max was never quite conventional. Still, I didn't expect the lacy panties under his suit. A flicker of worry passes over his features. I do the only sensible thing, kissing him deep and amorous as I knead the flesh of his ass through the lace. I tell him with my movements just how hot I find him, and this only makes it better. He told me he was a bit of a gender rebel, but I had no idea he was hiding such a sexy secret.

He responds by grinding more insistently against me, the hard evidence of his pleasure only makes me want this more.

I squirm, hiking up my skirt to bunch around my hips and grant Max access as he fumbles to get out our cocks. That's a feat, considering mine remains pressed flat to my body by several layers of tight panties, gaffing underwear, and doubled up pantyhose to minimize my bulge without tucking. It's still not super comfortable to be hard under all that constrictive fabric. I'll deal with it soon, but first, I want to see Max's dick straining against the sheer lace. Watch the color darken with wetness as his arousal grows.

Except that would mean we have to stop kissing long enough to separate, and I don't want to lose this momentum. If we slow down, or discuss what we're doing, I'll lose my resolve. This might be goodbye, but I want to remember it without the finality of saying it outright. Without the sheen of loss or sadness. Just this once, I want Max. Need this moment with all our pretenses shed as we come together.

Max pulls back, panting, gaze full of lust as he skims a hand over my chest. "Did you bring condoms?" he asks.

"Nope," I admit.

"Shit." Max slumps.

"That about sums it up, yeah." I sigh, but I will not let trivialities deter us from having a good time. I want Max too much to give up just because penetrative sex is off limits. "Get naked, we can still have fun without them."

Max frowns, but he removes his suit, setting each piece aside with care until he's standing in nothing but the yellow lace that cradles his bulge. He's just as pretty as I'd imagined, naked and straining against the lace in my favorite color.

"You like it?" he asks, his hands twitching with the effort not to cover himself.

I lick my lips. "Love it," I say. It would be easy to just run with the attraction thrumming between us and pretend I don't see all his insecurities, but Max means more to me than that. I can delay gratification if it means making him more comfortable. "You're so sexy in lace." I say, moving closer and opening my arms to him, Max steps into my embrace. We cling together until Max seems relaxed. Then I say, "You know you don't have to hide any part of yourself from me, right?"

"Yeah?" Max squirms and I release him. "Old habits, I guess." He retreats a step and won't meet my eyes.

"Old, like from when you were eleven and your mom left?" I suggest, knowing it's a risk to bring this up with him. This conversation could easily kill the mood.

Max crosses his arms. "She was my mom," he says, voice as small and lost as the little boy she'd abandoned. "Fuck, this is awkward to talk about when I'm half naked," Max forces a half-hearted bitter laugh, he scrubs a hand over his face. "I mean, mom-love is supposed to be this magical force that nothing can dent or break, but she didn't want me. I wasn't enough to keep her. And it seems like, other than my grandfathers, everyone else sees whatever she saw in me that isn't worth loving."

I figured it was something like that driving his insecurities. It might not be rational, but I wasn't particularly rational at eleven either. And that kind of wound festers. I should know, after hearing how I should hide myself repeated over and over for most of my adolescence into adulthood before I followed Celine to the city.

"You know your mom didn't leave because there's anything wrong with you, right?" I say. It was something wrong with her, but insulting her won't improve

Max's mood, so I leave that part unsaid.

"How do you know?" Max snaps, retreating further. I'm tempted to drop the subject, but he needs to hear it wasn't his fault.

"Max, you were a kid. There is nothing you could have done that any parent fit for the title would have stopped loving you over." Oops, so much for not insulting the dead woman.

Max scowls, shaking his head.

"Talk to me, mate," I implore. "What happened?"

"It's silly." Max blows out a long breath. "The week she left, I quit soccer. She wanted me to be this image she had in her head of a rough and tumble athletic son. I failed and she left. I rejoined the team, thinking maybe she'd come back if I was better. She didn't." He taps his temples. "I know here that it wasn't the reason she left. Grandad told me she made arrangements with him before that. They fought about it." Max moves his hand over his heart. "In here, it felt like I wasn't good enough. Like she saw that I'm not who I pretend to be, confident and outgoing." He gestures toward me. "Anyway, you hide, too. Under the baggy hoodies and the vest."

I swallow hard. It's a clear deflection, but turnabout is fair play. "Yeah. I told you why."

"It's not just anxiety though, is it?" Max presses, his voice gentle.

"No," I admit. He was vulnerable with me, I can offer him the same. "Sometimes it seems like the entire world is screaming that fat is unattractive. Let alone the fact that I don't even try to fit into their gender boxes." I step toward him, and Max reciprocates.

"If that's what they think, then the entire world is dead wrong. You're sexy, Si. I've wanted to feel your body pressed against me forever." He's close enough to touch now.

"Me too. So, you want to do this?" I reach out to cup him and fondle his cock through the wisp of fabric.

"Yes." Max covers my hand with his, pressing my palm more firmly against his junk.

"Want me to mouth all over your balls through the panties?" I ask, watching how he reacts as I rub the lace along his shaft.

"Mm," Max moans at my fingers brushing over his sac.

"Use your words, Max," I tease, rolling his balls gently in my hand. He clutches at my shoulders like I'm the only thing keeping him upright.

"Ngh, not yet." He gives a sharp shake of his head. "No fair, making me be the only one naked."

If he hadn't just assured me that he likes my body, I might have made excuses. I usually hate to be naked and vulnerable with guys. But this is Max and he's showing me his hidden parts, so I can be brave too. I make quick work of wriggling free of my vest and dress, draping the latter over my suitcase to minimize wrinkles. Fast, like tearing off a bandage. It takes a bit more effort to peel off my pantyhose. The gaffing panties I wore under the dress are a far cry from the sexy ones Max is wearing, but he's not looking at my discarded clothing. No, his gaze is fixed on me, as I kick my under-garments off in a heap on the floor. Hungry eyes, ready to devour me.

"What?" I demand, braced for any sign I need to go on the defensive.

Max shakes his head and licks his lips. "You're cute. All feisty and in a hurry to be naked with me."

"Not as cute as you. Can I taste you now?" I ask, ready to have him stop looking at me. All of me, with nothing to conceal or constrict my bulk. Exposed. I shiver.

"In a minute," Max pulls me into his arms, hugging me close. He hums low in his throat, like having my bulk pressed flush against his body is a turn on. Huh, from the rock hard erection pressing into my soft belly, he really does like just holding me. I pull his face to mine and kiss him. Trying to convey with my lips and tongue what I can't say with words right now. That what we've got is precious. That this moment of shared intimacy is so much better for knowing I can show him my insecurities and be met with not only understand-ing, but true passion.

Our kiss deepens, near frantic. Max moans into my mouth and the heat of his lace covered cock between us is too tempting to resist any longer. I break our lip-lock.

"Need to taste you," I insist when Max groans a pro-test. I pull away and go to my knees in front of him, nuzzling at his bulge. This is all about the buildup. The tease. I have no intention of simply sucking him off, which is just as well since we don't have condoms. I want to drive us both mad with longing as I press the lace into his most sensitive parts. Feel it moisten with my saliva and his pre-cum. Let him buck against the rough friction of it under my tongue. His hand rests in my hair as I take my time lathing his balls with languid licks.

Max moans and begs for more. He smooths his hand through my hair. I love the gentle possessiveness of him stroking me while I have my face buried in his crotch. There's a delicious burn of something humiliation-adjacent to the way he's petting me. Not the shame of someone seeing me as less for who I am. This is different. Something I've never trusted a partner I intended to see again enough to ask for.

I pull away from mouthing along his length. "Boss me around and call me your good little slut?"

Max's eyes widen and he searches my gaze. "You sure?"

"Please?"

"Yeah, okay." He swallows hard and then nods. He pets my hair again, drawing my mouth back toward his erection. "Get your pretty mouth back on my cock like a good fucktoy, Si," Max says experimentally. I get the idea he's trying this out to humor me.

His tone shifts a bit on the degrading words, like he's slipping into a character. He sounds like he did at their game session last night. It's endearing that he needs to try on a role to use me the way I want to be used. But then it occurs to me that springing this on him mid coitus is probably shitty. We haven't discussed sex because it isn't within the scope of what we agreed to. I'm showing him more of my vulnerable parts. Yet again, Max makes it seem easy to bare my soul.

I sigh and rock back onto my heels. I want nothing more than to slobber all over his cock while he says filthy things to me. But I don't want to taint the memory of tonight with coercing him into something he's not comfortable with later.

"Wait, sorry. Are you okay with a little light humiliation play?" I ask.

Max blinks at me. "What?"

"I'm sorry to spring it on you like this. I just like being called names while I get fucked. Not slurs or anything. Not stuff about my gender either. More like slut, and cum dumpster, that sort of thing."

"You want me to shame you over liking sex?" Max asks, hesitant. Like the idea has never occurred to him. Has he never watched porn? Then again, Max lives in mortal fear of anyone seeing him as less than perfect, of course he wouldn't get off on this let alone seek it out in his porn.

"Yep," I agree, bracing for him to reject this part of me. He wouldn't be the first. Doubt he'll be the last, either. I understand my kinks aren't for everyone. At my most cynical, I sometimes think no one can accept all of me. It's yet another reason I've been so reticent about pursuing anything more than casual sex. It's harder to get hurt if you don't hope for impossible things.

"If I say something that crosses a line, you'll let me know?" Max asks all earnest about not hurting me.

"Not a problem," I agree. Hope that I haven't scared him off blooms in my chest. Max must find whatever he's looking for in my expression. He smiles and strokes his thumb over my lips tenderly.

"Do you like to pretend other stuff? Or just slut-shaming?" Max asks.

"Just that and taking your load. You don't have to, if it's not your thing," I backpedal. I don't want to ruin this by getting too greedy. It would be better if he was into it, too.

"It's fine, my sweet darling slut," Max leans down, tipping up my chin for a kiss. There's a glint in his eye now. I can tell he's still playing with the words, but he's definitely not repulsed by the idea. I watch him as he pulls away to sit on the edge of the bed. He spreads his knees to make room for me to kneel between them, then pats his thigh. "Come here and show me how much you want my cum." He's getting more into it, which means that *I'm* getting more into it.

I scramble forward on my hands and knees to close the distance and Max moans, squeezing his cock like he's going to blow just from watching me. That makes my cock throb with desire, too. I wish we had condoms. Or that I dared risk going raw. I'm not a total pawn to my lust though. This is a one time thing, so I'm not going bare with Max, not even to swallow his load.

I can suck on his balls, though. Worship his hard

length through the spit-saturated lace as he pets my hair and calls me his good slut. Max tells me how much I'm making his balls ache, how greedy I am for his jizz.

"God, Si, I want to fuck you so bad," Max moans as he bucks against my tongue. "Give you every last drop. You're so greedy for it, aren't you, my filthy little slut?"

My needy moans are answer enough. Max is still petting me, his hands are heavier on my head, holding me in place more firmly as he thrusts against my mouth. He lets out a low, frustrated noise when I keep up the teasing licks through the fabric instead of sucking him properly. Then Max tugs at my hair.

"Get up here and hump me like the horny cumslut you know you are," he demands. Our eyes meet and there's a question in his, like, is this okay? I moan my encouragement.

I let Max pull my face to his for a lingering kiss. I hump against his thigh, letting him feel just how okay it is by the passion in our kiss and my hardness rubbing against him. His hand finds my erection, and he strokes me.

"Want you to fuck me from behind," I suggest between breathless kisses. That's a massive understatement. I'm aching to have him inside me. Want throbs through my entire groin.

"We can't. Now, be a good slut and let me get off all over you." Max presses his palm against my hip, shifting me to line up our dicks, so he can stroke them together. His firm touch sends shivers through me. I want him to manhandle me. Make me take every inch of him.

I shake my head. "Not in my ass, between my thighs. Spray your load all over my cock and balls while you fuck into me, breed me like I'm yours, please?" If he was mine, I'd want that for real. Beg him for it. But as things stand, pretending is the next best thing.

"Yeah, okay," Max agrees, nodding. He sounds wrecked.

"Fuck, yes. Breed your slut," I demand, rolling off of him and getting on all fours to present myself. Max stands behind me. It's his turn to tease now. He takes his time collecting a tube of lotion from his suitcase and shedding the sodden panties while I watch impatiently over my shoulder. He coats his dick in the lotion, the vanilla scent I've noticed on him before filling the room. It only amps up my desire for him.

"Max," I whine his name as he massages my ass. I shove back into his hands. "Please?" He pulls my cheeks apart and his cock brushes against me, a ticklish barely there touch.

"How much do you want it, slut?" Max asks as he slides the head of his cock between my thighs.

"More than anything, please, Max, let me have every inch of you. Empty your balls into me. I need you, so bad." I squeeze my legs tight around him, wanting to make this as pleasurable as possible, my soft curves accommodating him.

Max seems to appreciate my efforts. His slick cock slides into the tight channel I'm making for him. The head of his cock rubbing against the back of my balls has me riding the edge of an orgasm. I hold on tight, needing to keep my legs together so he can get off too. The challenge of it, of knowing he's getting off because I'm delaying my gratification does it for me. Max is using me like I'm just a means for him to get off and it's hot as hell.

"Max." I don't even know what I want at that moment. I just need to have his name on my lips. "Max, please."

"Oh, fuck, that's right, slut, milk the cum out of me. You're so fucking hot, Si! I need to fuck you, breed you, paint you in my jizz. Let me come all over you, my sweet slut." Max's words come out desperate and needy, no longer trying out the dirty talk or pretending. His raw desire for me spurs my need higher. I love that I'm driving him wild, that he seems as into my fantasy as I am, no longer just playing along like it's a role he has to fill to please me.

Max is the perfect blend of loving and filthy. He's using me to get off, and I crave every second of being debased by him. Because it's not really debasing, it's bliss. Sheer, perfect bliss.

"That's it, take every drop," Max groans, his weight pushing down on my back as he drives his dick into my balls. The hot wash of his cum over my groin tips me over the edge, too. Our bodies rocking together through waves of pleasure.

Afterward, we lay there panting and catching our breath until the cum under my belly itches and seems more gross than hot. I shove at Max. "Let me up."

"Sorry, Si, was that okay?" Max levers himself up to stand beside the bed. He watches me warily as I roll off the mattress too.

"Hottest sex of my life," I assure him flippantly. It's the truth. In part because he indulged my fantasies and partly because I'm not falling for him; I'm so far beyond falling that it's laughable. Max is everything I'd never dared hope for in a partner. Saying goodbye after this weekend is going to rip out my heart. I don't think I can stand here and pretend to be okay with our status quo.

"Yeah," Max agrees, "you're amazing. I... thanks. For you know, being you? And not making it weird. Some folks don't understand the panties thing. So, yeah."

I force a chuckle, clapping him awkwardly on the shoulder. "Their loss, mate. Your dick belongs framed in pretty fabrics. It was good for you, too?"

"Yeah, you're fucking fantastic."

"Good." We're standing so close, I only need to lean up to peck his cheek with a kiss. "We should get cleaned up and try to sleep. Got to pack. We're leaving in a few hours."

"Yeah, okay," Max agrees. His shoulders slump, and he looks disappointed. I don't have it in me to hold it together much longer. I turn to leave the room, not ready for goodbye. I only make it a few steps before Max's voice pulls me up short.

"Si?" Max asks, it takes an immense effort of will not to turn around and face him.

"Yeah?"

"Is this the end for us?" he asks.

"There never was an 'us'. Was there?" I retort, standing a foot from the door, still not turning back.

"I guess not." Max's voice wobbles on the last word. That's what does me in, knowing he's hurting too. "It's just, I'm not ready for goodbye."

What more do I have to lose by laying my heart on the line? I dare a glance over my shoulder. His expression gives me the strength to try.

"Why not? I mean, the wedding is over. You should get a free pass on set-ups for a while if you tell them I broke your heart, right?" I turn to face him, even though it means serving up this last desperately hopeful piece of myself. I brace for a rejection I'm not sure I can take hearing when everything else is already falling to pieces around me.

CHAPTER 30

Max

"This isn't about my friends," I insist, Si's bitter question ringing in my ears. It's only the truth; I'm off the hook and it only took breaking my own heart. And, judging from the tone of those parting words, Si's too. If that's the case, then it's possible I can salvage the situation. "Not anymore. I don't want to give you up, Si. Not if we might work as a couple."

"Even if it means carrying on long distance?" Si demands, hands shaking. Si seems poised to flee through our door. Something tells me if that happens before we hash this out, it will be too late to fix the mess I've made by being too scared to put myself out there for real. I want nothing more than to take my person into my arms and soothe away all the tension and worry. Si's lack of eye contact, slumped shoulders, and arms crossed tight give the impression of someone barely holding it together. I don't want to make the wrong move. I'm teetering on a knife's edge between getting everything I wanted and losing it for good. "You already told me you weren't keen on trying it with the guys your friends set you up with."

I shake my head, confused. "Long distance?" I repeat, stepping closer. The words still make no sense. Unless...

"Celine is moving in with her man. They don't need me crashing their love-nest, even if his swanky apartment had space for a third wheel."

"Your cousin is kicking you out on the street?" I ask, that doesn't sound like her. Si and Celine are as close as any siblings. Celine wouldn't turn Si out with no place to go.

"No, of course not." Si leans against the doorframe. "She's paid rent through the middle of January, so I have time to find a place. But I can't afford rent without her. Not even looking at crappy studios further from the city, and I'm too scared to risk living with some random stranger off the internet."

"Why didn't you say anything sooner?" I ask, horrified that Si didn't mention something so monumental. I thought we could talk about anything, so it's a shock to get left out of the loop when Si might end up homeless. Only, that doesn't explain the comment about long distance. Unless—realization hits me like a punch to the gut. "You're moving home?"

Si won't meet my eyes. "I can find work back home. Celine's folks have a studio apartment over their garage that I can stay in, just have to pay utilities and help around the house."

It's a relief that Si's aunt and uncle are offering a lifeline. From the stories I've heard from Si and Celine, that's far preferable to moving back in with Si's folks.

"But you hated small town life." My protest sounds weak, even to my own ears.

Si shrugs. "Sure, but I'd rather hate my life choices with a roof over my head and money for food than try living on the streets."

"Okay." I scrape my fingers through my hair, wracking my brain for solutions even though I'm sure Si must have thought this through. Then it hits me, Errol's looking for new tenants, and I'm not a random person off the street. I just have to ask in a way that doesn't sound like I'm only offering out of pity. "So, you said you can't afford Vancouver rents on your own, but you could with a housemate?"

Si's arms cross, brow furrowing in a scowl, "I already said—"

"Right, but you know I'm not attached to my place or my housemate, right? And Errol wants to rent out the two-bedroom unit above his place. It's nice. Nicer than my current basement abode, and the rent is about the same. Errol's a giant softie. I know for a fact he's asking well below market rent and he splits the utilities for the entire townhouse. His tenants pay a third of the costs. So, if you wanted, we could ask him about renting it? Rene even suggested it after the bachelor party, when you fell asleep in the car."

Si blinks at me. "Are you asking me to move in with you the morning we're supposed to be planning our fake breakup? Are you sex-addled?"

"What can I say? You're that good." I wink. Si's frown deepens. "Kidding!" I hold up my hands, hoping to stave off any offense I might have given. Then I lose control of my verbal faculties and words just tumble out on their own. "I mean, not about the sex. No lie, if we move in together I want more sex like that. And to date you for real. Honestly, the only part of this that felt truly fake was pretending not to fall for you. Because, Si, I'm really hung up on you. Or at least, that's how it's been for me. I've been dying to kiss you, only I was too chickenshit to screw things up before the wedding, which in hindsight was crappy of me. So, I get it. If it was different for you. No hard feelings, if you'd rather move in with your aunt and uncle and get your feet under you before making any big life choices. I'd still like to stay in touch and be friends, though. For real. If that's all you want. We can—"

"I don't want to be your friend," Si's words slice through me and I wince. That's enough to stop my verbal diarrhea, at least. I will not cry over this. Si doesn't need a big dramatic guilt-fest when there are obviously things I'm not aware of weighing on this decision. If that stings, well, it's only because I've read more into this than Si wants out of our relationship, such as it is.

"Okay," I choke out, keeping my eyes fixed on the ground at my feet. "Sorry."

"What?" Si's feet move into my field of view. Firm

hands grip my shoulders, Si's fingers tilt my face toward Si's. "Oh, Max, no, I mean, I don't want to *only* be friends. I want to be your datemate for real." Then Si's lips press against mine and I cling on for dear life, kissing like we might not get another chance. Even though we both just finally admitted to wanting all the chances to kiss.

"No kidding?" I break the kiss first, unable to contain all the hope and joy that making Si mine for real could be this simple. "You really like me?"

"I really like you. Like, *really* like." Si nods, then kisses my neck.

"That's a lot of liking." I chuckle, giddy with relief that this is going well. I twist to capture Si's lips again, more frantic needy kisses follow. When we pull back for air, Si is grinning at me.

"Yeah it is. So much like." Si kisses my cheek. "You get that I'm not comfortable around most people, right? But you not only see me, you seem to like what you see."

"No seeming about it. I more than like you, Si," I say, not quite ready for the other four letter l-word, even though it's there on my mind. I squeeze Si tightly, hoping to convey the depth of my emotions with touch.

"Right back at you. I mean it, you're the first person besides Celine that I'm comfortable enough with to be around without my compression vest on my Si days. You get that, right?"

I nod, because I couldn't help noticing that somewhere along the line Si stopped wearing the vest during our cooking lessons, but it was always on if we left the apartment or when Harvey visited. "So, does that mean you'll move in with me?" I check. Stepping back so we don't get distracted with more kissing before we sort out that detail.

Si hesitates, then nods. "Yeah, if we can find a place I can afford to pay my fair share, I'd like that. I don't want charity from your friends or to rush things with you because of my financial situation, though."

"Sure. We can talk numbers. And I'll ask Errol about the rent. We can look at other options, too." It's a practical decision, but my heart is still leaping at the idea of having Si with me every day. Of building a home together. It's faster than I ever would have suggested it otherwise, but I'm not going to let Si slip through my fingers. And I'm possibly already imagining merging our furniture and bathroom supplies. Like a dork.

Si pulls me into another kiss, and we end up back in bed, humping like horny rabbits who have dozens of missed opportunities to make up for. This time neither of us has the patience for teasing or drawing out our pleasure. We connect with months of pent up passion between us. The joy and relief of having nothing to hide or lie about. No more hidden truths to skirt, or guessing how the other person feels.

All our cards are on the table and Si feels the same as I do. I get on top, pinning Si under me. Neither of us is willing to give up our liplock to adjust, so it takes a bit of squirming and wriggling to get a hand around both our lengths and find the right rhythm and angle so that our thrusting hips drag our dicks together in surges of overwhelming sensation that blends with the euphoria of knowing I get more of this, more of Si. As much as we both want, for as long as we want.

I didn't realize what an onerous burden it was knowing Si would walk away after the wedding until it lifted. Si promised not to leave me behind. I'm floating among the clouds with the joy and relief of having everything I've been longing for in a romance. I don't feel alone, haven't since Si started to fill all the lonely places in my life with our running text conversation that never seems to run dry and our cooking lessons that have fed so much more than my body.

Words are still hard, and I can't quite convey how much this means to me, but it all pours out into the frantic friction of our bodies moving in sync. Hard dicks sliding together, our bodies pressed skin-to-skin as though if we rut together with enough enthusiasm we might merge into one flesh, mouths desperately sealed together like we can share one breath. I don't know who comes first, just that my vision is filled with Si and the bliss of getting off together. Being together.

We eventually make it to the shower for a quick cleanup. Then we retire back into our shared bed where I snuggle close to my love's soft naked body. Cuddling together in bed is better than sex in some ways. It's easy enough to find a person to give me an orgasm, but it's harder to find someone I want to stick around afterward. Someone it's easy to be naked and vulnerable with. Who fits against my body like we're two pieces of a puzzle. Si's sensual curves are perfect for snuggling; give me the yielding comfort of Si's belly over cut abs any day.

"You want to get tested when we get home?" I ask, idly stroking Si's hair.

"Hmm?" Si hums a sleepy response.

"Cause talking about fucking my cum into you was hot as heck, and I'd love to try it for real. If you want it, too?"

"You want to breed your filthy cum slut?" Si teases, turning toward me and tracing a finger over my lips. The shift in position makes the half-hard bulge of Si's cock an obvious endorsement of my suggestion, as if the words weren't enough.

"Yes, please," I agree. My dick twitches valiantly with renewed interest. My third orgasm in under an hour isn't happening. No matter how much Si arouses me.

Si notices, and grinds against me. "We should make an appointment first thing. Because, hell yes, I want that."

"Good. First thing. The lab on Lonsdale offers morning appointment slots, and we can get our results in time to christen our new place."

"Mm. New place and wild sex. Sounds like just the start to our new year, huh?"

"Definitely," I agree. "We're off to a perfect start, must've rolled a natural twenty."

"You're such a nerd." Si squeezes me tighter.

"Yep, but I'm *your* nerd."

"You are." Si cups my cheek and kisses my lips. "Goodnight, my nerd."

"Goodnight, my Si."

"Mm. I like when you call me yours." Si snuggles closer and we spend the rest of the night cuddled up under the covers.

CHAPTER 31

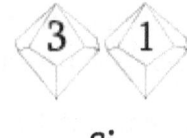

Si

Errol wakes Max and I up way before I'm at all ready to roll out of bed the morning after the wedding. We're expected to attend a brunch to send the happy newlyweds off on their honeymoon. They're sticking around Whistler for the next week. If it was me and Max, I'd want to go someplace more exciting than a ski hill. But, from what I know about the couple, they have a whole lot of staying in to have newlywed sex on their agenda, so maybe location doesn't matter for that.

Not that I blame them. Now that Max is officially mine, all I want to do is find excuses to get him alone and kiss him. And more than kisses. Too bad we're running late for brunch so there isn't time for a morning quickie.

We touch more during the shared meal than our

usual. Neither of us seems to have the slightest inclination to curb our affection. Besides, no one is paying attention to Max and I.

After food, we pack and head back to the city with Errol and his family. I don't hesitate to lay my head on Max's shoulder once we're on the road. He wraps an arm around me. It crosses my mind that Errol and Rene might notice the increased intimacy between Max and I, but I can't bring myself to care enough to stop.

Mo is cranky in the car until he falls asleep, I can't blame the kid for whining. The last thing I want is to sit cooped up in a car for hours either when I'm brimming with joyful energy that Max is mine for real. It's worse because I have to pretend like nothing has changed. As far as his friends know, we've been together for real all along.

"What's got the pair of you so smiley and loved up this morning?" Errol asks, after a few miles of blessed silence once Mo falls asleep from his motion sickness meds.

I tense at the question. We didn't discuss how much to tell everyone.

"Si agreed to move in with me last night," Max replies without missing a beat.

"Congrats," Errol and Rene say.

"You two wouldn't be in the market for a new place then, by any chance?" Rene asks, turning in their seat and flashing a toothy grin.

"We might be," Max says, shooting a glance my way.

"We still have to figure out our budget."

"That's fine, our upstairs unit should be ready for occupancy by the fifteenth, in case you're interested, right, Errol?" Rene says.

"If we don't run into any more issues. I swear the problems multiply like rabbits. Wrong parts, unexpected expenses, back-ordered supplies, and missing subcontractors," Errol vents. He has the air of someone who is thoroughly sick of renovations. I heard all about Celine's construction woes when she was getting ready to open the shop, so the complaints are familiar.

Rene snorts. "My cushy tub got installed last week. If you rent from us, you're welcome, by the way. They shipped us the wrong model the first go around, but our work crew dinged it up before we noticed, so they wouldn't accept the return. Long story short, we got a credit toward the correct model and the rental unit got the fancy jetted soaker tub that's only slightly less awesome than mine. Between the tub going in and the nursery drywall going up before the holidays, I'm fine with the timeline getting delayed a little here and there."

"Isn't Mo old for a nursery?" Max jokes.

"Well, shit," Rene curses, then glances into the rearview to check that Mo is still asleep.

Errol chuckles and rubs their knee. "Guess that's the cat out of the bag, huh?"

"Surprise," Rene adds. "We're expecting not long after Emil's due date. I'm a few months along. Didn't want to steal Emil's thunder at all, considering, and then with all the wedding festivities..."

"We were planning to tell the gang next weekend," Errol picks up where Rene left off. "Once Jude and Theo are back from their honeymoon."

"Sure, I can act surprised. I know Laura and Pia will never let you hear the end of it if they find out I knew before them," Max says.

"Huh? No need for that. You know I consider you as much a friend as them, Max," Errol says, a frown furrowing his brow.

Max shrugs. "Sure, I guess. But you've known them longer and all. It's not a big deal."

"You don't matter to me any less just because we only met a year ago," Errol insists.

"Huh. It's weird to me that it's been a year already," Max says.

"Right? Seems longer." Errol flashes Max a grin in the rearview. "Best slightly tipsy hiring decision I ever made." He winks. "You're one of the most motivated runners we've had in a long while. On that note, we need to handle your yearly review next week, can you schedule it when we get into the office Monday?"

"Of course, I'll squeeze something in first thing, fifteen minute block?"

"Go with a full thirty, I've got something to discuss with you," Errol says.

"Right," Max agrees, tone nervous and clipped. "I'll make it happen."

"It's nothing bad," Errol rushes to assure him, picking up on his anxiety about the meeting. If I know my guy, he's going to obsess over what Errol might say at this meeting until it's over. No matter how much Errol tries to reassure him at this point. Errol knows him too, because he sighs. "I promise your job is safe and I won't spring anything bad on you at our meeting, Max. Anyway, that got off track. My point is, you're important to me. If you doubted that, I'm sorry I didn't make it clearer."

"I mean, I guess if we weren't friends you wouldn't have much reason to drive my ass all the way to the North Shore after we go out. Then again, if I move into your rental unit, that would cut out the inconvenience factor. Is that your super secret evil plot?" Max teases.

"I would never!" Errol jokes.

"Uh-huh. Theo would give you disadvantage to that charisma roll. You're pretty sus," Max claims, eyes narrowing.

"Bluff check?" Errol suggests.

"Sure, whatever. The point is, I'm on to you and your games. Also, about this nursery, does it share a wall with our room?"

"No, the nursery is next to your washroom and the smaller bedroom's closet. And we put in soundproofing between the units. Plus, if this little nugget is as fussy as their big brother was, they will sleep in our room. We're not in the 'let them wail it out in the nursery' school of thought, so you shouldn't have too much to worry about," Rene supplies.

"Anyway, if you're serious about checking it out, you two can swing by to see the apartment in person anytime. I can message you with the details about average monthly utilities when I'm home and have all the records in front of me."

"Sounds good. Si's lease is up on the 15th," Max says.

"That works for us," Rene agrees. The conversation moves away from the apartment and Max asks how Rene is handling the pregnancy, and if they've thought of names.

I can't help comparing the situation to how Gina disappeared from my life when hers changed. His buddies aren't leaving Max behind because they have a kid and are expecting another. They're acting like Max will be a part of the baby's life and inviting him along for whatever comes next for them. That's what I want, friends who care through thick and thin. I'm still getting my head around the fact I might get to keep Max. Form genuine friendships with his friends. These people who never questioned or demeaned any part of my identity from the moment I met them. People who are like me.

Max's concern for them seems genuine, too. He offers support when Rene mentions extra sessions with their counselor and talking out flashbacks to their first pregnancy. It sounds like, this time around, they have a good support network.

I follow along with the conversation, but I'm sort of slipping from Si mode toward Simone. Rare as these midday switches are for me, it's always a bit of a trip, when it happens like this. Maybe it's from knowing I won't have to hide being Simone, as I've feared since Celine and Harvey announced their plans to move in together. It's safe to be Simone again, and my subconscious wants to assert that part of me. I was getting glimmers of the itch toward girl mode yesterday, so maybe it shouldn't be a surprise. I'd felt drawn to the dress rather than the suit, though going purely femme hadn't fit either. The mashup of vest and dress was the perfect compromise.

Today I'm dressed for pure comfort in my compression shirt and comfy worn hoodie. The compression garment is great for my anxiety on Si days. And I'm indifferent about it on Simon days. On Simone days, pressing my chest flat is a gnawing, aching reminder I'm not as busty as I might prefer on my girl days. I snuggle into Max more firmly. The creeping wrongness of my body makes this switch hard to handle when I'm trapped in the back of the car with no outlet to express it. My compression shirt is getting more oppressive with every breath I take.

"You okay, Si?" Max checks when I squeeze him a little too tight, like a scared kid with a teddy bear or something.

"Simone," I correct him. He tightens his arm around my shoulders, sussing out why I'm having a moment.

"That's a shift from earlier," Max observes.

I nod against his shoulder.

"Can I do anything to help you feel more comfortable?" he asks.

I try to think of some task to ease his concern. All I need is time to adjust to the off kilter sense of shifting mental gears. And space to be me, Max already gives me that without thought. "Dunno."

"Mo has some glittery lip stuff he didn't like the taste of up here, if you don't mind that he used the applicator once before deciding it wasn't for him. Would that help?" Rene holds up a tube of shiny pink lip gloss with cartoon princesses on the label. "He isn't a fan of fake cherries."

The gesture warms me inside, even if I am still sort of panicky at the sudden shift. I wish I could squirm out of the compression shirt. Then again, maybe I can.

"Help me pull off my undershirt?" I ask Max. Between the two of us, I wriggle free of the tight vest. My baggy sweatshirt is pretty neutral, so it's not the worst thing to be wearing, even if I would prefer one of my blouses. Mo's second-hand lip gloss gives me that pop of femininity I need to anchor myself as Simone. I get through the shift to girl mode with minimal dysphoria, secure in knowing that Max and his friends truly accept me as I am. They even try to help me feel more comfortable. Max and his friends are nothing like my old friends. In their eyes, I'm not a weirdo. To them, I'm just Simone. Max's datemate who sometimes happens to be Simon or Si, too, no big deal.

We chat more about the apartment once I'm over my initial anxiety about the flip to girl mode. There are plenty of details to go over, but I've already decided what I want, even before Errol confirms the absurdly low rent they're asking. I want to stay in Vancouver with Max. As my partner, no more lies. The possibility of keeping this newfound family spurs me to come clean to Max's friends.

"Max and I were faking," I blurt, then wince as it occurs to me I should have run this confession by Max first.

"Faking what?" Errol asks, glancing back at us in the rearview. Rene turns in their seat to offer a reassuring smile.

"Our relationship. He asked me to be his date to get Jude to lay off the matchmaking."

Rene slugs Errol gently in the arm. "Told you!"

"Hey, you just said it wouldn't surprise you if Max did something like that, not that you suspected he and Simone weren't an actual couple. You believed them until the bachelor party."

"Details." Rene flaps their hand in a breezy dismissal. "The point is, I was right. You all were coming on too strong for our poor Max."

"You usually are," Errol admits fondly. They exchange a besotted glance and Errol squeezes Rene's thigh before returning both hands to the wheel. "Why did you think you had to pretend, Max?"

"You all kept throwing every single guy you knew at me. And I kept going on all these painfully awkward dates so I wouldn't disappoint you, and it sucked. It seemed like if I didn't have a date, then I wasn't as welcome. I worried I'd get left behind once you all got sick of me. So, when Simone and I hit it off, I figured I could bring along someone I enjoyed hanging out with. It worked too. Everyone got off my back about dating, plus I got to hang out with Simone. No more surprise dates and I got all the perks of dating a person I really liked without all the stress of actual dating."

Max glances over at me, like he wants to check in that I'm okay with what he's said. I give him an encouraging nod. It's gratifying to hear my boyfriend admit he really likes me to someone I know he respects. And getting to call him my boyfriend for real now has a smile plastered all over my face.

"I'm sorry we made you feel less than welcome with us, Max. You're our friend regardless of your relationship status. I only joined in with setting you up because you talked about wanting to meet people and being lonely in the city. Jude said you told him you wanted a boyfriend."

"I told him that. But I meant someone like Gramps is to my granddad. A lifelong companion, not just a superficial relationship that's all about sex."

"That makes total sense to me. For what it's worth, I'm sorry we tried to smother you with our misguided attempts at showing you how much we care, Max," Errol says. "It seems like you found that for yourself with Simone, huh?"

"Yeah, I totally did," Max says. He's grinning as he twines our fingers together. "I found so much more than I was bargaining for when I asked her to be my plus one."

I lean in to kiss his cheek.

"Aw, Simone's your plus one bonus, that's a thing in your game, right?" Rene teases.

Errol opens his mouth to say something. Probably to explain the finer points of VentureQuest's die roll system. He's always got plenty to say about modifiers, advantage, disadvantage, and the dubious merits of the house rules Theo prefers versus the rules as written when we play. He must read the room because instead of explaining the game Errol says, "Yes, imzadi, that's a thing."

Rene's eyes are sparkling with mischief as they say, "I thought so. That's settled then. You two tricked everyone because Max is too sweet to just tell all you overbearing, meddling numbskulls to back off and leave his love life to him. And then you fell for each other? Do you plan to tell the others?"

"Do we?" Max asks me.

"Up to you, sorry to just blurt it out like that without discussing it first. I just didn't want to lie anymore, especially if we might live in their home." I gesture toward Errol and Rene.

"If you take the apartment, then it's your home," Errol corrects.

"Still, it didn't feel right to lie to you when you're being so generous. No false pretenses," I insist.

"That's admirable, but you don't owe us anything for renting to you. I mean, other than the rent and utilities, and a pet deposit if you get one. It's all laid out in the lease," Errol says.

"On that note, shall we swing by the apartment so you can look at it before we bring you home? I'm sure you're stressed about finding a suitable place to live if your current lease is up in two weeks, Simone," Rene offers.

We agree to the visit. The rest of the drive passes with good-natured bickering between Errol and Max about their VentureQuest campaign and work. The topic meanders back to Rene and Errol's new baby and how excited Mo is to be a big brother. Rene lists the pros and cons of potty training a new puppy while one is on parental leave with a new baby. That sounds like a nightmare combination of sleep deprivation and dealing with other creatures' waste to me. More power to them if Errol and Rene want a puppy. Maybe Max and I can dog sit. I'd enjoy a fuzzy friend.

After helping my folks with Becca, I'm content to play the role of doting aunty to other people's kids rather than having my own. Or for more general usage outside of girl mode, parsib suits me better, as in parental sibling. Hopefully Max is on the same page as me. I'll be the first in line to spoil any future offspring Celine has rotten. And I've been enjoying the time spent with Rain and Mo.

Somewhere along the line, I get drawn into the conversation as we rank our favorite sci-fi shows. Errol is a Trekkie, but I'm more into Red Dwarf and Dr. Who, my BBC preference kicking in again. I'm a sucker for a sexy accent. Max grumbles that fantasy is better, which I already knew from his shelves of painted minis reenacting scenes from his favorite books and movies.

Rene jokes they should make a show about hockey teams in space. Or space baking, which I agree would be cool, since stuff would react differently in an artificial atmosphere. I wonder what adjustments baking in space might require. Before I know it, we're pulling into Errol's driveway in the burbs.

The apartment looks as nice as Errol and Rene's home on the first floor, if less spacious. I've made up my mind before we get to the bedroom. I want to make my home here, with Max.

CHAPTER 32

Max

"So, I'll give you two a chance to explore without me looking over your shoulder. Let yourselves in through the kitchen door when you're done and I can drive you home," Errol says. He ducks out, leaving us to it.

We wait until the door shuts behind Errol to talk.

"Well?" I ask, "What do you think?"

"I can't believe we can afford this," Simone gestures around the well-appointed kitchen. It's all new appliances and fancy counters, and the rent is on the low end of what it should be, because Errol's a giant softie.

"But you can swing half, right?" I check.

"Yeah." Simone nods, gliding her fingers possessively over the shining countertops. "I can make it work. I want to. If you're sure you want to live here with me?"

It's not huge. The kitchen and living room both fit over the footprint of Errol's larger kitchen below. The two bedrooms are about half the size of the large ones I know are downstairs, but they're nice and cozy with new flooring and fresh paint. And Rene wasn't lying about the jetted soaker tub in the bathroom next to a stackable washer-dryer combo.

"Beats the heck out of my current lodgings, especially since my favorite feature of my place in North Van was sharing a commute with you," I say.

Simone grins at me. "So, should we ask to sign the lease? I mean, it's kind of weird to make our relationship official and then move in together the next day. I get it if it's too soon or you're having second thoughts now that the post-orgasmic glow has worn off—"

I step into Simone's personal space and cut off her nervous rambling with a kiss that leaves us both breathless. From the first time we spoke, I wondered what her lips would feel like against mine, and now that I know, I'm glad of any opportunity to kiss her. "The only second thoughts I've had about you were whether I should ever have suggested pretending when I was interested in the real thing. Pretty much from the second the words came out of my mouth. I've wanted you since you agreed to share my umbrella."

"Same," Simone agrees, which leads to more kissing. "I've wanted you since that day, too. No need to rush anything. It's a two-bedroom, so we can each have our own space, at least while we get used to being a proper couple."

"Hate to break it to you, but I think maybe we've been a proper couple for a while now. I mean, when was the last time you dated someone else? We cook and eat meals together, we flirt all the time, even when no one else is around. You back me cookies. We play games, and share our days... other than sex, how is that not a legit relationship?" I ask.

Simone gives me a rueful smile. "Put that way, I think we might be the only ones we actually tricked into thinking it wasn't real, just because we never fooled around. I'm glad you said something."

Simone kisses me again. This time it gets steamy fast. She pulls me close, and I'd love to take this a lot further than making out pressed up against the cabinets. We can christen the new kitchen counter before we even sign the papers, but Simone's told me before that she doesn't fuck in girl mode, so I reluctantly pull away.

"We should stop, before my dick gets stupid ideas," I say, holding Simone at arm's length. Not that I can't control myself, but it would be uncomfortable to ride home with blue balls if we keep up the kissing and touching.

She nods, slouching deeper into her hoodie and look-ing guilty. "Yeah. Sorry, don't mean to be a tease. Much beyond kissing with a side of light boob action does my head in on Simone days."

"I remember. You're not a tease, Simone," I assure her, cupping a hand to her cheek and wishing I could erase the suspicious furrow in her brow. "Everyone has boundaries, and I'll always respect yours. Always. I can totally do just kissing on your girl days. Anyone who thinks making out is only for foreplay is missing out big time."

"Yeah? You aren't just saying that, are you?" Simone asks, eyes narrowing, like she's heard it all before.

"No. I enjoy being close to you without sex on the table. I think the past few months established that, right?"

That gets a chuckle out of her. "Yeah, more than. I've lost count of how many times I wanted to push you up against the kitchen counters and ravish you at our cooking lessons, though."

"Well, tomorrow is Sunday," I quip with a wink. "Think Errol would let us move in this weekend so we can have a nice private kitchen for our lesson this week? Because I've wanted that, too."

Simone snort-laughs. "I doubt we can move in fast enough to have a functional kitchen by tomorrow, even if Errol and Rene agree."

"Don't underestimate the value of friends with cars. Alice's SUV fits a ton," I counter.

"Sure, but everyone is just getting back from the wedding, they won't want to move us tonight," Simone says.

"You're living out of a suitcase, Simone, how much stuff do you think you have?" I point out.

"I might surprise you. But what about you? I'd imagine it will take ages just to pack up all your miniatures so they don't get damaged. And don't you need to give your housemate some notice?"

"Yeah. Fine," I concede, knowing she's right.

Still, a hasty move would have been a perfect distraction from my upcoming performance review at work. Errol promised he has nothing terrible to spring on me at our meeting next week. I still can't help thinking of every screwup I've made at work since starting the job. It's like a worst hits reel in my head. Errol may be my supervisor, but he's not the only boss I answer to.

"I guess tomorrow might be an unrealistic goal. Unless I find someone to move in and take over my share of the rent, I'll still be on the hook for January's rent at my old place. So it's not like there's any great rush on my end. I'll talk to my housemate about it tonight. But that's fine. Maybe we can look at moving in time for next week's cooking lesson?" I suggest.

"I'd like that, or if not next week, then for the 16th, since I have to clear out of Celine's place by then. Besides, if we wait, we can get tested in time for our first night in the new place." Simone aims a comical leer my way and I smile back. I give in to the impulse to kiss her again, just a quick one, now that such things aren't off limits between us.

"That sounds like a solid plan. Come on, let's sign the lease." I offer Simone my hand. She takes it, stealing one last gentle peck on my lips before leading the way downstairs to make our future here official.

CHAPTER 33

Si

When I suggested getting our test results back in time to celebrate our first night in our new place, I might have been the slightest bit optimistic about getting our butts into the lab while coordinating a move. And how long the lab would take to post the results to their online portal. I've been refreshing that stupid digital medical chart a couple times a day since we got officially moved into the new place.

We considered waiting to have penetrative sex until the results came in, but then Max came to see me on our lunch break after his Monday performance review. He looked all aglow. Excited that Errol offered him a permanent employee contract as a production coordinator. That's the next step up the corporate hierarchy for him. I guess he's used to having to renew temporary contracts every few months or years. So getting offered a permanent position is a big deal to him.

I had big news that day, too. Paz came through with an official offer to apprentice with him. It means working long hours between the bakery and Celine's shop. But, in two years, I'll be a pastry chef. Celine crunched the numbers, and she thinks the shop might be ready to add in-house baked goods to the menu by then. She even suggested letting me buy into the business with her as a partner down the line. For now, I'm just ecstatic that I get to bake instead of solely slinging tea. If all goes well, I might even expand my repertoire and hang up the barista slash retail apron for good.

Max and I had a celebratory lunch together after sharing our good news. We stopped at a pharmacy to grab condoms on the way back to the tea shop after our meal. That night, I stayed over at his place after we fooled around, which cemented us sharing a bed, even before the big move.

Max was right about his friends pitching in to help us cart our stuff across town. With everyone grabbing boxes and loading them into cars and the U-Haul that Max rented for the day, we made quick work of things. It only took a few trips to move us both. Max had more stuff than I thought, taking most of his room's furniture and a hodgepodge of art supplies.

We had to make an Ikea run with the rented van to finish furnishing the new place, though we didn't need as much as I'd have guessed. Celine let me keep most of the stuff from her kitchen, since Harvey does most of the cooking at their place and he already owns his preferred tools. Max's full size futon is just the right size couch for our cozy living room. We had to get a new bed. That made for a memorable outing, testing mattresses together with the knowledge we'd be sharing whatever we selected.

Max got all excited about it, bouncing around and insisting on trying every option, just to be sure we got the perfect one. I think it was something he always wanted to do with someone else. Like grocery shopping together. The little details that make him feel less alone in the vast city. We've also discussed adopting a kitten once we're more settled. It's a long-term commitment, but I'm ready to be a pet parent with him. I'm happy to be Max's partner in all things. Mattress shopping, unpacking, and litter box training, and now that this freaking test result page has finally populated with a full panel of negative results, in fluid bonding, too. We've got the green light to fuck bare. The way we've been fantasizing about, without worrying about potential consequences.

Pretending is hot too, we've done that several times since moving in here, but I'm excited for the reality. I poke my head into the spare room where Max has his art stuff set up. The spare room sort of turned into a catchall space. I've taken over the closet in here. My wardrobes for my Simone and Simon days makes for a fair amount of clothing, most of it gathered over years of thrifting. I have my makeup and hair stuff in here, too.

Max even surprised me with the gift of a nice vanity with a lit up mirror like something out of my teenaged self's fantasy wishlist. It's weird and euphoric to have a dedicated place to store and apply my beauty products. It's the most thoughtful gift anyone's ever gotten me, and I can't help but smile whenever it catches my eye.

Max is currently working on unpacking and arranging more of his miniatures to his liking on their display shelves. His favorites are still in our room. With our friends having young kids, and more babies in the group's future, he explained he figures it'll be safer to put the rest of the collection in here. Where they'll be away from little hands, and no one can choke on them. Unlike if he set them up in the living room. I think it's a mark of personal growth that he's planning for people to visit us. It shows that he might finally believe they'll be there for him, the same way he is for them.

Max glances up at me in question when I barge into the room. I told him I was going to watch a show while he did his unpacking, since I've got some new episodes to catch up on. What with all the wedding events and our move keeping us busy for the past several weeks, I've fallen behind.

"What's up, Si?" he asks.

"Hey, Max, did you check the page?" I wave my phone at him.

He takes a second to parse my meaning, then he grins at me. "Not yet. Did you get your results? From that giant grin, I take it there weren't any surprises?" He pulls out his phone, and logs into his patient profile, then waits for his results to load.

"All negative, see?" I hand over my phone for him to read, Max angles his screen so I can see his results too, as they populate the screen.

"Same here. So. No more condoms?" he asks.

"No more condoms," I agree. I'm not sure which of us moves first, but our lips mash together in an ungainly, boisterous kiss.

"You're awful greedy for it, aren't you, Si?" Max teases me.

"So fucking greedy," I agree.

What we lack in finesse, we make up for in eagerness. Max palms my ass, squeezing my cheeks and pulling me tight against his body. I could melt into the way we fit together. This feels so right with him. I cup his face between my hands and kiss him until we're both panting for breath and moaning into each other's mouths. "Can't wait to fill you up, Si. Give you what you want, my sweet slut."

"Yes, Max, I want it all, every drop."

"I want you so bad," Max says, voice husky as I hump against him, rubbing our dicks together through our pants. "Bedroom?"

"No, here." I shake my head. There'll be plenty of time to screw in our big comfy bed, but right now, I want something different. "Fuck me up against my vanity, I want to watch your face in the mirror while you come inside me." I want to experience him loving me with his gift to me front and center. A big tangible reminder that he sees every part of me and loves me for it.

"Yeah?" Max asks, all breathy and eager.

"Yeah," I confirm. "Please."

In answer, Max draws me toward the sturdy vanity and strips off my baggy hoodie and the tight compression shirt underneath. He runs his hands and lips along the bare skin he reveals, touching me with all the reverence of a lover. I tug his shirt off too, wanting his bare shoulders under my hands. Max removes my pants and gets his mouth on my dick, sucking me as he fingers my ass with spit-slicked fingers.

I need little foreplay. Since I'd been rather hopeful the test results would finally show up today, I did some solo prep earlier in the shower. Max grins up at me, and I stroke his cheek.

"Mm, someone was an eager slut for me," Max observes when his fingers encounter little resistance.

"Always," I agree, "your horny slut."

"I want to finish you like this," he muses, lapping at the head of my cock without breaking eye contact.

"Ngh, yeah," I moan my assent to that plan.

"After I fill you up with my cum. You ready for me?" Max asks, standing.

"So ready," I agree. "But first, fair's fair. I showed you mine, now you show me yours."

Max gives me a shy smile. "I'm all yours," he says, dragging down his zipper to reveal a silky jock in bright teal and yellow poking out behind his fly. He shimmies out of his pants, making a show of it. I grin, hooting my encouragement.

"Work it, you sexy thing," I tease him.

The appreciation in my voice seems to bolster his enthusiasm. He gets into the act, his hips rolling to show off the bright yellow banana on the satiny fabric that's cupping his junk. It's fucking hot and silly and sexy and sweet all at once.

"Mm, that's one sexy banana I can't wait to peel," I tease him with a wink.

"Go for it." Max laughs.

Stroking him through the fabric makes his eyes roll up in pleasure and his dick twitch and leak in my grasp. The soft silky fabric forms a luscious contrast with his hardness. I let the head of his dick poke free above the waistband and mouth at him, tonguing his slit to taste his salty-bitter musk for the first time. Other than teasing along his shaft and balls on our first night together, I've only had my mouth on him with a condom. I like the way he tastes. I intend to suck him off sometime soon, but I want to feel him thrusting inside my ass more than I want to swallow his load. His erection bobs free when I ease the pretty underwear down his thighs.

"Tasty, but I think it's time for you to get inside me, Max," I say.

"Kneel up on the stool, then slut," Max suggests. I'm enough shorter than him that the stool ought to put us at the right height.

I turn my back to him and kneel on the wide, softly padded seat of the stool that came with the vanity. Once I'm situated, I lean forward to brace myself on the vanity's surface. Max takes up his position behind me, teasing his hard cock along my crack.

He reaches past me to grab the lube I stashed among my cosmetics when I was setting everything up last week. I arch back into him, loving the warmth of his naked body lined up behind me. There's a wet squelch as he squeezes out a glob of lube.

"Excuse me," he quips, and we both crack up laughing. Then Max slicks himself up and eases into me, slow and gentle. I sigh at the stretch of his initial entry and squirm a bit to angle him a little better. "You're so hot, Si. Love being inside you."

"Mhm, fuck me now, Max, want you to move. Fill me up and breed me."

Max doesn't need me to tell him twice. He shifts to grip my flanks, his steadying touch a comfort. Max moves slowly at first, finding just the right angle to make me gasp and clutch at the table edge under my hands. His thrusts get firmer then, rubbing me just right as pleasure sparks along my nerves, building inside me until I can't hold back anymore.

Our eyes lock in the mirror as Max fucks into me, pounding out his release in a heated burst deep inside me. I clench tight around him, milking every drop. I like the squishy noises of his release. Wet slaps of flesh on flesh, loud in my ears as he keeps thrusting through his orgasm. Max eases out of me when he's too sensitive to keep going. The hot trickle of his spunk down my thighs has my still hard dick twitching with want.

I watch Max in the mirror as he gathers up his mess with his fingers and reaches around me to stroke my erection with it. I pump wildly into his fist, mind tripping over the hotness of using his cum as lube.

Max has me right on the edge. Before I can come from the slick squeeze of his hand on me, he urges me upright. His stroking stops so he can turn me around. We stand facing, cum leaking down my thighs and making me feel wanton. Max crowds close to me to share a sloppy kiss. Then he kneels and his mouth engulfs me in sweet suction, his fingers find my hole, playing in the cum that's still filling me, marking me as his. Max takes me deep, his fingers pressing unerringly at just the right spot inside me. I blow at the thought of our next kiss being tinged with the flavor of our mingled release.

Max swallows around me, cradling me in his mouth until I'm utterly spent. Then he stands and gives me the kiss I crave, it tastes like us, the earthy musk of our sex.

In the past I'd laugh at stupid euphemisms about two becoming one and making love, but sex with Max is more than a physical joining. With us, being together like this isn't just sex. It's a baring of every part of ourselves and not just our bodies, it makes sex transcendent in a way I've never experienced with anyone else.

I love him. Love being with him and feeling our fluids mingling on my skin. It's like a promise that we can always have this precious connection that only the two of us share. Or maybe I'm just high on endorphins from phenomenal sex. Either way, Max is the only person I want to share this intimacy with. I'm staring at him, all sappy and lovestruck as I hold his face in my hands after the kiss ends.

"Love you," he says, echoing my thoughts. It's not the first time he's said it. Max tells me every day in a thousand ways spoken and not, but it still makes me all warm and tingly to hear aloud. He gives me one last chaste kiss on the lips before pulling away. "Come on, let's get cleaned up, then we can cuddle while you watch that show you've been saving all week, yeah?"

"God, I love you," I say, because that sounds perfect. Today is a good day. As if I needed further confirmation Max is my happily ever after.

Thanks for reading Plus One Bonus! If you enjoyed it, be sure to leave a review. If you haven't checked out the rest of the Table Topped series read about Max's friends at: https://www.amazon.com/gp/product/B08R6LM6YG

And if you're in the mood for a paranormal romance, check out my trans ghost hunter, Chad, and his vlogging boyfriend, Dan, in Hauntastic Haunts starting here: www.amzn.com/B07YSV2ZNQ

ABOUT THE AUTHOR

Alex Silver (he/him) grew up mostly in Northern Maine and is now living in Canada with one spouse, two kids, and three birds. Alex is a trans guy who started writing fiction as a child and never stopped. Although there were detours through assisting on a farm and being a pharmacist along the way.

Visit me online at:

http://alexsilverauthor.wordpress.com/

Join my Facebook group at:

https://www.facebook.com/groups/alexsalcove

Follow me on BookBub at:

https://www.bookbub.com/profile/alex-silver

Sign up for my newsletter for a free short story at: https://landing.mailerlite.com/webforms/landing/i2w6l7

And as always, consider leaving a review on Amazon or Goodreads if you enjoyed this book, reviews are of vital importance to independent authors, thanks!

TABLE TOPPED

Charisma Check

Gui's the best friend I ever had. I love him like a brother, too bad I'm falling for *his* little brother.

Jude is a walking talking temptation, everything I never let myself want. He's sweet as chocolate, wickedly funny, and he gets me. The sex, well, it's worth a repeat and that's something I never do.

When he visited Gui, I thought I could settle for a one night stand, but then Jude moves to my city to work at my studio. Gui gets him to join my gaming group and suddenly he's all I see. Now Jude's looking at me with hearts in his eyes and I'm terrified that I'm going to break his heart.

Charisma Check is the second M/M romance in the Table Topped series. It features Jude, a hopeless romantic with diabetes who makes animation and Theo, a commitment-phobic trans man with depression who runs tabletop games for his friends. www.amzn.com/B08R6J14VZ

CW: for severe depression, gender dysphoria, mention of past suicidality, surgical recovery, injection medications/needles (insulin dependent diabetes)

Saving Throw

Rene was my first everything. Best friend, first kiss, first love, first heartbreak.

Seven years after walking out of my life, they tear open old wounds with a single photo of a smiling little boy and the message they're coming home.

Mo has my smile and Rene's eyes. It kills me that I didn't know about him sooner. As furious as the news Rene kept such a major secret makes me, I want a relationship with my son more than I want to rehash old arguments. Besides, Rene has more baggage than the 747 they flew in on, and I swore off love the first time they left me heartbroken.

When I learn Rene and Mo need a place to stay while they settle into life in Vancouver, it sounds like a perfect opportunity. I've got a spare room. What better way to figure out co-parenting than living together? It's not like I'm going to fall for the ex who hurt me deeper than anyone else could. That would be ridiculous.

Saving Throw is the third M/NB romance in the Table Topped series. It features Errol, demisexual panromantic production coordinator who likes to be in control and his first love, Rene, a non-binary trans masc ex-hockey player turned coach.

CW: Past mentions of a physically abusive alcoholic parent and portrayals of trauma/PTSD related to that, secret teenage pregnancy and related gender dysphoria/difficulty with accessing medical care. Side characters struggle with infertility.

HAUNTASTIC HAUNTS SERIES

Dan's Hauntastic Haunts Investigates: Goodman Dairy (*Book 1*)

Dan's Hauntastic Haunts Investigates: Hawk Lake (*Book 2*)

Dan's Hauntastic Haunts Investigates: Ivarsson School (*Book 3*)

Drew's Haunted Hangout (*A Hauntastic Haunts Short Story 1*)

Rafael's Haunted Halloween (*A Hauntastic Haunts Short Story 2*)

Lee's Haunted Holiday (*A Hauntastic Haunts Short Story 3*)

Drew's Haunted Hangout

What if your imaginary boyfriend wasn't so imaginary?

Drew was no stranger to feeling ostracized from his peers. His obsession with the paranormal began young. When he befriended Toby, the dead boy who lives in his garage.

Drew was the weird unathletic kid everyone avoided on the playground. As a teen, he found understanding in an online community created by a paranormal investigations vlogger.

Falling in love with Toby only made Drew's interest in ghosts more intense. But when he discovered Toby's striking resemblance to an unresolved missing person report, he didn't know how to help his ghost boyfriend.

At a loss, Drew turned to his online idol for help. The truth could set Drew and Toby both free, or destroy everything between them.

This is a young adult paranormal MM short story. http://eepurl.com/dNcScQ

Dan's Hauntastic Haunts Investigates: Goodman Dairy

When ghosts reach across the veil, Daniel Collins is there to tell their stories.

Dan is a vlogging ghost hunter. He has devoted his life to documenting paranormal activity. In his converted van, he travels around the country exploring haunted sites. He loves the thrill of filming restless spirits.

Chad Brewer, skeptic, works for an insurance company. He doesn't believe in ghosts, but watching Dan's vlog is his guilty pleasure. The cute vlogger is accident prone. He has Chad's work extension on speed-dial. The two talk whenever Dan gets hurt during an investigation, a frequent occurrence.

When Chad loses his job for approving too many claims, Dan offers him a position as his personal assistant. The pair sets out to investigate a haunted dairy barn for the vlog's next video series. The catch is that they must live and work together in Dan's tiny traveling home.

As the paranormal activity at the haunted dairy ramps up, so does the romantic tension between the two men. Can the love between a skeptic and a social media sensation conquer a vengeful ghost?

Dan's Hauntastic Haunts is a paranormal MM romance between a gay vlogger and his trans personal assistant. Buckle up for a hauntastic good time. www.amzn.com/B07YSV2ZNQ

PSIONS OF
SPIRE SERIES

Shelter	Novella 0.5	February 2019
Bright Spark	Book 1	February 2019
Bold Move	Novella 1.5	February 2019
Keen Sense	Book 2	April 2019
Weak Link	Novella 2.5	June 2019
Quick Fire	Book 3	July 2019
Clear Sight	Book 4	March 2020
New Look	Book 4.5	July 2020
New Ground	A SPIREverse daddy kink standalone	November 2020

***

Links:

Shelter	www.amzn.com/B07NM9XL8K
Bright Spark	www.amzn.com/B07NZ8KPS6
Bold Move	www.amzn.com/B07YVGZXDM
Keen Sense	www.amzn.com/B07R6L8W91

Weak Link   www.amzn.com/B07T4J2LJZ
Quick Fire   www.amzn.com/B07VGTF3NB
Clear Sight   www.amzn.com/B07ZQP7BDS
New Look   www.amzn.com/B08F4GBK63
New Ground   www.amzn.com/B08NHQFJDZ

Shelter

Family is what you make it.

Former foster kid and abuse survivor, Elliott Sheffield, lost everything when he developed telepathy at twelve years old. He's used to not relying on anyone. There are worse things than being lonely and alone, even for a psion who craves closeness. He has plans for his life and nothing can distract him from proving that he can succeed. That will show everyone who cast him aside. Especially his former best friend Caleb Gaetz.

Pansexual, poly, psion, Caleb is comfortable with all of those labels. Life seems easy for Caleb. He has a supportive family and a vibrant social life. The future will figure itself out. For the present he plans to enjoy his university years to the fullest extent possible. He knows his hedonistic tendencies irritate his former best friend, Elliott, to no end. He just doesn't understand why Elliott takes Caleb's sex life so personally.

When life throws them both curve balls, they must adjust their visions for the future to one that will give them both a happily ever after, or risk their plans falling apart.

This urban fantasy romance contains an open M/M relationship, mention of past abuse, and positive HIV status. www.amzn.com/B07NM9XL8K

Bright Spark

Sometimes growing up means giving up your preconceptions.

Aaron Anderson and Jake Moretti were childhood sweethearts until Aaron developed psionic abilities that turned both of their worlds upside down and tore them apart.

Six years later they reconnect when Aaron returns home to work with a youth summer camp affiliated with SPIRE. Jake is at the same camp, along with his current partners, to protest the organization funding it. Sparks fly when the couple reunites and Aaron discovers hidden abilities that bring him to the attention of SPIRE.

Aaron and Jake have every intention of seizing their second chance at love. But once more, forces outside their control are at play. And the organization Aaron believes in is at the center of events targeting vulnerable youth.

This urban fantasy romance contains M/M and an open M/M/M relationship. www.amzn.com/B07NZ8KPS6

www.ingramcontent.com/pod-product-compliance
Lightning Source LLC
Chambersburg PA
CBHW020904200626
46814CB00001BA/165